LOVE WORTH FIGHTING FOR

Tangie had just decided on what to eat when "Mr. Tall, Dark and Handsome" introduced himself to her. She sat openmouthed looking up at him, stunned by his sudden arrival.

"Hello, my name is Eric Duval. I'm one of the partners here and you are? Mind if I join you?"

He had taken her open mouth as a yes and, before she could answer him, promptly sat down, extending his hand toward hers.

Tangie blinked several times to make sure she wasn't seeing things. Realizing how foolish she must have looked just staring at him while he carried on a one-sided conversation, she blushed and quickly extended her hand to shake his.

Eric, with a devilish smile, took her hand in his and raised it to his lips to gently brush it with a kiss. He let his mustache tickle her hand ever so slightly and enjoyed the reaction with which he was rewarded. Tangie felt little shivers travel up her spine as she blushed again.

Tangie leaned back into the booth seat.

"My name is Tangerine Taylor, or Tangie for short. It's a pleasure to meet you, Mr. Eric Duval."

With one eyebrow arched, she asked, "So tell me, is this the way yo̶u̶ ̶t̶r̶e̶a̶t̶ ̶a̶l̶l̶ of your customers?"

LOVE WORTH FIGHTING FOR

KATHERINE D. JONES

ARABESQUE

★BET

BOOKS

BET Publications, LLC
http://www.bet.com
http://www.arabesquebooks.com

ARABESQUE BOOKS are published by

BET Publications, LLC
c/o BET BOOKS
One BET Plaza
1900 W Place NE
Washington, DC 20018-1211

All Kensington Titles, Imprints, and Distributed Lines are available at special quantity discounts for bulk purchases for sales promotions, premiums, fund-raising, and educational or institutional use. Special book excerpts or customized printings can also be created to fit specific needs. For details, write or phone the office of the Kensington special sales manager: Kensington Publishing Corp., 850 Third Avenue, New York, NY 10022, attn: Special Sales Department, Phone: 1-800-221-2647.

First Printing: January 2004
10 9 8 7 6 5 4 3 2 1

Printed in the United States of America

For all those who question if dreams really do come true—
they do, and this is proof. Keep writing, but more
importantly, keep dreaming.

ACKNOWLEDGMENTS

After the first word hits the paper, you never quite know how the journey will turn out or where it will take you. I have to thank my family for their support during this, my first work. It was not easy, but it was worth it. To my mom, Mattie Jones, your love and encouragement were immeasurable—I owe you one, two, three . . . To my dad, Charles Jones, thanks for all of your encouragement, too. To my sisters Carla, Candice, and Kari, you guys were great. To my sons Ivan and Isaiah, what a blessing you are and part of my reason for being. Thanks for being so patient with Mommy.

To Linda Gill at BET Books, it has been a real learning experience. Thanks for hanging in there with me. To my editor, Demetria Lucas, and the BET Books family, thanks for the opportunity and leap of faith in this writer.

My agent, Cheryl Ferguson of Ferguson Literary Agency, thanks for the late-night chats and everything that you did.

A big thank-you to Kathryn Falk and *Romantic Times*, I cannot express how much I appreciate the confidence, connections, friendship, kicks in the rear, etc., that made this possible. Never knew one casual e-mail could change my life so completely!

A big thank-you as well to Joyce, Sybil, and Col. D. Anderson, for being excellent readers.

To my friends: Pam S., Amy D., Renita K., Karen M., Kim C., Sabrina K., Marquitta D., Wendy S., and Kim R., your friendship has been an appreciated and timeless part of the fullness of my life. My Hampton *fellas* in the book—don't take it personally; it just means I was thinking about you. Much love to William W., Avery, Russell, the other William, and especially Victor for technical assistance.

To my husband, we did it. You are my joy, my buddy, my best critic, and the hardest-working husband I know. Thanks for the late nights, doing the dishes, and keeping me on track. Keep loving me . . . without you this would not have been possible.

To my Lord and Savior, Jesus Christ, I thank and praise you daily. You put the right people in my life at the right time and for that, I am eternally grateful.

Chapter 1

LOCAL SPORTS HERO FOUND SHOT TO DEATH
By Kay Dawn, *Baltimore Post* Staff Writer

The body of James "Bubba" Fraser was found early this morning on Seventh Street in southwest Washington, DC. He was pronounced dead at the scene by the medical examiner. The cause of death was multiple gunshot wounds. A homeless man believed to be seeking shelter for the night made the gruesome discovery of the body at approximately 2:00 A.M.

Fraser was best known for his outstanding play as a basketball center for Mount Vernon High School in Alexandria. He had been named to the Virginia All-State team three years in a row. The Detroit Pistons drafted him in 1991, but he was cut from the team after what was thought to be a career-ending foot injury. After his rehabilitation, Fraser played two successful seasons with a Chilean league before returning to the United States in 1995.

Though he was unable to capitalize on a career with an NBA team, he found success in establishing his own sports consulting firm in

1996. His business helped young athletes prepare their personal portfolios before signing
with a team franchise.

He is survived by his parents, James and
Susan Fraser, and his three-year-old daughter,
Kenya Coles, by well-known model Tia Coles.

The Fraser family issued a brief statement saying that they were shocked and confused about
their son's death and they pray anyone who can
help bring their son's murderer to justice will
come forward as soon as possible.

Police say it is unclear why Fraser was in the
area at such a late hour. It is an area known for
drug activity and prostitution. They admit that
they have few leads at this point. Anyone with information is urged to contact the Crime
Stoppers Unit at (202) 555-STOP.

Tangerine had just glanced at the headline when the
phone rang. "Hi, Mom, yes, I was just looking at that."
Tangie remembered Bubba from her alma mater. He
was a couple of grades ahead of her in high school. His
picture was often in the local community paper for his
support of basketball camps for young children.

"I know you are busy. I just wanted to know if you
had seen the news about James," Hattie said.

Tangie sighed. "This is so terrible. Why would anyone want to kill James Fraser? He was such a good guy
and so down-to-earth. I even heard he was thinking
about running for mayor. He would've had my vote."

Hattie grunted in disgust about the news. The recent crime wave in the area had put a damper on the
District's charm. "Did you know him well?"

"Mama, everybody knew Bubba. He wouldn't have

known me in school, but I remember him well. He was a tall, handsome young man, even back in high school. I didn't know that he had kids though."

Hattie had gone on to the next subject already. "When you get back, I want you and Candy to come over for dinner. I haven't seen my two favorite girls in a while. I figure that between the two of you I should get a grandchild soon, huh?"

Tangie laughed. "Here we go again. I am going to have to tell Candy to count her blessings that she has her own mother to run to when you start this speech. I promise you, when the time is right I'll send over a whole flock of grands for you to spoil. Right now, I have to focus on my career."

Hattie relented. "Okay, I'll let you off the hook this time. I still want that dinner date though."

"You bet. I'll make some veggie lasagna for you. I owe you. Thanks for helping me prepare for this trip."

Tangie flitted around the room gathering clothes from several shopping bags to put in her suitcase. She didn't dare try to cut her mother off in order to finish packing; instead she listened like the dutiful daughter. Tangie appreciated all her mom had done. She wouldn't trade her for anything in the world—although they disagreed almost as much as they agreed. Hattie had an opinion on everything and she'd let you know it. Like it or not. But because of her strength and strong will, Tangie had always known she had someone in her corner.

During their nightly phone conversation, Hattie remarked, "Better you than me. I don't have fond memories of that place." She exhaled loudly over the phone. "You don't remember this, because you were just a little girl. It wasn't at all like I had expected. It just seemed weird, like it had a creepy aura all its own. I can't explain it. But, since I know you are looking forward to it, I want you to have a good time. You be careful though and stay safe, baby."

"You are too much, lady, talk bad about the place, almost scaring me to death, and then you say have a good time. I know I can always count on you for objectivity."

Tangie packed as she held on to the cordless phone. "Well, Ma, I gotta go, it's getting late. I'll talk with you once I get settled in the hotel."

Too much, yeah, that was her mother, she thought. Hattie Taylor had definitely graduated from the school of hard knocks. She was forced to raise two young girls by herself, one terminally ill. She had managed everything for a number of years before Tangie's older sister, Tammy, had finally succumbed to her illness when she was twelve years old. Tangie's father had walked out on them shortly after Tammy's diagnosis, saying he couldn't deal with losing his daughter. He couldn't watch her die. As a result, what he lost was a wife and two daughters. After that, Tangie and her father had never been able to repair their relationship. As far as she was concerned, she only had one parent. She would never forgive her father for what he had done to the family. And to Tammy.

In the years that followed, Hattie and Tangie had developed a closeness in their relationship like few mothers and daughters. They learned how to depend on each other and trust each other with everything. In Tangie's case, it was *almost* everything. There was Rodney.

Hattie didn't like the fact that Tangie would be spending a week in New Orleans, but she was extremely proud of her daughter's accomplishments. She only wanted the best for Tangie.

Her mother had been instrumental in getting Tangie ready for the trip. They shopped and ate like old girlfriends instead of mother and daughter on her mini shopping spree. She felt good walking into Hecht's and buying clothes without being restricted to a budget or the sale rack.

Tangie also felt good about leaving the plus-size clothes alone. She had achieved her weight loss goal in seven months. She reclaimed her figure, which for the past couple of years had been in a state of total rebellion. She was proud to be back to a size ten, an eight when she skipped dessert for a couple of weeks.

During the conference, Tangie would attend several meetings and workshops. She and her mother chose several short-skirted suits that would be acceptable in the business arena. They selected suits in black, gray, blue, hunter green, taupe, and power red; each with matching Evan Picone shoes. He was one of Tangie's favorite designers. Besides, what woman could pass up a good shoe sale? Balancing her checkbook from their little excursion, she realized she'd spent nearly four thousand dollars for a five-day trip. It was an investment in her future though. This trip was her ticket to promotion. She was a single woman who made good money, she deserved to splurge. Tangie was proud of her five-digit savings account and great mutual fund and stock portfolio. She had it all. Almost.

The morning of her trip she read the *Baltimore Post* as part of her ritual. Unfortunately, the news report

on James Fraser had become familiar territory for
residents of the nation's capital. The District rou-
tinely switched places from first to second as the
murder capital of the country. And though it was easy
to get jaded about crime, Tangie couldn't help feeling sorry for the family of the victim. Their hopes
and dreams of the future had been dashed by a senseless act of violence. Fraser had been one of those
Virginia boys who had made it big and then come
back to help the community. He was always promot-
ing some social cause for children.

Reading the article, she too wondered what he had
been doing in that neighborhood. Like the police.
Unconsciously she wrinkled her nose. It was not the
kind of place decent people wanted to be when the
sun went down. The drug trade and prostitution were
the only things now that the once thriving business
community offered. It was a neighborhood where
even the police shied away until they had to go there.

Glancing at the clock, Tangie folded the paper
thoughtfully. Despite the troubling news, she had to
focus on getting ready for her trip to the airport. She
put her dishes in the sink and washed them quickly.
The shuttle would be at her door before she knew it.
She was filled with nervous energy as she gathered
her bags. Tangie couldn't help being excited. She was
headed to one of her favorite places—and on the office dime.

Two hours later, Tangie could not stop a big goofy
smile from spreading across her face as she boarded
her plane at Reagan National Airport. This was her
first major business trip as department manager for
the company that she worked for. The idea of the trip
was made even nicer because she had always wanted

to visit New Orleans but had never found the time. Tangie looked forward to walking in the Garden District and seeing the picturesque homes and gardens. If she was lucky, maybe she could even take in a riverboat cruise or plantation tour. If time permitted . . . Tangie was so excited about visiting the city she had almost forgotten that it was a business trip.

The conference was geared toward upper management, which provided a golden opportunity for her advancement. She was practically assured the promotion to vice president of consumer affairs, with her selection to attend the conference over the others in her office. The thought almost made her giddy. It was a position that she had worked her butt off to get and one she had coveted since coming to the company.

She looked around at some of the other passengers. She wanted to smile again, but dared not—she didn't want to get hauled off the plane for looking suspicious.

She readjusted herself in her seat and pulled the book out she had been working on for the past few days. Maya Angelou's *I Wouldn't Take Nothing For My Journey*. She felt the same way about much of her life as the author did. It hadn't been easy but now she was starting to see results. Tangie had worked for the same computer company since finishing her internship ten years ago and now here she was, one of the company's fastest rising stars.

She couldn't help admiring Maya's willingness to take risks and do whatever she had to to survive. Maya had made it against all the odds, and today continued to reach new heights.

Similarly, with long hours and being responsible for several new projects each year, Tangie was certainly proud of herself for what she had been able to achieve. She had always been a hardworking, driven young woman, and now at thirty-two years old she was climbing rapidly up the corporate ladder. This trip could be just the beginning.

Tangie smiled to herself. Despite her personal set-backs, she was finally starting to achieve her professional goals. *New Orleans, here I come!*

An extra bonus was getting out of the rat race of Washington, DC, for five days. Most of her coworkers would call her a workaholic, but she knew how to let her hair down and enjoy herself. Since finding out about it three weeks prior, she had been fantasizing about her trip to New Orleans, especially the food and learning about Creole culture.

The food, the Quarter, the Waterfront, she was ready for it all. Since her dramatic weight loss two years ago, she had become a health and fitness nut, but not on this trip. Tangie planned to stray far away from her diet and experience as many culinary delights as she could stand. She was also going to experience all the sights and sounds that N'awlins had to offer. She hoped to take in some jazz or maybe even some zydeco while she was there.

On board she looked around her first-class accom-modations and thought, *Yep . . . life is good. You done good, girl.*

She started to pick up her book again, but put it down. She was enjoying her ruminating too much. Besides, a little introspection never hurt anyone. She thought about her life. Her mother had always been her stabilizing force. In her darkest moments, she could always lean on her. At times, she didn't like de-pending on her mom so much, but definitely appreciated being able to count on her. She looked

down at her hands. They were so much like her
mother's. Delicate, yet strong, capable, and hard-
working.

And ringless.

Tangie stretched again in her seat and idly watched
the puffy white clouds. She thoroughly enjoyed the
ride as the plane glided through the air. She loved
being in business class—especially courtesy of the
office—and though she wouldn't allow herself to get
seduced by success, she was sure enjoying life right
now. *I made it in spite of you, Rodney,* she reflected.

Smiling inwardly, she casually picked up her book
again and found that she was three-quarters of the
way through the novel by the time the plane landed
at the New Orleans Airport.

Her excitement bubbled to the surface again the
moment she deplaned. She was in love before she left
the terminal. Mom was right about one thing. This
place was different, but it was definitely not weird.
The sights, the sounds, and even the smells . . .

Okay, okay, she told herself, *just get the bags and* get *over
to the hotel.* So much for that air of cool sophistication.
Tangie made her way to the baggage claim area, where
she picked up her three Samsonite bags, and walked to
locate the hotel van area. Within minutes, she was on
her way to adventure and that goofy smile was back.

It took her only a few minutes to get settled in her
hotel suite in the French Quarter. Tangie inhaled the
smells of the city around her as she sat on the balcony. The weather was great, a little humid, but there
was a nice breeze blowing off the gulf. She was so excited she couldn't decide what to do first.

She methodically unpacked her bags, hung up her
newly acquired wardrobe, and then took a shower.

It was only 4:00 P.M., but she wanted to feel fresh and pretty before she went out to explore the Quarter. Her hair and nails had been done before traveling, so she decided to give herself a facial to complete the look. She had checked into going to one of those hot new day spas springing up everywhere in the District, but decided on the do-it-yourself approach instead. Besides, she had used and sold her favorite pink skin care products for years and they worked just as well spa products. People always thought she was younger than her thirty-two years with her near perfect complexion and beautiful skin.

Wrapped in only her towel, she felt both fresh and refreshed. She was ready to tackle the city, or at least have a good meal. Tangie sat on her bed and spread all of her New Orleans literature around her. The hotel was situated in a great spot in the French Quarter, which offered several great choices of eateries and restaurants. Along with those and the markets, the Quarter was also the starting point for many of the tours. She would decide when to take her tours after registration.

Shuffling through the glossy pamphlets and brochures, she noticed that Café Du Monde was only a short walk from the hotel, and there was the French Market, Aunt Sally's Pralines, and all of Bourbon Street to explore too.

Tangie thought about food. She had been watching several New Orleans–based cooking shows back home and couldn't wait to start her food tour, beignets, étouffée, napoleons, shrimp, authentic jambalaya, gumbo, and more. Emeril and John Folse had whetted her appetite for several delicacies as well as wholesome local fare. She couldn't wait to taste New

Orleans, and the rumble in her stomach confirmed she'd better find something soon.

She went to her closet to find something comfortable and most importantly simple to wear. After a few minutes, she selected a royal-blue short-sleeved silk sheath with matching sandals. The dress was simplicity itself and it hugged her curves nicely. She wasn't heavy anymore, but she still had it where it counted.

Mercifully, she didn't have to get up at her usual time—the crack of dawn. Registration for the conference didn't begin until 10:00 A.M., so she would have plenty of time for rest and relaxation. *I guess they don't call it the Big Easy for nothing*, she thought as she prepared to leave her hotel room.

Shrimp was on the top of her list to try while in New Orleans. She decided to go on a hunt for one of those famous New Orleans shrimp po-boy sandwiches.

She passed by the House of Blues on her way to find a restaurant and made a mental note to stop in later. It was much too early for the festivities. Another block down, she came to Johnny's Po-Boys Restaurant. The smells made her mouth water and her stomach grumble again. She chuckled to herself. *Guess I found my place to eat.*

After lingering over her food she walked over to a nearby bakery. Tangie stood over the selections eager to taste everything she could see. She chose a beignet, a napoleon, and two totally decadent chocolate-chunk cookies for later.

Tangie sat down at a table for two, eagerly anticipating her first bite. She bit into the napoleon with delight and let the rich chocolate and cream filling make sweet love to her taste buds. It was so good.

Only her home training prevented her from moaning aloud.

When she finally looked up, her gaze came headlong into the eyes of the most gorgeous man she had ever seen. He was drinking coffee and eating a croissant. He was the color of a mouthwatering Hershey's milk chocolate bar with big, exotically shaped mahogany-brown eyes and long black eyelashes she could see from three feet away. Tangie wanted to look away, but his gaze held her. Mesmerized. He was tall, she could tell by his long legs under the table. He had a full, expertly maintained mustache, thick, close-cropped black wavy hair, and ooh . . . those lips.

Her imagination was really starting to get away from her. She successfully resisted the urge to fan herself. The man looked good enough to eat.

Tangie flushed when she realized that he was looking at her with the same interest. *Oh God, he's smiling at me.*

Her hands were starting to feel moist and sticky, and not from the napoleon. As much as she had been looking forward to her dessert, she had lost her appetite. To make matters worse, she felt as if her heart was going to beat right out of her chest.

He smiled wickedly at her again.

It had been too long since she had played the dating game and she didn't trust herself not to behave like a total idiot.

His open appraisal of her caused her to panic. Not because she wasn't used to the attention of men, but because with this man she liked it. Tangie gathered her things and hurriedly walked the short distance back to her hotel. She refused to look back just in case he was watching her. She was trying hard to maintain her dignity. *Just keep putting one foot in front of the other,* she told herself.

Once settled into her room, she chastised herself for behaving like a scared teenager. Was she thiry-two or twelve? Her heart was still beating to a samba rhythm, but she was feeling better to be back on home turf and away from his heated gaze.

She thought, flopping down. *Oh well, it could have been worse . . . I don't know how, but it could have been worse.*

Tangie turned the radio on for a distraction. The soulful sounds of the singer Maxwell helped begin to relax her, but it wasn't long before "Whenever, Wherever, Whatever" began to play havoc with her senses. She fidgeted nervously on the bed, sexual tension increasing by the minute. Tangie groaned.

Anxious to take her mind off the stranger from the café, she quickly flicked off the radio and picked up her book, finishing the remainder within an hour.

Unconsciously, Tangie's mind drifted back to the man she had seen in the bakery—Mr. Tall, Dark, and Handsome, she dubbed him since she didn't know his name. She kept thinking about his sexy lips as a smile slowly crept along her own. She wanted to taste his skin. See if he tasted as good as he looked. Run her tongue along that hard jawline. She could just imagine his lips giving her sweet kisses down her neck, stomach, and even . . .

"Okay, Tangie, snap out of it," she said out loud.

Thankfully, the telephone rang just as she was coming out of her reverie. Tangie looked at the clock, and knew exactly who it was. She had been expecting her best friend's call. They traveled together whenever possible, but Candy was working on a major project at work and couldn't afford the time off for this trip. She made Tangie promise that she would fill her in on every detail while she was there. Tangie needed to calm her breathing before picking up the receiver.

"Hello?"

"Hey, big girl, how's N'awlins? Tell me what you've seen, what you've eaten . . . Come on now, give me all the details. Have you seen any of those fine Creole men?"

"Hello, little girl, how are you?"

They had been friends since their junior year at Mount Vernon High School. The friendship had only grown stronger when they attended college together as roommates. Their home by the sea had provided many challenges, and with each other's help they had both managed to graduate with honors. They had even both majored in business administration.

They did have their own individual interests though. Tangie was more practical and preferred the business clubs and activities. Candy was more into drama and theater, but the two young women shared a genuine fondness and love for each other. Candy helped fill the void left in Tangie's life by Tammy's passing. Candy was her sister in every sense of the word.

Tangie responded, "As a matter of fact, while sipping coffee and eating dessert, looking *tres chic,* I might add, I did run across a rather fine looking gentleman at the bistro."

Candy asked excitedly, "Ooh, girl, what did you say, what did he say, did you talk to him?" She was all too familiar with her best friend's antics and flare for the dramatic.

"Er . . . well . . . no, but that's okay. Just seeing him was enough," Tangie replied sheepishly.

She looked down at the fashion magazine she had been flipping through aimlessly. She could tell Candy's voice had taken on that lecture tone. Tangie braced herself for what was coming next.

"Coward! Girl, you are too tired. If you see 'Mr. Fine' again, do you think you could manage to get his name and maybe a dinner invitation? If Stella can, maybe now you can get your groove back too." She added emphatically, "How long has it been since you and Rodney broke up?"

Not bothering to wait on a response, she continued, "I'll tell you, it has been over two years. That's enough time to jump out there again. You're not getting any younger, babe. Remember, progress, not perfection. Maybe a swift, hot, torrid New Orleans affair is just what you need."

That comment sparked Tangie's attention. Brief and torrid was not her style.

Candy let out an exasperated breath. "Tangie, at least see what's available—and no, you don't have to sleep with him. Just see what the brother is about. You might be pleasantly surprised."

Tangie sighed as she listened to the barrage. Candy would continue until she was finished. Sometimes Tangie got a word in, sometimes she didn't. She would wait to see. . . .

"I'm not trying to beat you up. I am just concerned, that's all. Life is for the living and you need to start getting out there again.

"Well, dear, Siddiq is waiting for me so I've got to go. I was just calling to check up on ya, and even though I am extremely jealous of you going to New Orleans without me, I'm glad to hear you're doing okay. I'll holler at you tomorrow and yes, I am expecting a full report on everything that you see, hear, drink, and eat. Love ya. Bye."

"Love you too, you crazy woman. I promise I'll fill you in tomorrow. Tell whatshisname hello for me. Talk to you later."

Tangie enjoyed chiding Candy about Siddiq. They got along well, but she never missed an opportunity to kid her buddy about him. She teased him about his long name, the result of his Muslim heritage. He was a great guy and Tangie was happy that her friend had found a serious relationship; however, it only partially helped to keep her out of Tangie's business. The girl found the time and energy to butt into her life whenever it suited her. Their bond was a strong one that had stood the test of time.

No matter what they did or pursued, they kept enough room in their lives for each other. Candy was never one to hold back or let you get a word in edgewise, but Tangie loved her. She had helped her through some pretty rough situations, especially when she and Rodney first broke up. If it hadn't been for Candy, Tangie knew she probably wouldn't have made it. Candy refused to let depression take over her and kept pushing Tangie to deal with her feelings and find other interests. They developed a workout routine that guaranteed relief of stress and anxiety and had helped Tangie not revert to food for comfort. At her worst, Tangie had ballooned past two hundred pounds—food would not become her emotional crutch if Candy could help it. Eating, especially when you enjoy food, is such an easy way to deal with emotional stress.

Rodney had been Tangie's whole world, but Candy wouldn't let Tangie just give up and believe life was over just because he had moved on. Candy had hovered over her like an overprotective mother hen until she felt Tangie was ready to move on too.

Tangie continued to flip through the magazine. She cringed when she thought of Rodney. She knew she never wanted to experience that kind of pain again. Unfortunately, talking to Candy had brought up unwelcome feelings. The hurt and betrayal she had experienced were almost too much to bear. She was very reluctant to let another man have the chance to reject her heart—and two years had done little to make her want to trust love again.

She stopped flipping through the pages now. Her mind was on what had been. They were both young and in love. She would have given her very soul just to be with him. Maybe that was her problem? Had she had sunk herself so far into the relationship that she couldn't see straight?

She must have missed the signs that indicated they had problems. Maybe she gave him too much credit. She had counted on him a lot and thought it only natural that he would always be in her life. In retrospect, there had been plenty of good times in their relationship, but toward what she realized was the end, things had changed, and everything had become about Rodney Johnson. If she was to be honest with herself, maybe things weren't always so perfect.

Bitterness welled up in her from her very depths as she thought about the day that he left. Weren't she and Candy supposed to be planning their weddings by now? Something had gone terribly wrong, but she didn't know what. Didn't know why Rodney had cheated on her and never looked back. Thinking about that night, Tangie felt as if a weight were sitting on her chest, pushing the air out of her lungs.

Tangie was angry with herself. Before now she had managed to keep her emotions on an even keel, for the most part. She had a social life, great friends, and a career where there was job mobility. She couldn't afford to continue to let her emotions run amok—she had too much to do in her life to be bogged down by old memories. Tangie sat in her room thinking about her next moves. She could waste all her time in New Orleans being miserable or she could take advantage of the opportunity that she had been given.

Nervous energy told her it was time for action. She was restless in more ways than one. And judging from her body's reactions lately, celibacy for over two years was getting to be real old. She looked at the clock on the nightstand. It was still early, but if she didn't want to crash before enjoying some of the New Orleans nightlife, a nap was in order. She undressed, figuring on a short rest before having to decide what to do about dinner. It was a typical early summer New Orleans day, and although the air conditioner was pumping, she decided to slip into the cool, inviting sheets without pajamas. The silky, cream-colored sheets felt like pure heaven next to her bare skin.

Tangie felt unusually comfortable in the hotel bed; she loved her bed back home and had anticipated having trouble falling asleep. Snuggling deeper in the sheets, she saw that handsome face smiling at her with those gorgeous, inviting lips. She began to feel warm and tingly all over her body. He'd had on a white short-sleeved shirt and blue well-fitting trousers. His broad shoulders, exquisitely tapered waist, and muscular legs even his dark blue pants couldn't hide garnered an unexpected reaction from Tangie. Why was she so drawn to the man? He wasn't the first handsome face she'd noticed in New Orleans.

Was the room getting warmer? Her body heat began to rise as she imagined his strong hands caressing her. They were soft and gentle and knew all the right places to touch. Soft moans escaped her lips. The touches felt so good. It had been too long since she had been so passionately stroked.

Tangie's eyes flew open, her heart pounding in her heaving chest. She looked around the room to make sure she was still alone. She was. She had fallen asleep and at thirty-two had had a wet dream. The dampness between her thighs and the familiar ache at her core confirmed it. Tangie sat up in the bed, pulling the rumpled sheets up to her neck . . . She was embarrassed. Why was she suddenly being reduced to an overly hormonal adolescent?

She hated having erotic dreams and the feelings of wanting she felt afterward . . . She was left with just raw heartache and exposed need.

Tangie was so confused. She had every reason in the world to be happy, a great job, money in the bank, and great friends. Nevertheless, there was something missing. She was lonely.

But then, no amount of loneliness, or in her immediate case, horniness, would allow her to forget the pain of Rodney. She would have to be crazy to take a chance like that again. Wouldn't she?

Her stubbornness prevented her from ever truly giving a new relationship a chance. She had all but forgotten what the dating world was about, since she had been two years without a real date. When she went out it was always with a man she knew well. She had her selection of male friends, but they were just that, men who weren't looking for a relationship and they knew she wasn't either. They could hang out, but there was no kissing and certainly no sex. She wasn't exactly the ice woman, but pretty darn close, and the men she loosely dated knew the rules of the game. This was not exactly the bravest way to behave, but it was certainly the safest.

Her conversation with Candy had brought up all sorts of memories that Tangie hadn't wanted to deal with. *What are best friends for?*

She sat there, waiting for the painful memories and uncomfortable feelings to subside. *Damn that Rodney.*

She had been doing all right until today. She really hadn't been thinking about relationships or being made love to until seeing the stranger's beautifully sexy, bewitching lips.

Crazy as it sounded, did she dare consider a brief and torrid affair like her friend Candy had suggested?

She turned and looked at the clock when her stomach started to grumble. Surprisingly, her power nap had been almost two hours. It was close to 8:00 P.M.

Tangie hung her outfit up on the closet door. She was mentally going places that she really didn't want to go. Again. . . .

Chapter 2

Tangie had to do something; the dream had left her feeling flushed and in need. She decided to take a lukewarm shower, hoping to extinguish her burning physical desires. After a few minutes, the water started to take the edge off her nerves. Her breathing returned to normal and she wasn't quite so wound up. She concentrated on the flow of the water and let her troubles go down the drain, to mingle with the bubbles from her cucumber melon bath gel. She inhaled its light fragrance and started to feel better. She would be all right after a while, she thought.

Sitting on her bed wrapped in her soft, cozy terry cloth robe, she sorted through her brochures again. She was looking for something in particular. A nice quiet spot for dinner. The Quarter had so many choices. There was a restaurant and setting for everything. Maybe the Court of Two Sisters, which she had heard so many good things about.

Nah, probably full of tourists. She was in the mood for solitary dining so that she could begin to sort out her feelings. Maybe just a nice quiet out-of-the-way spot with good food and good atmosphere. She put lotion on her body vigorously as she went through her normal post-shower routine.

Her peace of mind had been thoroughly interrupted and she had to find a way to get back on an
even keel. Uncomfortable thoughts of Rodney had
been swirling around in her head today too much for
comfort. It was time to move on, even if it didn't
mean forging a new relationship with someone. She
just had to get over the breakup and get him out of
her system for good for her own peace of mind.

Tangie resolved that she was not going to allow
herself to waste this trip to New Orleans. What was in
the past needed to stay there. Besides, she had too
much to look forward to. There was no sense in continuing to look backward. Her mother had raised her
to be stronger than this anyway. Achieving this trip
was a signal of her future success. She was on her way
to making it in life, and she was going to have a darn
good time getting there.

*Why come all this way to mope, girl? You could do that in
your condo in Virginia. New Orleans is about having fun!*

Tangie decided on a restaurant that advertised a relaxed, quiet atmosphere and was only four blocks
away from her hotel. She dressed in a casual peach-
colored silk pantsuit with comfortable walking
sandals and headed out. She was pleased to see that
it was everything the brochures said it would be, small
and dimly lit, and the smells coming from the kitchen
were positively divine.

It was a little after 8:00 P.M. and it looked as if only
the regulars were there. There were no cameras and
no odd-looking outfits. The atmosphere was very
New Orleans laid-back.

Maybe the tourists overlooked this place. Tangie
certainly hoped so. She had a feeling it was going to

be one of her favorite spots. If the food tasted half as good as it smelled, she would be in heaven.

Although she was alone, she was seated in a booth and given ice water and warm, fresh French bread. She wondered if the bread and butter were low-fat. *Fat chance*, she thought. She studied the well-worn menu with a slight smile on her face. She couldn't decide between the shrimp, the shrimp, or the shrimp.

Tangie was too engrossed in the menu to notice a very good looking man walk into the restaurant. He had an air and confidence about him that would make most men jealous and most women do a double take.

His wavy jet-black hair was close-cropped. He and his barber had a close relationship. He had smooth skin, the color of milk chocolate. The new growth on his chin and jawline gave him a masculine, almost swarthy appearance.

He seemed very familiar with the place and warmly greeted both staff and customers. Tangie may not have been very observant, but he noticed her right away since she was not a regular. He took the time to check her out, while she wasn't paying any attention to him. Eric Duval liked what he saw. He could tell from her well-developed arms and legs that she was athletic, or at least that she worked out on a regular basis. He enjoyed the sexy glimpse of leg peeking out from under the table.

She wasn't particularly big or small but to his mind was comfortably shapely. Not skin and bones and definitely not too much to hold on to.

Just watching her for a few seconds sent his hormones over the edge. *Damn, I don't even know her name. That's quite an effect you have on me, young lady.*

He continued to watch her as his imagination ran

away. He daydreamed about holding her in his arms. All of a sudden, he felt an uncomfortable tug in the groin. He chastised himself for being so shallow. *High school was twenty years ago, man.*

Looking at her very closely, he got the impression that he knew her—she was familiar to him.

Eric contemplated his next move when he realized she was the same woman he'd seen earlier in the afternoon.

Is she somehow involved in this business—a plant by McCollum or Avery or just a tourist?

He walked confidently over to Tangie's booth. If she had been looking, she might have thought it was a swagger.

She had just decided on what to eat, when Mr. Tall, Dark, and Handsome introduced himself to her. She sat openmouthed looking up at him, stunned by his sudden arrival.

"Hello, my name is Eric Duval. I'm one of the restaurant's owners, and you are? Mind if I join you?"

He had taken her open mouth as a yes and, before she could answer him, he promptly sat down, extending his hand toward hers.

Tangie blinked several times to make sure she wasn't seeing things. He was the same gorgeous man from earlier in the day.

Realizing how foolish she must have looked just staring at him while he carried on a one-sided conversation, she blushed and quickly extended her hand to shake his.

Eric took her hand in his and with a devilish smile raised it to his lips to gently brush it with a kiss. He let his mustache tickle her hand ever so slightly and enjoyed the reaction with which he was rewarded. Once again, he felt an uninvited slight stir in the groin. Tangie felt little shivers travel up her spine as she blushed again.

She leaned back into the booth seat. "My name is Tangerine Taylor, or Tangie for short. It's a pleasure to meet you, Mr. Eric Duval."

With one eyebrow arched, she asked, "So tell me, is this the way you greet all of your customers?"

Eric made himself comfortable before he replied.

"Only the beautiful ones," he responded with a wink. "I assure you the pleasure is all mine. I love your name. What was your parents' inspiration?"

Tangie smiled at him. "That's a question that I get all the time—no, it wasn't a fruit fetish, more of a musical tribute. They loved Sinatra's version of the song 'Tangerine.'"

Eric laughed. The sound wrapped around Tangie in a warm embrace.

He told her, "Ah . . . named after a song. That's original. I like it though. So what brings you to N'awlins? Listening to your voice I'd say you are from the East Coast, Virginia, Maryland, or DC? Am I right?" He gave her an electric smile, showing perfectly dazzling teeth.

He is charming, I have to give him that. I love that laugh and that voice. . . .

He made eye contact with a waiter and he came right over to take their order. Eric gave her his winning smile again and proceeded to order for her and him.

Tangie listened and was slightly annoyed at his arrogance. He had totally taken over her nice quiet dinner *alone*.

Oh well, she thought, maybe the distraction he provided would be worth it. After all, she had five days of possibly boring workshops ahead of her on how to do her job better. She might as well have a little fun tonight. She listened as he ordered the wine.

"Are you always so helpful with your customers? Maybe you should find out if they have food allergies or something like that," she said, the merest hint of annoyance lacing her tone. She wasn't truly upset, but she needed to set some boundaries.

"I assure you, if there is anything not to your liking I will take care of it personally. So am I right about your origins?" he asked.

Tangie nodded her head gently.

"Yes, actually I am from northern Virginia. I went to school in the Tidewater area though, so sometimes I sound a little southern. How about you? You don't exactly sound like one of the natives."

"I'm not permanently posted in New Orleans but I've spent a great deal of time in the city and am intimately acquainted with all the best spots in town. This restaurant was a friend's idea and I agreed to a not-so-silent silent partnership."

When dinner arrived, they continued to enjoy light conversation. Tangie told him about her conference, her best friend, Candy, and her job. "This conference I'm attending is a real opportunity for me. I like the work that I do, but I'm ready for more of a challenge. I am vying to be the vice president of my division. I should know in a couple of weeks if I'm selected. Other than that I am a pretty simple person. I love to read, work out, spend time with my buddies. I am not a party-goer and can't remember the last time I went dancing. I guess I am kinda boring when you think about it."

"Boring? Never. I think most folks around our age are more settled now than they used to be. Who has time to run around playing games? For most, it is work, work, work, and occasionally you can throw in some quality time with wife and kids.

"That's something I hope to avoid when the time is right though."

"The wife and kids?" Tangie asked with a smile.

"No, the work, work, work part. I want to be a real part of my family life. My dad has always been there for me. I want to do the same for my kids."

He told her about his job as an insurance investigator and his many travels looking into cases of fraud. "I enjoy the restaurant business though, so when I'm in town I do the best I can to help out. If that means dining with beautiful young ladies, then I suffer through it," he said with a shrug of his shoulders in mock exasperation.

"Yes, I can see that you work so hard."

"Tangie, since you are new to this area, I have a deal for you. I suppose you haven't had a chance to see much of my fair city."

She was intrigued. "Yes, Mr. Duval. What are you offering?" Tangie didn't even recognize the little vixen that she had become flirting with him.

"As a seminative I'm prepared to give you my special reduced-rate New Orleans tour. But you have to call me Eric."

She felt herself melting under his power. She loved his voice and the way he said her name. He had an East Coast accent too, but with a slight lilt. She accepted his invitation before even asking what the reduced rate was.

"On one condition, you let me pay for tonight's dinner," she said.

Eric smiled. "The moment I sat down our bill was settled, but thanks for the offer." He reached for her hand in an intensely intimate gesture.

Tangie let him caress the back of her hand in small circular motions. She felt warmth suffuse her entire body. "That was unnecessary, but very nice of you, Eric. How can I possibly repay you for your generosity and time?"

Eric looked at her suggestively.

She continued, ignoring the heat that arose between them. "Well, if nothing else, can I invite you to my hotel for coffee? The food and conversation have been excellent and I'd like to repay the kindness."

For the first time that evening, he looked at his watch, and she noticed that it was a Rolex.

"I really hate to turn such a tempting offer down. Coffee sounds great, but I can't tonight. I've got some business to take care of so I'd love a rain check, if you're still offering?"

They were having such a nice time together that Tangie couldn't help being disappointed. She steeled her expression and said, "Sure, no problem. I understand." However, she really didn't understand, as it was very nearly midnight. They had talked and eaten for over three hours. Tangie found him intriguing.

Warning bells went off in the back of her head but she pushed them away. She liked Eric and she wanted to enjoy his company while she was in the city and she definitely wanted to come back to his restaurant.

Eric left a generous tip for the waiter and they left.

"Where are you staying? I have time to give you a lift," he offered.

"Thanks, but I am very close by. I've chosen to go to spots where I can get to on my own steam. I love New Orleans, or should I say N'awlins, from what I've seen so far?"

"You say that like a real pro. You sure you don't have any Louisiana blood in you?"

"Perish the thought. My mom would have a fit if she heard that. I can't imagine why, but she doesn't think much of your fair city."

"You'll have to bring her back with you, so that I can give you both my special behind-the-scenes New Orleans tour."

They continued walking and talking and before she knew it, they were back at her hotel. When he got to the door Eric kissed her lightly on the lips, and told her he would call her in the morning to arrange their first touring site.

"I'm in room 506, just buzz me around 6:00 P.M. Don't worry yourself with calling in the morning."

The kiss was chaste at best, but her lips still tingled several minutes later and the blood rushed to her face. Tangie could not believe it as she stood there blushing like a schoolgirl again. What was it about Mr. Eric Duval that had her experiencing all these feelings anew? She had met plenty of handsome men before, been on plenty of what she called dates before, so what was going on here? Tangie practically floated back to her room.

Once there, she went directly to the veranda to look out over the city. She felt light as air. Her chance encounter felt so right.

When she could calm down, she would go about the business of getting ready for the conference. Early registration was between 8:30 and 9:45 A.M. Regular registration was at 10:00 A.M. She wanted to get her information packets early and scope out the best place to sit. Sorting through the suits she'd bought, she finally settled on the taupe one with the midlength skirt and cream shell.

She was still smiling when she disrobed and got in bed. She fell asleep with no problem. She was too tired for dreams, pleasant or otherwise. It had been a long day.

Chapter 3

Tangie awoke at 7:00 A.M., feeling invigorated and eager to get through the day. After her twenty-minute shower, she noticed she had received a delivery. There were a dozen long-stemmed red roses on her table! Tangie was flabbergasted. She rushed over to read the card.

Enjoyed last night immensely, looking forward to seeing you again. Eric, it read.

The goofy smile was back. Tangie dressed and went down to the lobby for the conference. She managed to make it through the welcome and subsequent workshops without knowing what was said. Her mind wandered all day. She imagined what life would bring with Eric Duval. Hmmm . . . Tangie Duval, Tangerine Taylor-Duval. They both had a nice ring.

She couldn't believe how juvenile she was acting. Yes, he was handsome beyond measure, smart, witty, a good conversationalist, but something about that man made her feel like a schoolgirl with a crush.

She thought about the roses upstairs in her room and she had to put a lot of effort into not smiling like the Cheshire Cat. It had been eons since she had received such a lovely bouquet. The whole situation was very pleasant, if not just a little unnerving at the same time.

Finally at 5:15 P.M., after making pleasantries with her fellow conference mates, she escaped to her room. She would have just enough time to freshen up before meeting Eric at 6:00 P.M.

On the way up to her room in the elevator, she thought about what to wear. Should she be casual, sexy, or somewhere in between? The nights were pretty warm here this time of year. She realized after her first outing that sweaters were optional. Even with a breeze off the gulf, the temperatures stayed above eighty.

Tangie settled on a sleeveless silk summer floral dress in neutral colors of beige and green with matching green silk panties. The beige dress highlighted the sable color of her hair, which she bumped lightly with a curling iron. Tangie smiled at her reflection in the mirror. She had always loved the feeling of pure silk next to her skin.

She wanted to feel sexy, so decided against wearing a bra. "Thank you, *Firm* videos," she said to her reflection. She was in her thirties and still able to go without a bra without the threat of arrest for indecent exposure.

She didn't know how her evening would turn out. Would Eric want to kiss her again? She didn't know, but she certainly hoped so. She flossed her teeth before applying Confidence lipstick. The color was perfect for the dress because it did not overwhelm her appearance. Then she turned her attention to her nails.

Tangie applied fresh coats of Iced Cappuccino nail polish on her fingers and toes, and once satisfied with her appearance, settled down to wait. She tried to quell the feelings of anticipation she had by reading the latest *Essence* magazine, but she just couldn't concentrate. Everywhere she looked, she saw that incredible smile and felt those sweet lips gently kissing her.

Tangie knew she could be in real trouble with this guy. All of her previous efforts to protect her heart seemed to be melting away under the heat of this man.

She had been lonely for so long she had almost convinced herself that it would be her lot in life. However, this Mr. Duval seemed like a good candidate to fill the void in her life.

Intuition told her to go slow, but her hormones said, *Forget that!*

She had some questions for Eric though. She couldn't remember where he said he was from, how long he would be in Louisiana, or what company he worked for. All she remembered was that it had something to do with insurance.

Insurance sounded about as exciting as Rodney's job with UPS, she thought ruefully. Eric's job obviously allowed him to eat well, dress well, and live comfortably. She supposed being part owner of a quaint New Orleans restaurant didn't hurt either.

Sitting down to let her polish dry brought to mind several other observations. In fact, the more she thought about it, there was a lot missing from their conversation last night.

Her mind kicked into high gear. The questions she had were becoming uncomfortable. She didn't even know if he was an only child, anything about his family, or whether he had a family. Had he been rushing home to a wife last night? Tangie don't read more into this. The man said he wanted to be there for his family, like his dad had been there for him.

Thoughts over what to do continued to war within her. Seven minutes until 6:00 P.M.

There was a lot that needed to be said this evening; otherwise tonight would be their last outing together. She still had some of her senses about her.

Five minutes to go. She tried to push that niggling voice out of her head. The one that said, *Watch out!* They had talked a lot about what they wanted in the future.

She stood up to look out of her window. She didn't know why. Since he had walked her back to her hotel, she didn't even know what kind of car he drove.

She smiled as she pictured that delicious body behind the wheel. She figured he drove something, red, shiny, and sporty. . . .

Tangie was unceremoniously jarred out her daydreams by the ringing of her telephone. Thinking it was Eric, she answered the phone in her best sexy voice. "Hello, this is Tangie," she crooned.

"Tangie? Tangie . . . Oh, girl, you have a lot to tell me and you'd better start talking!" Candy demanded, noticing the change in Tangie's voice immediately. Her friend was having a very good time.

Disappointed, Tangie said, "Oh, it's you. Hi, Candy."

"Doggoned right it's me, but I guess I'm not the one you were expecting, eh? Not with that sexy come-hither voice you pulled out of the closet. Come on now, out with it, what's his name and where did you meet him? I want all the details, my sistah."

Tangie glanced at her watch; it was 5:59 P.M. She said hurriedly, "Candy, girl, you know I love you, but I've got to go. I promise I will call you tonight, no matter how late it is, and fill you in. Bye."

"Tangie, Tangie, Tangerine Taylor!" Candy huffed into the silent phone line. She was very worried about her friend now. Candy was concerned that Tangie had not been in a relationship for so long and now she was extremely vulnerable. Candy hoped Tangie's Mr. Wonderful was also Mr. Right. She could not bear to see her friend go through the hurt again that she had had with Rodney.

Candy had watched Tangie become so wrapped up in Rodney that she didn't live for anything or anyone else. On the other hand, she was also thrilled for Tangie. It was about time she got excited about someone; she had cut herself off from the male species for far too long. Candy certainly didn't want history to repeat itself.

Sipping her warm cider, she mulled over the situation. Tangie deserved to be happy, so she just had to trust that Tangie knew what she was doing. She hoped she wouldn't rush into anything too quickly. She thought, *Let's just hope the ever practical Ms. Taylor is the one in charge, not the free-spirited Ms. Taylor.*

Chapter 4

Eric knew in his head that seeing Tangie was wrong, but it felt so right in his heart. Ever since he'd seen her at the bakery, he knew there was chemistry. It was more than physical, he felt a oneness with her that he couldn't explain. He had wanted to make love to her, make her his from the first moment he saw her. He could name a dozen reasons he wanted to pursue a relationship with her, but the bottom line was he just wanted to be with her.

Eric could tell she was comfortable with him, but more importantly, with herself. He didn't like dating a woman who always had to prove she too could wear pants. A woman like that never lets her guard down and is too quick to talk about how much she doesn't need a man!

Most of the women he ran into of his age group were either so busy being "men" themselves they couldn't recognize a good one if they were bitten by him. Or they had so many problems that a day with them felt like a year and he was emotionally spent at the end of the date.

Tangie was different; he felt he could trust her and he didn't get the feeling that she was bringing all sorts of hang-ups to the relationship, but why now?

He was working on such a serious case and she could get hurt. Was it God or the devil that brought them together where neither one belonged?

He knew this dalliance could be his undoing, but if he didn't see her he would regret for a long time not pursuing whether or not it could work. He made his way to a lobby phone and dialed her room. The line was busy so he sat down for a couple of minutes.

He called Tangie's room again and as soon as he heard her angelic voice, his spirits lifted and he knew exactly what he was doing. He hoped that the flowers this morning hadn't been overkill.

He noticed her long before she saw him. The woman actually blushed! How long had it been since he had seen that? he thought and smiled to himself. He already knew she was smart, very good looking, self-confident, but not aggressive. She allowed a man to be a man, and that appealed to him. When he had ordered for both of them, she didn't object or make a scene over paying the bill. Eric was finding himself way more attracted to her than he should be.

The look Tangie gave him and her smile when they saw each other were confirmation enough. She was definitely the one, Eric thought.

He was a real clotheshorse; he could make a potato sack look good. Eric wore a cream-colored brushed silk shirt and linen-blend pants. He was the epitome of casual elegance. She was very pleased with the man standing before her. They greeted each other with genuine warmth when they embraced and he directed her to the valet stand. It only took a few minutes for his car to arrive. Tangie was pleasantly surprised. It was a black Cadillac Seville STS, a car she'd always loved. Tangie liked to drive most times, but traffic on the beltway took the pleasure out of the experience. She had settled for a Nissan Altima at home. It handled well and the gas mileage was good.

She liked the speed and freedom of an open country road whenever she could get to one. Fortunately for her, there were many beautiful places in Virginia to explore.

Looking around, she noticed how immaculate the interior was. It even still had that new car smell. She was reminded of the golden oldie television show *Banacek* and wondered if Eric played it fast and loose like the main character did.

Eric watched her as he slid into the driver's seat. He could just imagine how she would feel in his arms. He felt his temperature rise a few degrees just thinking about her. Before his thoughts got too carried away, he'd better start making conversation. "Don't be impressed with this car, it's just a loaner while I'm here. It actually belongs to the company. One of the benefits is we have access to any car they have available in the fleet. I like this one because it handles well, even though it is a little more car than I need. My car at home is an Acura NSX-T."

Eric made that last remark as glibly as he could while navigating the traffic along the busy New Orleans streets. He waited for a reaction, and not noticing one, he figured it was safe to continue. "Are you ready for dinner now?"

Tangie responded, "I could eat now, but I am not starving. I'll follow your lead since you're the tour guide," she teased.

"Well, while in N'awlins you must hear jazz and not that raggedy stuff they play on TV shows, but the real deal. I think most shows do New Orleans a real injustice. Every show or movie must have that staged funeral procession. Everyone uses the same street, with the same four black people and the same music. That cracks me up," he said wryly.

"They should give people more credit," he continued. "But anyway, there is this spot I love to go to just to get some great down-home food and clear my head. I love my restaurant too, but this is all part of your tour. I want you to see the real New Orleans. When we get there, though, don't let the outside fool ya, it's a great place to eat, and of course I would never let such a pretty lady get botulism."

"And we thank God for small favors," she teased right back.

Another ten minutes and they were entering what looked like a glorified shack. It was dimly lit, but true to his word, it was clean and decent. The booth they were escorted to provided them with an excellent view of the stage. The band was playing classic jazz tunes and though the members appeared a little long in the tooth, they were excellent.

Tangie soon found herself caught up in her surroundings, tapping her foot to the music and feeling completely and totally at home. Maybe it was the atmosphere, maybe it was Eric. How could she feel so comfortable with a man she'd only known for two days? Tangie wondered to herself.

"This place is great. How did you ever find it?" she asked.

"When in Rome . . ." he replied with a smile. "Actually Big Mama, the owner, is a third cousin or something. I've known about this place all my life, but I don't get here nearly as much as I like to because of work and other obligations. So bringing you here wasn't as altruistic as I led you to believe, I must confess."

"Oh, Mr. Duval, you wound me."

When the band took a break the food was served. She guessed the proprietors didn't want a conflict of interest, or maybe just no slurping, burping, or smacking during the performances.

Eric had told her the food was plentiful and exceptional, and so far he had been right about everything. She saw no reason to doubt him now.

"Do you know what you want?"

Tangie looked puzzled. She hadn't been given a menu when they walked in.

"I don't know, do you have some suggestions?"

"Yeah, everything, what's your pleasure?" he said slyly.

"Okay, since you are so good at it, I'll let you order for me again, or maybe I'll just share your plate."

"Oh no, you never get between a man and his food. I'll order for both of us," Eric hastily responded.

"All right, now I am really curious. Big Mama must really know her stuff, if you draw the line at common courtesy. I thought I could at least count on you to keep me fed."

Tangie learned that there was no menu. Big Mama served the same food every night and everybody knew what she cooked. When customers came in, they just ordered the *usual.*

"You can, just not by my food. You can count on me for much more too," Eric said, slipping her hands into his.

Tangie noticed that they were warm and comforting. She felt a tremendous sense of security sitting there with him and to her it felt good. For the mo-

ment, the persistent doubts that she'd had in the
hotel were banished.

She thought she would burst by the time the band
came back "onstage." She had tasted and sampled
enough food for an army. The seafood gumbo, fried
fish, crab legs, fried shrimp, boudin, macaroni and
cheese, collards, and red beans and rice were
scrumptious, but she had to draw the line at crawfish.
She wasn't going to suck the brains out of any crea-
ture's head no matter how good they were purported
to be. She watched in feigned disgust as Eric devoured about a pound of the steamed creatures.

Their conversation had dwindled while they were
eating and listening to the music, but now after getting full on great food and music they were able to
concentrate on each other once again.

Eric looked deep into Tangie's eyes, reveling in
their soft brown color. He could get lost in those eyes.
With mock seriousness he asked, "Did you have a
good time?"

"Yes, I know I overdid it a bit, but this place was well
worth it. Big Mama, your fifth cousin ten times removed, sure knows her way around a kitchen. I didn't
know it was humanly possible to eat so much!"

Eric chuckled. "Yeah . . . I was checking you out.
You did kinda put a Sumo wrestler to shame."

Tangie poked him in the shoulder across the table.
"Hey, it's all your fault and now because of you I have
gained ten pounds in one night."

"I know several ways to work off all this food, if
you're interested."

"Yeah, I know several ways too and I am going to do
one of them as soon as I get back to my room," she
teased right back.

"Aw, all by yourself?" he said, mock petulance lacing his tone.

"Yes, Mr. Duval, all by myself. So you, sir, will just have to help another damsel in distress."

Tangie had made a vow never to tip the scales above 150 pounds after her weight loss, but this trip was trying to threaten her resolve. Back in her room she would have to do a twenty-minute workout before she would allow herself to go to sleep; besides, she was so full she could hardly move.

Okay, he is nice, considerate, a lot of fun to be with, looks and smells great, and he's successful, Tangie thought. *What's the catch?* Did he have a wife and six kids at home? A girlfriend, or worse yet, a boyfriend? A bad habit or two, sell drugs, beat women, or have some incurable, communicable disease?

Something had to be wrong. She liked him too much, and she enjoyed their easy way of talking to each other and his sense of humor. Tangie could never be with a man who couldn't laugh at himself, some stuffed shirt who took himself too seriously. Eric was easy on the eyes and easy on the heart.

They had eased into another amiable silence before he broke into her reverie. "Are you ready to go?"

His question rousted Tangie from her musings.

"Tomorrow I have some people to meet with pretty late, but I would love to see you again if you don't mind. I know your conference wraps up in a couple of days. Could we plan on Thursday night for dinner and dancing?" Eric asked.

"I don't want to show you up or anything, but I might be able to show you a couple of things. The club is in the tourist area, but if we go early we will be at home before the parties get rowdy . . . or any other place you'd like to be."

Tangie started to tingle all over just looking at him. The words *we'll be at home* stuck in her mind.

In her best slow and sexy voice, she said, "Sure, that's fine."

It was time to say good night, but neither Tangie nor Eric moved. They continued to sit in their own private part of New Orleans oblivious of everyone else around them.

Tangie sighed. "You know, Mr. Duval, this conference is informative, a great networking opportunity, and I'm learning a lot, but for some strange reason I find that I am thankful to be here for much more personal reasons. I was so excited when my boss first gave me the opportunity to come, and now the furthest thing from my mind is work. So how in the world did that happen?"

"I have a confession, you have the same effect on me. I have a lot to get done, but spending time with you seems to be taking over my motivation."

Tangie felt emboldened by his admission. "Eric, if you are ever in the DC area, please look me up. I'd like to spend more time with you, if you're available. I've enjoyed your company tremendously."

Eric had been listening quietly and intently until her last statement. Suddenly his eyes lost their twinkle. *Is this the kiss-off?*

He looked at her with a pained expression. "Tangie, I like you a lot, probably much more than I should for such a short relationship. Is there a reason you don't want to see me . . . give us a chance? I would never have asked to see you if I didn't want more. I'm not that kind of man, Tangie."

Eric raked his hands through his hair. "We have plenty of time to get to know each other better. There's something special about the way you look at me. You know as well as I do that we've got something going here."

"Eric, it's not that I don't like you or I'm unwilling to explore where we can go. I just don't want to get hurt. I was so wrapped up in my other relationship that I didn't know if I was coming or going. Forgive me if I'm just very protective of my heart. Can you understand?"

Tangie pulled her hands out of his. "If you just want something physical, I'm not the one. I have to have more than that. I know we didn't talk about this kind of stuff before, but that's the way I feel."

"I don't mean commitment now, I'm not rushing things."

Tangie was flustered now and felt like she'd really stuck her foot in her mouth.

Eric looked down, then looked at her. All he wanted to do was run his fingers through her hair. "Tangie, I know how rough it can be. One thing I've learned though is that we can't go on living in the past. Tangie, all we ever have is today."

He paused. "A very good friend of mine convinced me of that during some pretty dark moments in my life. It's a long story I'll tell you about one day soon."

Eric looked away for a moment. His mind seemed to be racing a mile a minute and his chest felt constricted. He didn't want to lose Tangie already—they were just getting started.

"I'm almost thirty-five years old. I know who I am and what I want. Please don't take me for one of those strung-out, confused brothers. I make decisions and stand by them. I'm not an alcoholic . . . a drug addict . . . I don't have a girlfriend, and I don't have a wife or kids!"

Eric was on a roll now. "My HIV test six months ago was negative and although I am celibate right now, for the record, I don't make a habit of engaging in unprotected sex. My last confession was late last year, and yes, I love my mother and my country."

Tangie was taken aback by his tone. Should she kiss him or slap him?

She wasn't trying to pick a fight with him. She'd fully expected that he wouldn't mind the out that she was giving him. How could they pretend to have a future in a long-distance relationship?

Tangie started slowly. "Eric, I am extremely attracted to you, way more than I should be for a guy I've known for less than a week. Believe me, I fully understand that you are a man and I'm not questioning your masculinity or manhood, but where do we go from here?"

She sighed and started looking around her. Most of the other patrons had left and the band was now packing up. "Okay, so I'll see you on Thursday after you conclude your business and then I leave here on Sunday. Tell me honestly, will I ever see you after that?"

She knew she was getting in over her head, but she had to be realistic. What kind of future does a week-old long-distance relationship really have?

Eric looked at her and nodded. His anger had dissipated, but he remained firm in his position. "That's a legitimate concern, Tangie, one that you might have voiced instead of just trying to dismiss me. I don't like being toyed with and I don't like games," Eric said evenly.

"To answer your question though, as two successful people, where we go from here is entirely up to us. I can come to DC or we can meet here in New Orleans, Atlanta, or anywhere else for that matter. There's always the Internet, e-mail, snail mail, or even the telephone. My company has a branch office in Virginia and I'm willing to relocate if I know that you are going to give me a chance. Don't shut me out, Tangie," he pleaded.

"You know, you really are cocky. Are you this self-assured and this passionate when you are pursuing insurance defrauders or whatever you guys call them? Aren't you supposed to be in the stage where you're trying to woo me? I'm feeling a lack of wooing here."

He blew out an exasperated breath. Would she always get to him like this? he wondered.

Eric was contrite. "You're right and I apologize. Let's not waste precious time fighting. I want the time we spend together to be meaningful. I want to spend all my time figuring out what pleases you, then doing it. I guess it's my job to make you feel as comfortable and cared for as I can."

He gave her a carnal look. "In my defense, if you didn't look so good in that dress I might be able to think straight."

Eric reached for her hands again and noticed that they were shaking slightly under his touch. He spoke low and intimately to her. "Right now all I know is that I don't want to lose you. This could be the start of something really special between us. You may be afraid of totally losing yourself in someone, but for me it has been so long since I cared about someone that I relish the thought of you becoming more important than my job. I do want to get lost in you."

Tangie remained silent, not wanting to break the spell of his hypnotic words.

"Tangie, you are so beautiful. I love the way you fit in your clothes, and I must admit my overactive imagination wants to know how you look out of them as well. I love your hair, your soft skin, your mouth, and even your toes poking out of those sandals you're wearing.

"Don't get me wrong though, the attraction is definitely more than physical. I just wanted you to know how much you make me sweat." Another stroke on her hand.

"I'm going to have very lustful dreams about you tonight." Eric was searing her soul with his eyes.

Did the temperature just go up a few hundred degrees? Tangie thought if her body felt tingly before, after listening to Eric just now and seeing the look in his eye, she was on fire. Embarrassed he would know what was on her mind and how the ache was back in her feminine core, she remained mute. She needed some time to collect herself. Eric had put all of her senses on overload.

Eric misread her lack of response and thought he had been too offensive. Chagrined, he said, "I'm sorry, I ugh . . . What I mean to say is . . . Tangie, I didn't mean to be insensitive. I just want you to know what's on my mind. Will you forgive me?"

Tangie recovered quickly. "I'm okay, you didn't offend me, and I . . . uh, just have a lot on my mind."

They got up together and headed toward the exit. The staff seemed relieved that they were finally leaving. No one wanted to be there all night.

When they reached Eric's car, he looked at her with twinkling eyes and a devilish grin. "We can cancel coffee, but I won't cancel this."

Before she could react, Eric's lips were on hers and his hands were gently caressing her bare arms and shoulders. He pulled her closer to him so he could taste her sweetness. Tangie's body responded without hesitation. Their kisses became more passionate and they become lost in the wonderful sensations. Unbidden moans escaped Tangie's lips—her traitorous body was giving Eric the reaction he wanted. Passion swelled between them.

Tangie's nipples distended, pushing up against the fabric of her dress. She let out soft cries as Eric's tongue plunged deeper in her mouth. His kisses bruised her lips and sent heat flowing along her chin and neck in the trail he was making down her soft skin.

Soon there would be no turning back as his hands began to explore her forbidden areas. Tangie arched her back as she felt the soft touch of Eric's hands against her breast caressing her hot flesh.

She pressed toward him, wrapping one leg around his to feel all of him. Her hips swayed gently as she pressed into his aroused bulge. She knew she was playing with fire now and she was at the point that she didn't care.

This time Eric groaned. He kissed her deeper and pulled her close. His need for her was growing by the second and he didn't know how much of a gentleman he could be if they continued much longer.

There they were in the parking lot of the restaurant acting like two love-starved teens and neither seemed to care a bit.

Eric was the first to regain his composure, though it took every bit of his willpower to do so. He wanted to be inside her, making love to her. But he wasn't sixteen again and he knew better.

"Tangie," he said, releasing a deep sigh, "as much as I want you right now, I think we'd better stop. In a few minutes I won't be responsible for my actions."

They finally pulled away from each other, panting for air and flushed with excitement.

Tangie should have been embarrassed by her wanton behavior, but something about Eric Duval brought out the vixen in her and made her want to take chances. Her earlier objections and questions about their relationship seemed to evaporate when he touched her.

For Eric, being with Tangie was a dream come true. The timing was awful, but he knew that he had found a woman he could treasure. It was the mix of what she did to him emotionally and physically that made her so appealing to him. She made him feel alive.

While he had to admit that it had been a long while since he had made love to anyone and he didn't know how much longer he could wait, he knew that he wanted it to be with Tangie.

Eric chastised himself for his current behavior because he usually had his thoughts of physical need under control, but being with her made him want to lose all restraint, loving her through the night. He wanted to please Tangie, giving her everything that she wanted. He would be fulfilled just being with her, waking up next to her, but knew that would have to wait. He wanted Tangie when she was ready for him and he knew it was too soon for her, no matter how much they wanted each other physically.

Eric wanted to make sure that they were on solid ground. Tangie was going to have to learn to trust him and be willing to give herself to him completely. He didn't want her to be afraid of anything with him.

They needed more time to be with each other and he also knew that they had much more to find out about each other. There was the stumbling block of his job, something that would have to be overcome before he could truly give of himself to her. After he finished the case, then he would explain everything to her. The thought was making him anxious to get it over and done with.

Tangie straightened out her dress as best she could. It would be hopelessly ruined in some places. *So not only does he stop me from eating my delicious dessert, but now he ruins my wardrobe,* she thought.

She eased back into her seat, still looking flushed and feeling flustered.

Why was he so damned attractive! He was weakening her resolve with every minute they were together. She couldn't make love with him and leave.

They looked at each other and smiled a sheepish, slightly embarrassed, *what are we doing?* smile.

"Are you okay?" he asked

She nodded and soon they were again gliding through traffic in his car. They made the drive back to her hotel in relative silence. Tangie watched the city from her car window, which was slightly cracked, letting a tantalizingly warm breeze wash over her. She was beginning to see why people fell in love with New Orleans. The city had a soul and an energy about it that couldn't quite be described.

In what seemed like no time at all they were back at her hotel.

She had resolved to calm her hormones down and not have a repeat of the restaurant scene. She leaned over to give him a light peck on the lips good-bye, but mischief got the best of her and she gave him a pas-

sionate full-mouthed kiss instead. Then she opened
the car door to leave, but not before she heard a
barely audible moan escape from his lips. She was still
smiling when she reached her room.

Once inside she noticed her message light blink-
ing, but was too tired to be bothered. She figured it
was probably Candy or her mom, but they would have
to wait until the next day.

Tangie lay down spread-eagled on the bed and
thought about Eric. He made her ridiculously giddy
and stirred passion and emotion in her that she
thought was long since buried.

She noticed that her nipples yearned for his touch,
and her mouth missed him already, his kisses burned
in her memory. Moreover, her new silk panties were
ruined!

When the phone rang twenty minutes later, Tangie
answered on the first ring. "Hello, Mr. Duval, I see
you made it home safely."

"Oh, is that you, Tangie? Guess I must have dialed
the wrong number."

"Eric, you are such a rat. I had a good time tonight."

"Me too, thank you for going out with me. I'm
sorry that things got a little hairy earlier. I want to
be with you, Tangie, and not just in a physical way.

"I know my schedule has been crazy and I really appreciate you hanging in there with me. I don't want
you to think that I'm taking you for granted." Eric
sighed. "I would love to talk with you all night, but it's
late, so go ahead and get some rest. I'll be thinking of
you."

Tangie felt warm and tingly again. She knew she
would be thinking of him too. It seemed as if he were

permanently etched in her brain now. "I'll be thinking of you too. Good night, Mr. Duval."

On day three of their New Orleans tour, they spent time exploring the French Quarter. They listened to music at one of the record stores, a passion they both seemed to share, ate praline samples at the Cooking School store, and walked down the historic cobblestone streets.

Tangie loved many of the African artifacts she found at an open-air market. The woodwork and detail were exquisite, from letter openers to door statues. She ran her fingers over the wood carvings, the images giving her the feeling of connection to her ancestors.

Eric watched Tangie as she went from baskets to maracas to chairs. She was beautiful, he thought to himself. He watched the way her eyes shone when she was really excited about a piece, the way she tucked errant hairs behind her ears, and especially the gentle glide of her hips when she walked.

He felt that familiar pull in his groin as he watched the sun dance lightly on her hair, leaving sparkling brownish red highlights to tantalize his senses. He liked the way she had styled it today. He could just imagine running his fingers through her silken mass of curls. When she looked up at him and smiled, Eric thought he would lose it.

Eric and Tangie continued their stroll up and down the streets of the French Quarter, from Charles to Bourbon and what seemed like every street in between. They stopped in quaint little shops and for lemonade. The weather was typical New Orleans humid, and by the time they reached the hotel they were both overheated and exhausted.

"You want to hit the lounge? As usual when I'm around you, I find myself quite parched. You really do something to me, lady," Eric teased as he headed in the direction of the bar.

"Is that a fact? I seem to notice the heat always goes up a few notches when I'm around you too. How about some margaritas?" Tangie suggested. "No alcohol for me though. I don't want to get too light-headed in all this heat."

Their walking tour had been wonderful, but the early summer New Orleans weather was taking its toll. After last night, they decided to play it safe and keep to public places. They didn't want passion to win out over common sense. It would be very easy to let the relationship become physical before the emotional was truly explored.

Eric mused when he looked at her, *There is something to be said for leaving common sense aside.* He watched her mouth, wanting to kiss her lips and revel in their lush sweetness.

They talked for hours until Tangie decided to call it a night. She wanted to spend as much time as she could with Eric, but she also knew she had to be awake for her conference in the morning.

He couldn't possibly know what he did to her whenever she looked at him. Tangie was going to have to figure out a way to get her libido to cooperate. She was too old to start acting like some love/sex-starved teenybopper. She needed to try to stay in control of her physical desires. At least until she got to know him a little better, she thought. Ohhh, but he did make it hard for her, especially when he looked deep into her eyes and called her name with that sexy voice of his.

Eric didn't want the evening to end either, but he knew they both had responsibilities. He, for one, was working on one of the biggest cases of his life. He needed to think about what exactly he was doing. Tangie had him thinking foreign thoughts like wishing he were working a regular nine-to-five. Like wishing after the case was finished, he was coming home to her. Like wishing she would be his.

Chapter 5

Tangie was exhausted by the time she got into bed, but she still slept fitfully. She had spent a wonderful evening with Eric and felt good about where they were headed. Yeah, it had been rough for a minute, but they had worked it out and for now they were going to take it slow. She dreamed of making love to Eric, then Rodney, and then things just became a blur.

When she woke up at 4:00 A.M., she felt weird. She didn't understand why she kept thinking about Rodney. The thought of making love to Eric was pleasant, but what did the rest of it mean? Her grandmother interpeted dreams. She wished she could call her to find out what this one meant.

That thought brought a smile to her face and she started to settle down. She went to sleep again with comforting thoughts of her family on her mind. She needed to call her mom. She hadn't spoken with her since she'd arrived in town. She needed to let her know the city was everything she had expected and more.

Tangie drifted into a deep sleep, never noticing the dark figure on her balcony.

* * *

Tangie was the subject of intense scrutiny at FBI headquarters, where several men sat in a conference room.

"So who is she?" Agent Spates asked.

"As far as we can tell, sir, no one really. Just some woman from Virginia, here for a geek conference," said Agent Jordan.

"I see cultural diversity training was a waste of money for you."

"Sorry, sir, the agent in question and the subject were first sighted together near Johnny's Po-Boys in the Quarter and then again tonight."

"Here, these are the surveillance photos," said Agent Jordan. "Other than some serious kissing and some touchy-feely stuff it doesn't appear that there is much to the relationship. We don't think they knew each other prior to this contact. She's two years his junior and everything about her checks out in Virginia."

Agent Jordan opened a manila file folder. "Here's the information that we've gathered so far, driver's license, birth certificate, Social Security card, right down to her library card. On the surface she appears clean and not involved in the operation."

Jordan paused after putting all the information on the table. He knew he had messed up by being insensitive. Agent Spates was next in line for a high-profile promotion if he didn't retire, and he usually mopped up the floor with agents who did not perform. Jordan's palms were sweaty as he waited for the butt chewing he assumed was coming.

Spates regarded the young agent coolly. Sometimes fear was the best punishment. "Good, let's keep it that way, we don't want any civilian casualties. Keep the surveillance on her until she leaves. When she returns, have the Virginia boys watch her for a week. If those two don't make contact, close her file."

Agent Spates's tone became more serious. "Now fill me in completely on what our man is doing. Where is he and has the meeting been set up yet?"

Jordan cleared his throat nervously. "As far as we know, sir, everything has been set. There, uh . . . have been some minor gaps in the surveillance. We do know that he has also been driving his personal vehicle and that all tracking devices have been removed. Nonetheless, we have been able to track his movements; an Acura NSX-T is not that common a car, even in a big city like New Orleans. We expect to know what is going on soon."

Agent Spates snorted, "Ninety-two thousand dollars for a car? I can't believe that crap. Almost a hundred grand for aluminum," he said incredulously. "If I didn't know him so well, I'd start to believe his press too."

"Sir, Eric is a good man, all of his accounts are in order. We all know he is a stand-up guy. Otherwise he never would have been brought in for this assignment," Agent Jordan reminded him gently.

"Easy, easy, I'm on your side. I've known Eric and his family for years. I guess I'm a little edgy because I don't like this case. Cops are supposed to serve and protect—not serve up a scapegoat like these clowns are doing."

"I want to see the reports that you have on Avery and Williams again. There's more going on than meets the eye. I can feel it. Eric needs to stay close and keep us informed. Get a message to him to come in or tell me what the hell is going on."

"Yes, sir. Do you want me to use the regular channels or go out of the zone?"

Spates rubbed his chin. "No, let's not do anything

in the routine. If he has run into trouble, I don't want to give his position away. Let me know the minute you hear from him."

"This case gives me the creeps because it makes you wonder about other cities. How widespread is the corruption?"

"If this thing goes sour, I don't know if we can get to him in time. Duval is virtually on his own and with some of the dirtiest cops that New Orleans's finest has to offer. Keep me posted and, Jordan . . . I don't expect any more surveillance gaps."

"Yes, sir!"

Spates sat at his desk again when Agent Jordan left. Eric had always been one of his favorite agents and he had a soft spot for him. Eric was dedicated, hard-working, and dependable, but more than that he was like a son to him. Spates was always more concerned about members of the Special Corruption Unit. He liked to keep close tabs on his agents when they were working on cases. They rarely played by the rules and definitely had their own way of doing things, which got results, but always caused him great stress.

His agents playing fast and loose was totally different from the information in the case files sitting on his desk. Several members of the New Orleans Police Department were engaged in illegal activities and under suspicion. So far, the FBI had been able to uncover a network of at least thirty officers in and around the state, mostly within a five-county area. It appeared that they were collectively responsible for the beatings, deaths, and rapes of several people. They had also contributed significantly to the drug traffic and trade as well as money laundering by local Mafia groups. These officers were a disgrace to the force, but it took more than suspicion to bring them down. Their tentacles spread throughout the city like a virus, and the unit had to tread lightly in order to pull off the operation.

Eric had been called in as a drug dealer with connections all over the East Coast. He was sent to make a deal with the officers for one of the largest drug hauls that had been seized in police history. This was major and only the mayor and the upper echelon of the FBI were aware of the sting. No one at the police department was told because there were too many suspects involved.

The information indicated that Detectives Avery and McCollum were the main targets. They were involved in a casino scam that made the Gambino network look like child's play. The Bureau was going with the sure case though. The casino scam was so big, they weren't even certain who was involved. Attempts to infiltrate the organization had been met with good cops turning up dead and missing informants. Eric, through his persona of Eric Duval, emerging drug lord, had been able to negotiate a very big drug shipment. He was just waiting to find out when the deal was supposed to go down. His contacts at the police station had been very cagey, never providing him with details and always questioning his ability to get the merchandise.

Avery and Williams had been identified as the culprits in two of the city's most heinous crimes, and their network was spreading. This sting was about more than just dirty cops, it was about redemption for the force.

Chapter 6

Tangie woke up at 7:30 A.M. to get ready for her conference. She decided on a gray two-piece suit. She always liked the look of gray, it made her look sophisticated. Next, a red silk shell to add a punch of color. Pleased with her appearance, Tangie prepared to attend the first workshop, motivation and recruitment.

But despite her best efforts, by the time she made it to the workshop area all she could think about was seeing Eric.

The last two days had been a blur. She had attended all the sessions, but all she managed to accomplish was a few doodles on a notepad about Eric.

She would have to pay better attention in the workshops for the remainder of the conference so that she would be able to tell her boss Cliff that she had learned something while she was away. Thankfully, Tangie had always been a good note taker. Today she promised herself that she would place special emphasis on whatever the speakers had to say, no matter how boring.

Tangie studied what she had written and hoped sincerely that it made sense. Throughout the day she zoned in and out of the sessions. The Franklin Covey session had been informative and she found very useful time-management tips she could use with her staff.

Promptly at 5:30 P.M. Tangie was excusing herself from her colleagues. She had done better than expected and she had even managed to carry on intelligent conversations with a few people.

She had been thinking about him so often that she'd forgotten that she wasn't going to see him tonight. She could still feel his hands caressing her and those thoughts sent chills up and down her body. "Get a grip, girl," she said aloud. The woman in the elevator stared at her cooly. "Oh no, not you, I'm just talking to myself. Excuse me."

Tangie didn't quite know whether to stay in or go out and see the sights. She still had some of her New Orleans brochures sitting in her room. Eric had been a wonderful guide but there was still so much to see. A week was definitely not enough time to see the city, probably not even three weeks.

Before meeting Eric, she had planned on taking pictures and buying souvenirs. Now was a good time to do that and spend some quality time alone.

She spread the brochures out on the bed and pored over each one. Several minutes later Tangie decided on the Natchez Riverboat tour. It was perfect, she could take pictures, eat, and collect a few trinkets to take back with her. She called the concierge to arrange for her tickets.

With an hour to relax before her outing, she put on her favorite robe, pushed the mess over, and just plopped down on the bed. After about ten minutes of resting, Tangie started to feel guilty about not checking her messages. There were four—a check-in call from her mom, two from Candy, and one from a

deep-voiced, sultry-sounding Eric telling her he
missed her and wanted to say hello. She loved the way
he said her name.

He was so attentive to her and made her feel so special . . . much more so than Rodney ever had. Of
course, Eric and Rodney were two different people.
She wondered why Rodney was on her mind so much!
It had been two years since she had set eyes on him.

When they broke up, they stopped traveling in the
same circles. Whenever her friends wanted to give her
the ex-boyfriend update, she would change the subject.
Now all of a sudden, she thought about him more on
this trip than in the last several months, and to make
matters worse she had even dreamt about him. Candy
would have a field day with that one. Tangie chuckled
to herself. She had been harping on Tangie to let it go
with Rodney. What would she say if she knew Tangie
was dreaming about him now? That would probably
send her on a tirade for about a week.

No, she thought, Rodney was no longer a consid-
eration in her life, he had been unfaithful. He had
another life. She hoped he and the other woman
were very happy. Tangie didn't owe him anything.
Furthermore, she deserved to be happy. She would
follow this relationship with Eric to the end of the
line. She owed it to herself and Eric to see if they
could make it, and that brought up a whole new set
of issues. Where would they make their life?

She had to consider what changes she was willing
to make in herself for him. Her job was nice, it was secure, but it didn't excite her anymore. If things didn't
work out with the promotion, maybe it was time for a
change of scenery. Especially if it included the sexiest
lips and body known to man.

Tangie laughed to herself. She was always projecting a whole story from the smallest thread of evidence. She mused, maybe she should be a writer. She'd always had a pretty vivid imagination and could fabricate a story on the spot. She and Candy used to take turns trying to fake each other out. Tangie usually won because she appeared to be so serious and Candy always believed her no matter how outlandish the tale.

Tangie's thoughts meandered back to the dinner she and Eric had shared. He sounded so sincere, but was she really up for a long-distance relationship? Tangie knew that they needed to talk more and she wouldn't feel comfortable until they settled some things. There was still so much she didn't know about him, and that worried her. After what she had been through in the past, she wasn't going into this relationship blindly. She told herself, *This is why you have to take it slow—too much gray area in relationships.*

Tangie looked at the clock. There was just enough time for her to change and dash out the door.

Chapter 7

Eric Duval, Eric Johnson, Eric Scott, Eric Stevens, Eric Williams . . . He had so many aliases he wasn't sure who he was anymore. He was sure of one thing though, Tangie. He had to protect her from the world that he worked in. Most agents he knew were on their second marriages, or worse yet, second divorces. They couldn't bring the job home, but somehow it always managed to be there.

How could he explain that he had not been honest with her? That he had lied to her and if they continued in their relationship, it would always have to be that way? He sensed something in her. She was vulnerable and he would never forgive himself if he hurt her.

The adage *you always hurt the one you love* ran through his mind. He didn't want to be responsible for adding to her pain. Eric knew people well. He could tell when people were hiding something or covering up the truth, but with Tangie he sensed something different. *Pain.* She had been wounded.

How could he explain to her that he was part of an elite group of agents who traveled the world cleaning up corruption? That they assumed roles in order to catch criminals, often blurring the lines themselves?

True, the relationship was new, but if things didn't

start out well, it would have no chance for survival and growth. What would she think of him if she knew he had hidden so much of his life from her? Was he being fair to her?

Ironic, how you can't find love when you're looking for it, but it will sure find you when you aren't.

There was so much that he wanted to share with her. He was very proud of his career with the Bureau. Growing up as a State Department brat, he had lived on five of the seven continents.

He spoke four languages, traveled extensively, had an unlimited expense account, and owned a car that cost nearly a hundred grand. His aptitude for languages, combined with his other skills, had made him a prime recruit. The Bureau had contacted him during his final year in law at Georgetown University, which had made his dad, a career diplomat, extremely proud.

Eric was on the fast track at the Bureau. He had an excellent record, closing over 95 percent of his cases. It had only taken him nine years to make a name for himself. Four years ago he was handpicked for the Special Corruption Unit, SCU. In just three years, he'd excelled through the SCU ranks to become team commander. Everyone could see Eric was destined for a plush office with special agents as his beck and call.

In the beginning of his career, everything seemed to be falling into the right places. He was having great success in his work, was recently married to a beautiful young woman, and had a newborn daughter, Erica. Eric's life was a dream come true until one day, tragedy struck on a bright sunny day in Springfield, Virginia.

There was a horrible accident involving his wife and child. His wife, Rebecca, and Erica were on their way to

Springfield Mall to find his first Father's Day gift, but they never made it there. Witnesses said she had her turn signal on and had safely negotiated two lanes, but as soon as she made a move to enter the third lane, an eighteen-wheeler sped up and practically bulldozed her. It clipped her left side, slamming her car into the dividing wall. Rebecca and Erica were killed instantly.

Eric had been overwrought. He didn't want to continue without them and it was a struggle to make it through each day. Suicide had come to mind several times, but he couldn't take his own life. Rebecca had always loved life. She believed in living to the fullest. No, he had convinced himself not to do something so destructive because he knew that Rebecca would never approve. He continued for her.

When the offer came to join the Special Corruption Unit, Eric withdrew from his family and friends and threw himself into training. The next twelve months were a blur. He was on automatic pilot. He rarely showed emotion and completed all tasks with deadly precision. Eric was the perfect agent except in one area. . . .

His psychological evaluation showed he could be wrapped too tight, a ticking bomb. He was passing all the training milestones, but his superiors weren't sure what he would do under extreme emotional stress. No one knew what could trigger a break, and that worried the senior officers.

Agent Spates, his senior agent, watched his progress carefully. Finally, a decision was reached regarding his future in the agency.

Eric's Quantico leadership practically dragged him to see Dr. Wendy Rose, noted psychiatrist. She had been able to save the careers of many officers after they had suffered work-related traumas. Her specialty was in the area of posttraumatic stress disorders.

Her work with Eric had been a tremendous professional challenge. After several painful sessions, she was finally able to crack his armor. Losing his mother, Rebecca, and Erica had created such a hole in his heart that it had taken enormous patience to make progress with him.

Dr. Rose successfully helped him work through his abandonment issues and learn how to trust again. Through intense therapy, he learned how to express emotions other than anger. Doc Wendy, as he called her, became his lifeline, helping him rejoin the human race.

Eric was no longer afraid of his pain, but instead used it as his motivation. After his return to duty, in only six months he finished his first case. He had more than proven himself capable and an integral part of the Special Corruption Unit team. He had established himself not only as part of the team, but also as a leader. He was often allowed to handpick his team members, especially when a mission required several personnel. They sometimes played it fast and loose in order to get things done, but they always got the job done.

Eric was annoyed. . . .

After dropping Tangie off at her hotel he looked across the street and noticed a suspicious-looking parked car. The two occupants weren't doing a good job of being inconspicuous—which meant they probably didn't care if they had been made.

Eric had been in the undercover game too long to be fooled and he could tell they weren't Bureau. He had to assume that they were the target. He had been working this case for over a year and a half and it was finally ending. They were checking him out as much as he was doing the same to them. Communications with his team and the Bureau would have to be limited. Playing it smart was the only way to make sure the people he cared about wouldn't get hurt.

So why did he feel so uneasy?

He couldn't let anything to happen to Tangie.

He felt boxed in and didn't dare make contact with his superiors. The time for the meet had been changed unexpectedly and there was no time to establish a backup plan.

Eric didn't want to play hardball with the officers for fear that their suspicions would call a halt to the deal. He would have to deal with consequences the best way he knew how. He was flying solo on this one and he just prayed it didn't get him killed.

He dismissed the car and drove toward the meeting point. They knew where he was going and would have no trouble keeping up. Eric would have to think fast. He blew out a tense breath.

He made it to the meeting point in enough time to formulate his plan. He didn't see anyone, but he knew that they were probably still watching him. Hence, here he was sitting in a dark alley by himself pondering the idea of giving up his career for Tangie. Could he really work a nine-to-five again, drive a Volvo, pick up kids from soccer games, and go to the theater? He didn't know if he could believe in the white picket fence again.

The loss of the first time was much too painful, but for Tangie he would try anything.

Chapter 8

Tangie sat on her balcony watching the stars. The air was warm as it wrapped around her like a comfortable blanket. She was really starting to enjoy the thought of Eric being in her life, but there was no point in starting the relationship with secrets and lies. They would have to be totally honest with each other to make things work. Tangie would have to take the chance that Eric was an understanding man and that he wanted to be with her no matter what.

As painful as that thought was she would have to tell him about one of her greatest fears.

She made up her mind. They would talk as soon as the time seemed right. She sipped on her lemonade, more from nervousness than from thirst.

Years later, her memories of Rodney still had the same effect. It was almost impossible to think of loving someone like that again.

Her subconscious didn't listen though. The floodgates of that night had been opened, and it seemed they had a mind of their own. She couldn't stem their tide, and once again she was transported to years ago. Chills ran down her body as she thought about that night. Whenever she thought about her ex, it was the same reaction. Tangie couldn't shake the funk that would surround her.

So much had remained unspoken between them that there was no closure. His silence toward her had nearly been her undoing. There were so many questions and only he had the answers. She had never known if the breakup was due to her medical condition or if he had simply fallen out of love with her.

Tangie shivered. Rodney's rejection had shaken her to the core. Three years was a long time to throw away.

Now, here she was contemplating her future with a wonderful man. She needed to tell him that there was a possibility she could never give him children. She hoped it wouldn't destroy the prospects of their newfound happiness.

Tangie breathed deeply. She listened to the sounds of the Quarter. There was life everywhere. Couples and groups meandered along the streets laughing and talking. Occasionally she would hear loud voices or strained whispers. Lovers' quarrels, she surmised. The tears were gone now . . . She told herself she needed to leave the past in the past and just trust in her future.

Maybe now, with someone to share her life, she could get past those old demons.

Slowly the realization hit her—she loved Eric. She couldn't stand the thought of losing him.

His words echoed in her head. "Right now, all I know is that I don't want to lose you."

"I hope you mean that, Eric," she whispered into the darkness.

Tired from her long day, Tangie slunk to bed. She prayed for sleep, not wanting another restless night.

She just had to trust him. She loved Eric Duval and that was all that really mattered. This had turned into some trip—the conference, the promotion, and Eric. She adjusted her two pillows again and this time, slowly drifted off to sleep.

Chapter 9

Eric chastised himself for being distracted. He would have plenty of time to think about Volvos after this case was finished, he hoped. But for right now he had a case to close. Checking his watch again, he realized that he had less than thirty minutes to get to the right pier, so he would have to move quickly.

Breathing deeply, he got out of his car and leaned against the hood. All thoughts of Tangie were out of his head. He was Eric Duval, totally and completely. He took out a pack of cigarettes, lit one, and smoked it very slowly, never having developed a taste for it. This was all part of the role he was playing—the persona of Duval.

Butterflies danced in the pit of his stomach. He felt more than just the usual adrenaline pumping. He knew this case was one of his more dangerous, and his senses were heightened as he waited for the show to begin.

As he lingered, warm air beaded sweat across his brow. This was a typical New Orleans night. Hot, humid, and steamy.

After a few minutes, his eyes became adjusted to the dark and he noticed shadows moving around. Through years of training he sensed them rather than saw them. Eric figured there were at least two men on the tin roof of the warehouse, probably expert marksmen, two farther down the pier, and probably two more at the exit. He knew for sure that he was boxed in.

The plan had come to him as he was driving to the meeting point. Without backup, he had to improvise. Spates would be furious, but he had no other way. Eric wasn't in control of the timeline. They had told him when to meet and he didn't want to jeopardize the deal. He knew he had to be ready when they called; they weren't too sure about him, and hesitation might be cause for suspicion.

He waited patiently as four cops approached him from down the pier. Even though they didn't come into full view until about twenty yards away, Eric knew they were coming. One of the officers even had the audacity to wear his uniform.

They approached Eric cautiously. He recognized two of the four, and he guessed the two new officers were just for a show of force. His main targets, rather his contacts, were Avery and Williams.

The Special Corruption Unit had been called in to bust a ring of dirty cops. They were veteran cops who, fed up with never having enough money, time, or resources to fight crime, turned to it. Jaded and without proper leadership, they turned to the very same types of crime that they were supposed to abhor. They had all become willing participants in it and Eric was sent in to make a drug deal. He had been playing the role of an out-of-town major player. He was believable because he had enough local connections to make him less of a stranger. The thought of them and the illegal activities they had been involved in made his stomach churn. He wanted Avery and Williams off the streets for good.

The crew of officers turned out to be the biggest thieves, rapists, murderers, and drug dealers that the city of New Orleans had to offer.

Eric noticed that it was Williams in uniform. He supposed that was in case things went sour. It would be his job to take Eric down officially and get a nice collar for the drugs and the money.

Avery, obviously in charge, spoke first. "Ah, Mr. Duval, prompt as usual. I assume you came ready to play?"

The younger two men, Bullock and McCollum, were being initiated tonight. This was a how-to-make-a-deal night for them. The network within the police department was becoming deeper and more dangerous. Police corruption and police brutality were almost as commonplace as crime and criminals. It was the job of the SCU to investigate those tarnishing the name of police work and bring them to justice. The investigation had been long, painful, and hard on everyone involved. Eric would be particularly pleased to get out of Louisiana and be finished with the case. He loved what he did too much to tolerate those who took advantage of their position; officers like Avery and Williams disgusted him.

"I'm always ready to play." Eric looked around and asked coolly, "Expecting trouble?"

"A smart man always expects trouble and is ready to handle it," Avery replied with a slight Louisiana drawl. "Bullock, pat him down. I don't like surprises."

Officer Bullock nodded and approached Eric.

Eric gave him a cold glare. "Make it quick. I don't know where your filthy hands have been."

Bullock winked. "Don't worry, sweetheart, I promise not to enjoy myself too much."

Avery watched in amusement. "But enough of this small talk, we are all very busy men. What do you have for us, Mr. Duval?"

Eric contemplated his cigarette. "Didn't your mama ever tell you patience is a virtue?"

Eric took one last drag on his cigarette before tossing it to the ground. He painstakingly ground it with his shoe. Then he gave them a humorless smile and gently eased back to the trunk of the car. He opened it and produced two black nylon duffel bags that were full of cash.

Eric had been driving around the city with $1.5 million in large bills in his trunk for most of the evening.

The officers had specifically asked for large bills because of their very efficient money-laundering scheme through the local casinos. Avery and Williams were connected to half a dozen gambling establishments; the money changed hands so frequently that there was no way for the Bureau to trace it.

Williams spoke for the first time, saying, "Show me the money" with a rancorous laugh, like in the *Jerry Maguire* movie.

Eric had had enough. He needed to get out of there before things went terribly wrong, and the longer the meeting lasted, the more at risk he became. He shifted his stance so that he could keep an eye on everyone. Then he looked pointedly at the quartet and his voice turned to ice.

"Detective Avery, these bags are filled with C-4 explosive and if you want to live to slap your old lady around another day, follow my instructions to the letter. Have those two clowns on the roof drop their weapons to the ground and then come down here where I can see them better."

He pointed down the wharf. "Have the two on the pier and blocking the exit get into that trawler and set out on the water."

Avery looked at Eric in incredulity. He didn't know whether to believe him or not; nonetheless he started slowly moving as Eric told him to.

Eric continued in the same even tone, "Have your two protégés get back into your vehicle and you two come with me.

"Avery, since you seem to be the HNIC, I will hold you personally responsible for any slipups. I hope I am making myself perfectly clear, because I don't intend to repeat myself. Oh, did I fail to mention that I'm the detonator?"

Eric opened his lightweight jacket to show them his proof. "If you lay a hand on me, we all go up in a blaze of glory and this wharf will look like the Chinese New Year was just ushered in. Any questions?"

Eric looked around to see what the men were doing.

"Move!" he barked.

The four men looked at each other, then Eric, and Avery decided by the look in his eyes he wasn't bluffing. He narrowed his eyes and spurted out in anger, "You're a dead man. You think you can come to my town and walk all over my organization. You're dead!"

Avery then signaled to his men to follow Eric's orders, and in ten minutes they were where he had told them to go. When Avery and Williams were seated in his car and the cocaine and money in his trunk, he knocked them both out with the butt of his .38 and radioed Senior Agent Spates.

"We've got containment. Sir, I need a team at Pier 17," he told him.

Eric drove the two policemen to what the unit referred to as "the warehouse" where they would be questioned. The details of their organization would be discovered and the two officers would never be heard from again. That's the way the SCU worked. No loose ends.

In his report Eric would let brass know that he'd had to think fast once the meeting began. There was no C-4, but the case had gotten away from him and he had to regain control quickly since he was working without his usual backup. Avery had called the meeting before he could set things up properly and call Agent Jordan to report his status. He didn't delay because he hadn't wanted the officers to become suspicious.

In the debrief he would catch hell, but he couldn't worry about it. He only had one thing on his mind. One person, that is.

It was ten o'clock the next morning when Eric finally finished his report, and he was exhausted. He had to stay focused long enough to talk with his superior officer.

The senior agent called him into his office after he read the report. He was seated in Agent Spate's office ready to discuss the case.

Eric could tell by his demeanor that he was not pleased.

"Okay . . . what the hell happened? All of a sudden you're the lone friggin' ranger?"

The pain in Eric's head began just behind his left eye. He knew he deserved the butt chewing he was about to get.

Spates continued, "You didn't follow procedure at all

during this entire operation and you could have compromised not only yourself, but this entire unit. You were outnumbered and outgunned! If you or the bags had been searched . . ." He blew out a ragged breath.

"Look, I know you've been distracted lately, but that's no excuse for almost getting yourself and others killed. Did you ever stop to think what would have happened if they hadn't bought it? It could have gone very badly. You know as well as I do how serious this business is. We have never been able to locate Officer Owen's body."

Spates sat on the edge of his desk. He looked at Eric somberly before continuing. He didn't want to continue down this path with Eric, but he had a responsibility to the greater good. If he lost Eric, he would have to make the adjustment.

"You need to decide right here and right now where your priorities are. We don't fly solo unless under orders. You are either with this unit or out of it. We can't afford it any other way!"

Eric sat pensive for a few minutes. The thoughts were coming so fast that he didn't trust himself to speak.

He looked at Agent Spates. He wouldn't try to defend his actions. He had gotten the job done, albeit not the way he was trained to and certainly not the way that was in the best interest of the team. The bad guys were put away, the case solved, and really, wasn't that all that mattered?

No, Eric knew it. The time had come.

He began slowly, deliberately . . .

"Sir, this unit has been my life for the past six years. I have given it my all, and now I figure it's time. I guess I didn't want to admit it to myself, but I'm ready, I want out. I want to be reassigned."

The two men looked at each other in silence for several minutes. Agent Spates softened his approach. This wasn't quite what he had had in mind. He'd just wanted Eric to become more focused. "Is this what you really want, son? You know the consequences of leaving the unit."

Eric looked down before continuing. "Yeah, I know I need to debrief at Quantico and that our relationship will have to be severed, but that's the way it has to be. There's another part of my life that I need to focus on right now, and I realize that after yesterday's performance I really can't have it both ways."

Eric sighed loudly, understanding the enormity of the decision he just made. He knew it was the right thing to do, but doing this was more scary than dealing with the supposed bad guys. He really hoped Tangie cared about him the way he did her.

Spates looked at his "second son" fondly. "I respect your decision . . . and I wish you two all the best. I know how hard it is to make a relationship work in this business."

Eric looked at his mentor curiously. Yeah, Spates probably knew everything by now. *He probably knows more about Tangie than I do.* Eric had accepted that he didn't really have a life while undercover, but all that would change now. He was about to embark on a different journey. He would allow himself to have a real life for the first time in years. The SCU had been his safe haven while he recovered from his past hurt and pain. Now it was truly time to enter a new stage in life.

Despite his disappointment Spates was proud of him. He smiled at him. "You're a different person from the day you first landed here with us, Eric. I'm going to miss you, but I'll go ahead and make your transfer arrangements. I guess I always knew. Always hoped this day would come. Meet me Friday at 11:00 A.M. to discuss the final arrangements. I need to make some phone calls. They're going to love having you back at HQ.

"Good luck, buddy. I hope she realizes what a good catch she has." Agent Spates stood up to clap Eric on the back. "This young lady of yours must be pretty special."

Eric looked at him, his eyes shining brightly. "Yes, she is. I would never consider making this transition unless I had a good reason. You know that I respect you as much as my own father, sir. Your faith in me has meant everything. Nevertheless, I think we possess that internal clock that lets us know when the time has come. I can tell you though, a year ago I could never have predicted this."

Chapter 10

Tangie woke up feeling sore and out of sorts. The emotional upheaval she'd experienced over the course of the past two days was beginning to take its toll on her both physically and emotionally. She didn't like the feeling . . . it reminded her very much of her time with Rodney. Things would have to be different this time. She couldn't go backward. She rolled over in the bed and looked at the clock. She was supposed to meet Eric soon, and at the rate she was going she'd never make it.

"So much for being on time," she said aloud. "Where are you, Eric? I need to see you!"

Eric was driven to the Marriott Hotel by one of the younger agents. It was policy not to return home after the closure of a case for forty-eight hours in case of security leaks. He didn't dare make contact with her, but he felt better just being close to her. He knew the surveillance would continue until he returned to Quantico.

With the case over, he could check in as Eric Duvernay. He was now minus the fancy clothes, cigarettes, and player attitude. His fingers itched to call Tangie, but he was so exhausted he couldn't begin to hold a conversation with her.

Besides, all he really wanted to do was hold her in his arms. He carried that thought with him to bed. After the young agent checked out the hotel room, Eric slipped under the covers and slept fully clothed for the next few hours.

In the darkness, he awoke with a start; he was still a little disoriented and had to remember where he was and why. He looked at the clock. He hoped he could still catch her in the room. His heart was in his throat as he dialed room 506.

His voice was still thick with sleep when he spoke. "Tangie, it's Eric, I'm sorry I'm calling so—"

"Eric, is that you? Oh, thank God, I thought something terrible had happened to you. I thought I would hear from you before now. Where have you been?" Tangie demanded.

Eric noticed that her voice sounded shrill as she talked. "So this is how you sound when you are worried. Glad I found out now. Baby, could you put a little more bass into it?" He knew she was serious, but he couldn't help himself.

Tangie was fuming. "Eric, that's not funny! I was worried something heinous had happened to you— I've had this sinking feeling in the pit of my stomach all evening. Where have you been?"

Repentant, Eric responded, "I'm sorry, Tangie, truly I am. I closed out that case that I was telling you about late yesterday. I didn't call because I was exhausted, but I don't want to talk about that now. I missed the sound of your voice. Did you really miss me, Tangie?"

"You are the most cocky, most irritating, most—"

"Okay, okay, I get the picture, but you know these

things are all part of my irresistible charm. Do you mind if we have a late dinner in the lobby restaurant? I'm sure they make a decent blackened catfish or red snapper. I'm starved for both food and you."

Tangie relented. "Yes, I missed you. I haven't been able to stop thinking about you. I'd like to talk to you about something important when I see you."

Eric took a deep breath. Yes, they would have a lot to talk about before she headed back to Virginia.

"Now that this case is over, I can concentrate all my considerable energies on you."

Noticing the flirtatious tone in his voice, Tangie backed down more and softened a bit. "Okay . . . you win, but don't get too used to it. I'm just glad you're all right. I had the strangest feeling about you and I was so worried."

Eric couldn't resist the urge to tease her more, now that her mood had improved. "By the way, young lady, no more stunts like you pulled the other night. I have you to thank for another sleepless night. Next time you do something like that I may have to turn you over my knee."

"Promises, promises. Besides, I'd say we're even, Mr. Duval, especially after all you put me through yesterday and today. Now, my only regret is that I didn't do more to you."

"Evil woman. Are you trying to make me putty in your hands?"

Tangie wanted to see him, and soon—she needed to feel his arms around her. She wouldn't feel whole again until he gave her one of his pounding, soul-stirring kisses.

She continued, "Fish sounds great. By the way, you still owe me a napoleon since I couldn't finish mine the day I met you. You had me so distracted that I couldn't even finish my dessert. Are you close by?" she asked, smiling into the phone.

It was Eric's turn to smile. "Yep, I'm two floors down in room 310. I'm staying in the hotel for a couple of days. I'll explain when I see you. By the way, I chose two floors away because I couldn't trust myself to be any closer to you. I also didn't want to give you an opportunity to exploit my virtue."

"You wish, Mr. Duval, you wish."

"I was exhausted when I first checked in, but I am raring to go now. Do you think you can keep up with me?" he teased.

Tangie was curious about what was going on, but decided to hold her doubt in check. She wanted to give Eric a chance and besides, she was sure that there was a perfectly good explanation for all of this, so she would be patient and listen to it. "Remember, old man. I'm younger than you are. Do you think you can hang with me? Just let me freshen up a bit and I'll meet you in the lobby in twenty minutes. Leave the cane though, I promise to be gentle."

Tangie laughed softly. Eric loved the sound of her laughter. It was lyrical, and light. Music that he would love to listen to every day.

He couldn't help thinking about his recent job decisions. He prayed he was making the right choices, but as long as he could be with Tangie he knew he would be all right.

Tangie hung up the phone and hopped in the shower, the water nearly scalding, just the way she liked it. Feeling better, she set out to find the perfect outfit. It was late, but she didn't want to be too casual. She chose her all-purpose little black dress, which was made of silk and rayon. It felt heavenly next to her skin. Underneath she wore a black teddy. She put on black silk panty hose, midheeled black pumps, and was ready to go. She decided to leave her shoulder-length hair loose for a sexy, sophisticated look. She would make Eric pay for keeping her waiting.

Tangie was proud of the reflection looking back at her. Although her diet hadn't been the best since coming to New Orleans, she wasn't doing too badly. A dab of Sangria Red lipstick and she was ready. Eric seemed to bring out the tease in her and she wanted to be sexy and beautiful for him.

In exactly twenty minutes, she and Eric met in the lobby. "Wow" is all Eric managed to say. Tangie was also duly impressed with Eric's ensemble. He was looking oh so suave in fitted black leather pants and a gray silk shirt. This time no Rolex, just a simple black-banded Bulova watch. *He must be dressed down tonight,* she thought.

She inhaled deeply. Umm, he smelled absolutely wonderful. His Tuscany cologne made her want to throw her arms around him in reckless abandon. She licked her lips unconsciously. A gesture that did not go unnoticed by Eric. He smiled inwardly.

Before they could devour each other in the lobby, they moved toward the restaurant, where they were seated quickly in a secluded booth and given menus. She had been hungry before seeing Eric, but now had things on her mind besides food.

How could he make her tingle all over without even touching her? she thought.

He cleared his throat and said, "I really like your hair that way, you look fantastic. That dress . . . Well, it makes a statement."

Before sitting down Tangie twirled around to give him the full view. "Oh yeah? What's it saying?" she said coyly.

"It says 'I am fine and I know it,'" he replied with mock seriousness.

In her best southern belle impression Tangie said, "Why, Mr. Duval, you are positively trying to make my head spin."

They both laughed and some of the tension abated. They began to look at the menu in earnest. Since it was already very late, they decided to eat light. They ordered grilled chicken Caesar salads and white Zinfandel.

As they ate and drank, their conversation was natural and they both laughed easily, but they knew they were avoiding important issues. There was much that needed to be said, but neither was in a rush to broach an uncomfortable subject.

Eric had made up his mind. Tonight he would come clean. "Now that your conference is finally over, what are your plans? Tangie, I have been thinking about us and I want to know if you think we have a future. You need to know that I really care about you." He looked at her with such intensity, she thought she would be burned by the fire. "This is no passing fancy to me, Tangie, I love you."

Tangie listened intently. These were words that she longed to, but was afraid to hear. "Eric, I have done nothing else but think of us and I have to admit that I have very strong feelings for you too.

"I've decided that if you are serious about giving us a try, then I am willing to leave Virginia, to be with you. I am very satisfied with my life, but I'm willing to relocate. I've worked hard to get to where I am, but

I think you're worth it. Nothing matters as long as we are together."

Eric was pleased, but he was slightly disappointed that she hadn't told him that she loved him. *I know I'm doing the right thing,* he told himself.

Eric sensed her nervousness before he noticed the gesture.

She tugged gently on her bottom lip before continuing. "I don't want to shack up though, and I plan to pay my own way. I will find a job and want to maintain my own place. We need to see where this is going before we make a more serious commitment."

Eric's heart plummeted in his chest. He was ready to give his all, but obviously she wasn't in the same place. He remained silent. He wanted to hear her out.

She continued, "By the way, where would I be moving? You've never told me where you live when not in New Orleans."

He knew exactly what he wanted, but he was afraid of overwhelming her. He wanted her to be Mrs. Tangerine Duvernay.

Eric breathed slowly. "You're right, there's a lot we need to discuss before making plans. Do you want to talk here or the room?"

The tension they had managed to keep at bay crept back into their secluded space. They were both putting it on the line.

Tangie debated over going to the room. She didn't want to be distracted and didn't trust her hormones to cooperate if they were in too intimate a setting. They had too much to say to each other. "I am comfortable here," she responded.

She slipped her feet out of her black pumps and leaned closer to Eric.

He was momentarily distracted, but the seriousness of their conversation brought him quickly back to reality. He decided he would start at the beginning. She needed to know all about him, before she made a commitment to him. He started to tell her his story. He hoped that she would do the same for him.

"I am the son of a foreign service diplomat. My dad and I have traveled all over the world. What I haven't seen with him, I've experienced with my current job. My mother died when I was ten. She was the most beautiful, caring woman I've ever known, and still to this day I miss her."

A momentary flash of pain came over his face, but Eric continued. "I went to Georgetown and during my senior year, the FBI recruited me. I was married to a wonderful woman named Rebecca and we had a beautiful child, but they were both killed in a car accident a few years ago."

Again, a momentary flash of pain and Tangie listened with a heavy heart. She didn't interrupt as he spoke, but reached out for his hands and squeezed gently to show her support.

"I have been working on a high-profile case for several months. The insurance investigator role was just that, a part I was playing. I have had so many aliases that sometimes I don't know who I am supposed to be! My last name is Duvernay. My full name is Eric Christian Duvernay."

He showed her his Virginia license to prove it. He went on to tell her that his home of record was Manassas, Virginia. Tangie noticed that they were probably only twenty-five minutes away from each other. Her gut twisted with every word; this was not what she had expected. She had fallen in love with a man she didn't even know.

"My eccentric aunt Kari left me money, cars, and a condo. She was always my home base whenever Dad and I came back to the DC area. I stayed with her while my father trained for his next assignment. She was a show-tune fanatic and by the time I was five, I knew every song from the 1940s forward." Eric smiled at the memory. "I loved her very much, even her quirky ways." He knew he was giving her a lot of information, but he couldn't stop, she needed to know.

He confided, "For the past several months my dad has been keeping up appearances in Manassas. He takes care of my condo and two beagles, Joe and Freddie. Those two really help me keep some sense of normalcy in my life."

Eric took a deep breath; he was starting to get nervous about Tangie's silence. "That's me in a nutshell. This was my last undercover assignment. I plan to go back to headquarters—probably as an instructor. I am looking forward to a nine-to-five job and something that doesn't have me constantly looking over my shoulder. I don't want that for us."

Eric waited until she would meet his gaze before he continued. "Tangie, meeting you has made me willing to want to live like a real person again. I want to feel human, not like I'm watching my life unfold on a movie screen."

He sensed the need to be quiet.

Maybe it was late. Maybe she was just tired. Confusion started to grow in Tangie and she wasn't sure anymore about what she should do. He was being honest now, but he had led her on. His whole life had been about lies and deceit. Would he know where to draw the line? Could she trust him, or would he turn out to be another Rodney? Intellectually, she knew she shouldn't compare them, but her heart was having a tough time telling the two men apart.

She took a long, slow sip of her wine. Emotions warred within her. She was feeling let down and betrayed again. She sat back in her chair and closed her eyes before responding. "I certainly wasn't expecting all this. It's better than a game of *Truth or Consequences*," she said dryly.

Her subconscious taunted her. *He's no better than Rodney.*

She studied Eric's features for a moment. Her breathing was becoming labored, and she felt on the verge of a panic attack.

Tangie finally found her voice. "Eric, to tell you the truth, it's late and I am feeling a bit overwhelmed."

She felt backed into a corner. Should she trust him? Would there be more to the story later? "It is getting pretty late and I think I just need time to mull things over for a bit. My flight doesn't leave until 3:00 P.M. on Sunday. Let's meet after we've both had a chance to get some sleep."

Tangie stood up, kissed him lightly on the cheek, and hurried to the elevators. She didn't want him to see the tears that had begun to fill up her eyes.

Eric resisted the urge to go to her. He knew that he needed to let her work things out. He had to believe that it couldn't end like this. The sick feeling in his gut intensified as he watched her walk away.

She made it to the room just in time. The tears came with abandon now. Hurt and pain dogged her every thought.

Chapter 11

Tangie woke up at 6:30 A.M., took a shower, and dressed quickly. She had spent most of the night trying to decide what to do, and somewhere in the wee hours of the morning decided she needed to put some distance between her and Eric. She needed time away to be objective. Her decision on whether to continue with the relationship was too important to trust to a whim.

Talking with Candy wouldn't help. The girl was a hopeless romantic, but Tangie needed her shoulder about now. She never pulled any punches, so she'd make a good sounding board.

Tangie called the airline to change her ticket, and at 9:45 A.M. was boarding a plane back to Reagan National Airport and away from Eric Duvernay.

Four hours later she was loading her baggage into the trunk of her Altima. Tangie took the long way home on purpose; she needed to clear her head. To say she was emotionally exhausted was an understatement after being on such highs and lows in New Orleans.

Tangie gripped the steering wheel, rolled down the windows, and drove with relish. It was surprising how good it felt to be behind the wheel of the car. She took I-395 South to Duke Street and drove the miles back to her town house in Fairfax, Virginia.

She didn't care that this route was full of street-lights; she needed to feel in control. Concentrating on driving made her feel better bit by bit. But, try as she might to avoid it—all thoughts turned to Eric. Should she be ecstatic or depressed about their love? Did they even have a relationship?

Tangie had such strong feelings for him. Was it the moment, the place, the man, or a real emotion? He had admitted that he loved her, but she didn't know if she could trust that either. She was so engrossed in her thoughts that she didn't notice a blue Chevy Caprice following her. The car had kept a respectable distance since she'd left the airport parking lot.

Forty-five minutes later she sighed heavily as she drove into her parking space. By the time she reached her doorstep, she had started to feel more like her old self again, the tension beginning to seep out of her weary bones.

After picking up her mail, she plopped down on her couch. Fifteen minutes later she was asleep, still holding the mail in her hand. She fell into a deep, ex-hausted slumber.

Six hours later the continuous ringing of the phone awakened her. Groggy, Tangie finally answered, "Hullo. . . ."

A mixture of relief and irritation dotted Eric's tone when she finally answered. "Well, at least I know you are safe. When the front desk clerk said you'd checked out, I wasn't sure whether to be scared or annoyed."

Tangie listened silently. She knew she had acted

impulsively, but she wouldn't back down until she was sure of how she felt. Besides, she wasn't ready to deal with him yet. Tangie wanted a few days of peace to collect herself.

Truth be told, she wanted to be in Eric's arms at that very moment. But she couldn't, not yet.

Eric continued, "I'll be in the hotel for three more days. If I don't hear from you, I'll know your decision." His tone was still harsh, but there was no bite to his bark.

He hesitated, unsure of what to say next. "Tangie, I know I sprang a lot on you and I hope you can forgive me for having to be dishonest, but I was undercover. I had to protect the mission. I also had to protect you. I don't know what I would have done if they had somehow come after you." He blew out a tired breath. "Can you understand how important my secrecy was? I need to hear from you soon. I . . ."

Eric wouldn't tell her how much he loved her until she gave him some indication that she felt the same way. He hoped he wasn't making a fool of himself.

Tangie held her breath while she listened to Eric. Her heart made that familiar racket whenever she heard his husky deep voice. She didn't know what to say. She wanted to be with him, needed him to hold her and tell her that she was safe with him. Her heart was melting, listening to him, and part of her wanted to throw caution to the wind and tell him how much she loved him and wanted to be with him—but she couldn't.

Eric didn't know what to make of her silence and he didn't trust that he wouldn't make a complete dolt of himself by begging, so he decided to give her space. He gently placed the receiver in the cradle and sent up a prayer. He had trusted love and he hoped he wasn't making a mistake. He wanted to spend the rest of his life with Tangie and he didn't want to lose her now.

Tangie had listened to the sincerity in Eric's voice. Hot tears were threatening to spill over her long lashes. She closed her eyes, holding on to the phone, ignoring the blaring tone that indicated the connection had been broken.

No sooner had she hung up the phone than it rang again. She answered cautiously. "Hello—"

Her mom interrupted impatiently. "Tangerine, I called the hotel, but they told me you checked out very early this morning. The other day you told me that you were going to stay a couple of extra days. I figured you came home early, but couldn't you have called? I might have been able to meet you at the airport."

Hattie noticed the protracted silence on the phone. "How are you, baby? Was the trip okay?" she asked, worriedly. Her mother radar had gone on high alert.

Relief flooded Tangie's voice when she realized that it was not Eric. She didn't trust herself to talk to him again. "Hi, Mom, I'm fine, just tired. The conference was okay, although I don't feel any more 'effective' as I was led to believe the conference would do for me. New Orleans wasn't bad. I went off my diet and splurged a little, probably not as much as I wanted to, but the food and music were enjoyable." Tangie struggled to keep her tone light and noncommittal.

"I came back early to get settled in before work. Thanks for all your help, by the way, we'll have to do it again soon. Hey, how about I take you to lunch at the Pavilion?" she asked.

Hattie nodded in self-satisfaction. "Sure, that way I

can check you out for myself. Mothers always know when something's bothering their children."

Hattie wanted to drop everything and run over to Tangie's place, but her daughter was an adult. She would give her some time and space. "You sound like you need to go. I guess you don't want to talk about it now, and I can wait. I'm looking forward to lunch, sweetie. I love you."

Tangie groaned. Despite her attempt at nonchalance, she hadn't been able to pull it off. Her mom could always read her like a book and knew something was wrong.

"I love you too, Ma, see ya later."

Realizing the pattern that had started, she hung up the phone and quickly called Candy's number before the phone could ring again. The answering machine picked up.

Tangie groaned again before leaving a message. She was definitely back.

"Hi, Candy, I'm back. Give me a call, you know who. See ya."

Tangie went into her room to unpack. Taking out many of her new acquisitions, she didn't realize how much laundry she would have to put in the dry cleaner's.

As she closed her bedroom curtains, she noticed a blue car parked across from her house. She thought it was odd because it looked like one of those funky undercover cars on television—a Chevy Caprice with too many antennas. Her thoughts floated back to New Orleans.

The two agents in the car realized that they had been made when they saw her watching them out the window.

Tangie openly watched them as the car pulled away a few minutes later. She was tired of thinking about Eric. She turned on her DMX music system, blasting it as loud as she could stand, and started to clean her already spotless town house. She didn't feel like going out again and didn't know how else to release her pent-up energy. She started in the guest room.

Tangie always enjoyed being at home. She had decorated the room with her current fantasy, which she called neoclassic. The room was furnished in a Queen-Anne-style high four-poster bed, an armoire, and a lowboy. It was completed with a sitting area, vanity, and writing desk. Each piece had a dark cherry-wood finish. After catching a white sale at Hecht's she'd decorated the room in the complete set of navy Amalfi. It was a rich pattern that didn't make the room either too feminine or masculine.

Tangie liked Almafi so much that the pattern was coordinated from the bedroom to the trash can in the bathroom. It was a lovely sight and Candy, her frequent guest, loved it too.

Over an hour later she was still restless. Cleaning had helped, but what she really needed was an ear. She hadn't heard from Candy all day, which meant she and her boyfriend, Siddiq, were probably spending time together.

She tried Candy's number one more time anyway, then went into her exercise room. Knowing she needed to get back into her old routine, she did 350 crunches and walked on her treadmill for about an hour. The sweat soaking her back and chest felt good. The more she exercised the more in control she felt. Two hours later, her muscles screaming from weight lifting, she decided she'd had enough. Now she was ready to relax.

She took a bubble bath in her favorite cucumber melon scent and luxuriated until her skin was wrinkled. Afterward she changed into loose-fitting sweats and sneakers. She packed her lunch, took out her clothes for work, and settled in to read. For the moment, she wouldn't think about Agent Eric Duvernay, she would just enjoy some peace.

Under his cool demeanor, Eric's breathing was erratic and his pulse racing. He was seated in his senior officer Agent Spates's office about to totally change his life. All of the arrangements had been made for his transfer, and Eric would be leaving immediately for Quantico, Virginia. As requested, he was being reassigned to a teaching position. He couldn't help thinking about Tangie.

Agent Spates said, "I can't think of a better way for you to give back to the unit than to help train young agents, making them as good as you."

Eric took the sentiment as a compliment.

Spates gave Eric a copy of his transfer paperwork and new orders. Eric looked down on what would be his new life.

Spates gave him a chance to review the papers before telling him about Tangie. "I'm satisfied with Tangerine Taylor's background check. She appears clean and the tail we had on her showed nothing unusual."

Eric seethed inside, but kept the same pleasant expression on his face as he said evenly, "Chief, Tangerine Taylor is an innocent. She's had nothing to do with this case from the beginning, so I don't see why you were concerned. If there had been any problems, certainly you could trust that I would have handled them. Sir, I believe my record speaks for itself."

The chief wasn't fooled by Eric's manner, he knew his agent well enough to know he had hit a sore spot. He could tell by the expression in Eric's eyes. "Take it easy, Agent Duvernay." Spates looked at him intently. "You know that this is procedure, has been since Hoover, and it's probably saved a few agents' lives too."

The senior agent couldn't be angry about Eric's attitude. He knew the hell that Eric had been through. He reached into his drawer and withdrew a manila envelope. "Here's your plane ticket. You know the drill; after the lab cleans it, your car will be delivered to you."

Eric had recovered from his initial outrage. He knew Spates only had his best interests at heart. "Sir, you know I appreciate everything you've done for me. You had more faith in me than I had in myself and that helped carry me through some pretty rough times."

Spates smiled. He reached into his desk drawer. "Here's your bonus check. It wasn't S.O.P., but it was damn good work. Now get out of here. Tell you the truth, I'm anxious to get back to DC myself—too many damned mosquitoes here. Good luck, man, and take of yourself. I'll probably see you at Quantico, or maybe after retirement." He said that with a wry smile.

He and Eric both knew retirement was a lifetime away. Too many SCU agents were killed in the line of duty before they could collect any benefits. Eric nodded. Satisfied with the arrangements, he stood and gave his mentor a warm handshake and left.

As soon as he exited the SCU building in New Orleans he blew out a long, satisfied sigh of relief.

He packed hurriedly when he reached his hotel room. Absentmindedly, he had only one person on his mind. Tangie. His flight was a late one, so he had plenty of time to focus on the object of his desires. He would eat, do some quick shopping, stop by his restaurant, say good-bye to his partner, and then plan how he was going to get her back in his life for good. He paced around the small room until a plan started to germinate.

He began by writing down the numbers of the shops he needed to call. He called room service, ordered a house salad, steak, and baked potato for a late dinner. Eric thought about it for a minute and called room service back. Tonight he would splurge on some of the finest New Orleans turtle cheesecake the city had to offer. He had earned it. It had been a rough week!

Eric knew once back at Quantico, he would be part of a vigorous training regime and there wouldn't be too much opportunity to go off the exercise schedule. At thirty-four years old he was six four, 195 pounds, and in superb shape.

He reflected on the events of the last few months. It had been a long, lonely journey in New Orleans to close the case. The only bright spot had been falling in love with Tangerine Taylor.

Eric still had the phone book in his lap. He stopped daydreaming about Tangie long enough to get back to the business at hand. He would have to work quickly; he hadn't meant to come off like some Neanderthal bully during their last conversation.

Even as he ordered a dozen long-stemmed red roses to be sent to her house, he couldn't help thinking about the unbelievable transformation in his life. But the ache and longing for her in his heart were very real. He didn't want to lose Tangie and he just hoped that they could get past the negativity of the last conversation. Even he had to admit to his impulsivity. He should never have issued an ultimatum. No matter how long he'd known her, she was in his blood and it was certainly going to take longer than three days to decide what to do. After the florist he called the balloon shop, candy store, and . . .

Tangie was just about at her wits' end when the doorbell rang. She needed to talk, but she didn't know if she was ready to face her feelings about Eric yet. She knew immediately who it was by Candy's signature ring. That woman practically lay on the bell. Tangie thought on her way to open the door, *Why doesn't she just use her key?* Ordinarily this bugged the heck out of Tangie, but she was so happy to see her friend when she opened the door that she gave Candy a big bear hug.

"Dang, Tangie, someone would think that even though you didn't call, you'd actually missed me," Candy said with her slight southern lilt.

"Oh, shut up and get in here! I need the company right now."

Candy looked at her closely. "Company, huh? Are you hungry? We could go out and get some low-fat Buffalo wings and a decreased-calorie strawberry daiquiri."

"Girl, you are so crazy! Or we could order some veggie pizza and have some juiced carrots," Tangie countered.

Candy wanted to say something more typically sarcastic, but sensing something was not quite right, she tried to be more agreeable. "Okay, you win, pizza it is. How about Super Supreme from Pizza Hut, though, and cranberry-apple juice loaded with sugar?"

Tangie looked at her friend. She really wasn't in the mood to fight and besides, she was already getting back into her routine. One more sugar-filled day wouldn't hurt, so she conceded. "Okay, okay, brat. So how have you been? It took you long enough to get in touch with me. As I recall—my phone call to you was several hours ago. How's whatshisname, by the way?" She had barely taken a breath before she was asking more questions. "Go ahead and catch me up on life in the metro area. I haven't bothered to turn on the news or read a paper. I haven't been able to concentrate on much."

Tangie was talking fast out of nervousness, a habit the friends shared.

Candy looked at her speculatively.

"You ready for something to drink? I have some wine, Kool-Aid, and homemade cranberry-spice juice that I made. Let's go to the kitchen."

Candy fell in step with her and had to move quickly. She was a little concerned about her because Tangie didn't look so good. Certainly not after that dreamy tone she had used on the phone in New Orleans. Maybe this wasn't such a good time to tell her about Rodney.

"Well, if it's another Tangerine Taylor original I simply must try this recipe. Lord knows you've used me as your guinea pig for just about everything else," Candy said, smiling.

She gave Tangie the thumbs-up sign. "The place

looks great. I see you have been doing some redecorating and cleaning. I was just here a week ago and already it's different. By the way, I was thinking about going out to Potomac Mills next weekend, you want to go? I need some new fake greenery. You know how I murder the real thing."

Candy tasted Tangie's recipe. "Umm, this juice is pretty good."

After Tangie put the pitcher of juice back in the refrigerator, they sat down at the kitchen bar together. "Sure, that sounds good to me, but I'll call you on Friday night or early Saturday to confirm just in case you and your shack-up make new plans—you know how you two are."

Despite their best efforts, the tension was growing thicker by the minute. They sat sipping their juice in silence for several minutes.

Finally, Tangie blurted out, "Okay, Miss Candy Carlson, to be Mrs. Candy Mohammed one day before we both get old and gray, out with it! I know you've got something to say. You are procrastinating, which means it's bad news. Talk to me—we've known each other too long for games. Just spit it out."

Candy looked at her friend pointedly. "I could say the same thing to you. You are wound up about something, but you're right, I do have something to tell you," she confessed.

Candy let out a long breath. She didn't quite know how to break the news to Tangie. She reached into her purse and pulled out the same newspaper clipping that Kim had given her, as well as a more recent one. She handed them both to Tangie gingerly.

The paint on the walls all of a sudden became more interesting as she waited for Tangie to read the notices. She fidgeted nervously, anticipating her re-action to the news.

As she handed her the paper, Candy's behavior put Tangie on edge. Dread snaked through her as she read the simple, heartbreaking words. The clipping was from Florida and it was Rodney Johnson and his fiancée's marriage announcement.

Unbidden tears welled up in her eyes. Feelings of betrayal threatened to overwhelm her as she read the details of her ex-lover's impending nuptials. It was her wedding to him that should be in the announce-ment! She felt the sting of rejection almost as a physical wound.

She sat back hard in her chair, her eyes glistening with unshed tears as the meaning of the words sank in. How could he have done this to her? Didn't she deserve better? Her body trembled as she succumbed to the tidal wave of emotion that swept through her. Candy reached for her and hugged her friend close as the tears continued to flow.

Several minutes later Tangie was able to compose herself. It seemed for the moment that she had fi-nally run out of tears. Candy brought her tissues and waited for her to be ready to talk.

The delivery arrived and the pizza provided them with the opportunity to change their focus. They chose not to talk about Rodney. They ate in relative silence, only conversing when necessary.

Tangie had a lot to deal with, and Candy didn't quite know the best way to help. When they were fin-ished with dinner, she suggested another activity. The watched one of their favorite movies, *The Preacher's Wife,* for the umpteenth time. Tangie was always soothed by the sweet gospel sounds in the movie.

Later that night, neither felt like sleeping so they spent most of their time in Tangie's living room talking.

Tangie nodded off twice while talking. Her eyelids felt as if they weighed a ton. Finally, she said, "Okay, enough for one night. I'm really tired now and I have a lot to think about. Call Siddiq and tell him where you are so he won't be worried. I know you aren't planning to drive home now, it's almost 4:30 A.M."

Smiling, Candy said, "Not to worry, I knew when I got here I was staying. Siddiq already knows. I'll just go get my bag from the trunk."

Tangie stood in the doorway, calling out to her, "And you say I'm a brat!"

When Candy returned, the two talked while they cleaned the kitchen together and went upstairs to bed. Thankfully, they had the weekend to catch up on sleep. Neither was known for being an early riser, and this late night would take its toll.

Candy slept in Tangie's guest room, which she jokingly referred to as her own as often as they did sleep-overs. The room looked like a magazine layout or a room featured on HGTV. Fortunately, Tangie and Candy shared the same taste. Candy loved sleeping in the bed and spent the night at least once every couple of months. She knew Tangie's house almost as well as she knew her own.

Later that morning, Tangie woke up to a big clanging noise, nearly jumping out of her skin. Her body went rigid when she heard strange movements downstairs in her kitchen.

Chapter 12

"Shoot, shoot, shoot," Candy huffed, dropping pans out of Tangie's cabinets.

Tangie lay back down in her bed and chuckled to herself. *What is the girl doing in my kitchen? She knows she can't even boil water.*

So much had happened in the last week, hell, so much had happened in the last few hours, Candy thought grimly. She didn't want to be unfair about the situation, but there was more news to tell her friend, and she wasn't sure if the timing would ever be right.

Tangie listened to her friend muttering and dropping things for five more minutes, then decided she'd had enough. She bounded down the stairs ready to beat a confession out of her.

Watching Candy destroy her kitchen, she barked, "Step away from the oven, put all utensils down, and move away with your hands up."

The look on Candy's startled face was priceless. Tangie broke into peals of laughter as her friend dropped the dish she was holding.

Wiping flour off her face, she protested. "You think you're pretty funny, huh? I was just trying to make us a nice breakfast."

"If you're trying to cook for me, I know something

is up. If you need to talk—talk!" Tangie said in mock exasperation. She had assumed her friend was still concerned about Rodney.

Candy didn't know how much longer she could hold out. She blew out a ragged breath. "Okay . . . I know you've had a lot to deal with lately. I hate to add to your burden, but I feel like I'm gonna burst!"

Tangie groaned inwardly. "All right, girl, spit it out, you've never had that trouble before."

She looked directly into Candy's eyes and said, "I'm okay, Candy, really . . . tell me what you've got to say."

Tangie went to her kitchen bar stool and sat down heavily. She was tense, preparing herself for the worst.

Candy gave up on preparing her culinary delight and brought Tangie a cup of coffee. Nervous energy made her blurt out, "Whatshisname asked me to marry him and I don't know what to do. Whew! I said it."

She lowered her eyes in anticipation of Tangie's re-action. She felt so selfish dumping on her, yet she trusted her friend implicitly and she needed her shoulder.

Tangie was silent, giving Candy the go-ahead.

"Tangie, can you imagine me as Candy Mohammed? I've got to admit it is pretty hysterical. Ugh . . . Tangie, what should I do? I love him, but marriage? I've been pretty comfortable leaving things the way they are." She shrugged her shoulders.

Tangie just smiled as she waited for Candy to run out of energy or breath, whichever came first.

"It's such a big step and I'm not sure that I can do it." Candy was on a roll now. "What if he kidnaps me to The Gambia—will you come save me? I'm being face-tious but you know what I mean! I don't think I'd be any good at that traditional wife stuff. I mean, what if he takes all that honor and obey stuff literally? Honor, sure . . . obey, we may have some problems there."

Candy took a moment to inhale. "Girl, you've read the stories. These mixed marriages have so many problems. Remember that movie with Sally Fields, *Not Without My Daughter*? That could be me. Okay, well, he's not from the same country, but you know, it could happen. And yes, I know I haven't been to Mass or confession in about a year, but I'm still what I was raised to be and that's Catholic! I have no intention of converting to the Muslim faith. I wouldn't mind being Mrs. Siddiq Abdul Mohammed, but I admit I'm nervous even after dating for two and a half years."

Candy looked at her plaintively. "I feel guilty talking about this now. I just wanted you to know."

Tangie listened thoughtfully. Sighing, she responded, "Oh, Candy, you are still the queen of melodrama! You love him and he loves you. Has he asked you to be a traditional wife? Are you pregnant or even planning to have a child in the next year? Has he ever mentioned going back to his homeland? Have you two talked about anything other than the proposal? Sweetie, just slow down. It will be okay."

She shifted on her kitchen bar stool and toyed with the idea of finishing breakfast. "We've always been there for each other. We're not going to stop now. Just talk to the man. I'm sure he has some of the same issues. He didn't make the proposal lightly, so that means he has been examining the relationship for its deeper meaning too."

Candy sighed again, listening intently.

Tangie pounced on the opportunity to continue. This was one of those rare occasions when Candy chose to listen rather than talk.

"Religion is such an important part of life. Ask him what he wants to do before you project your little pre-conceived notions onto the silver screen. Just step back, give yourself some room, and talk about your fears openly.

"Sometimes you do go to the limit . . . that imagination of yours is almost lethal. But that's okay, I still love ya and so does Siddiq. See there, I didn't even call him whatshisname."

Tangie exhaled. "Now why would you feel you are dumping? This is great news and we knew one day it would happen—by choice or by shotgun."

She gave Candy a smile of reassurance.

"Thank you . . . I think. I just felt bad knowing I needed to come over here and give you the bad news. What a mixed message, huh? Be sad, your ex-boyfriend is marrying the bimbo he cheated on you with, but be happy for me, I am getting married. Helluva weekend, pal."

Tangie sighed. "Well, that's not the way I am taking it. The Rodney situation will take care of itself. I mean, it's over now. We are going to deal with the present day and be thankful for what we have."

Candy listened to the sage words from her friend. "I knew I could count on you—always the serious-minded thinker among our crew. What would we do without our Tangerine?"

She reached across the counter and patted Tangie's arm. "After all this business is done, should we ask Kim to an outing next week? She might enjoy a little time away from the twins—like a mother's day out."

Tangie said, "Yeah, that sounds good, I haven't seen Kim in a while. I still can't believe that girl didn't tell us about Rodney! He is going to be her cousin-in-law and she actually kept that information through all the planning. Remember in high school, we used to call that girl a bad refrigerator? She couldn't keep nothin'. Now look at her."

Candy was feeling better now that she had gotten everything out. "Okay, enough about me and Siddiq. What the heck happened in New Orleans?" she asked breathlessly.

It took Tangie another hour to recount the details of her trip and her time with Eric. Smiling, she said, "He looks like that fine brother from the singing group Groove Theory, you know, the one that was in Toni Braxton's *You're Making Me High* video, only better. Smooth, chocolate skin, silky mustache, wavy jet-black hair, and smoldering mahogany-brown eyes. I won't even tell you about those lips. Ummm, just thinking about him makes me want to eat him up."

Moaning, she continued, "But . . . Candy, after what I've told you, how can I trust him? I don't know if I can decipher between the lies, half-truths, and the genuine truth. He has been so circumspect about everything that I just don't know anymore. Intellectually, I know that he had to keep his cover. But in my heart, it still doesn't seem right to me. Why couldn't he just leave out the other stuff instead of making it up? I don't know if I would have liked that better, but being lied to makes me feel so violated. I know that I just need time to work it out. I know that I don't want to give up on us. I just have to work it out in my mind."

She shrugged. "Seems where men are concerned, I'm a terrible judge."

Candy shook her head emphatically. "Don't even think that way, Tangie. What you and Rodney had was special until he messed it up. Furthermore, Rodney and Eric are two different men."

Candy tried a different tack. "Sounds like Eric is so polished and suave, I don't even know if I can eat with the brother, he'd probably have to show me the proper utensils. More importantly, it sounds like Eric is really serious about you; otherwise he wouldn't have told you everything, and you have to admit he didn't have to. He could have just tried to get into the panties and left all the rest. I'm sure he has come clean now; otherwise he would run the risk of losing you permanently."

Candy continued with an exaggerated wave. "Talk to him, Tangie, and follow your heart, not that methodical head of yours. This is not some computer problem where you analyze the data and solve the problem right away. This is real life," she said emphatically.

"I know what you are saying is right, but I've made quite a mess of things. I should have stayed so that we could talk again. Maybe this wasn't the best time to get impulsive. I guess I was pretty juvenile to leave, huh?"

"Well . . ."

"You don't have to answer that, Candy!"

"Okay, let's clean up this disaster zone that I made of your kitchen and then we can continue this some more."

Hands on her hips, Tangie responded, "Us clean up the kitchen? I don't remember making this mess. When I went to bed in the wee hours of the morning, this place was spic-and-span."

"Aw, come on, bud. What's yours is mine and what's mine is yours. That's what friends are for."

Tangie was just about to swipe her friend with the dish towel when she was interrupted by the chime of her doorbell. Her first instinct was to ignore it.

Who was ringing her bell at 9:30 A.M. on a Saturday?

Annoyed, she looked out her window and saw that it was a flower truck. She made herself presentable and went to answer the door. She signed for a huge bouquet of red roses and walked back into the kitchen.

Casually she said, "Since we're up, do you want some bran muffins? I froze some last week. They should be good warmed up with this coffee."

Candy replied, "Umm . . . sounds good. Breakfast of champions."

Candy had had her back to Tangie. Her eyes widened in surprise when she noticed the bouquet.

"Those flowers are gorgeous. I suppose they're from Eric? What does the card say?" she asked excitedly.

Candy handed her friend the muffins from the freezer and sat down at the breakfast bar.

Absently Tangie turned her attention back to the flowers. She knew they were from Eric, but she didn't know if she was ready to deal with him yet. She pushed those thoughts from her mind, took the card from the bouquet, and read it to Candy.

It said TANGIE, I'VE NEVER KNOWN ANYONE AS SPECIAL AS YOU. I LOVE YOU MORE THAN LIFE. PLEASE COME BACK TO ME. ERIC.

Tears sprang to Tangie's eyes as she read the words. What was she going to do?

She didn't have long to ponder. A minute later the doorbell rang again.

She looked at Candy, who just smiled and shrugged her shoulders.

This time when she returned to the kitchen she was holding a twelve-balloon bouquet. The balloons simply read *I Love You*.

Candy gushed, "This is soo romantic . . . Come on, girl, give it another chance. If you don't, I'll take the brotha!"

"And mess me out of being the bridesmaid? Never!"

Before they could continue their banter, the doorbell rang for the third time. This time it was a twenty-pound basket from Harry and David. It was filled to the brim with fruit, nuts, one of their signature cheesecakes, and lots of candy. At this point Tangie was starting to feel overwhelmed. She looked at her kitchen full of gifts that Eric had sent, feeling a mixture of pleasure and pain. The what-ifs were killing her.

The doorbell rang yet again while the two were eating muffins and Candy was rattling on aimlessly about romance.

Tangie groaned as she walked to the door. *What could it be now?* she thought.

She opened the door to a nice-looking young man dressed in a tuxedo.

"Tangerine Taylor?"

"Yes?"

"This is for you." He was there to deliver a singing telegram from Eric. In a beautiful tenor voice he sang, "Roses are red, violets are blue. I love you so much I don't know what to do. If you leave me now, I'll just shrivel up and die. Please, Tangie, please don't make this grown man cry. Say you love me too and we'll know what to do."

When the song was finished, she laughed, then cried.

Tangie gave her songbird a nice tip after Candy

took pictures of him. "Remind me to sleep over more often. This is better than television or Danielle Steele. Well, Miss Lady, I'd say that you don't need to question his sincerity anymore, what do you think?" Candy said, when they were finally able to settle down for some peace.

"Ugh . . . now you know why I fell head over heels for him in a week. I want to be with Eric, but I'm just so scared!"

They walked back to her living room to sit down again. Tangie's shoulders felt heavy from the weight of such a big decision. "Eric called when I first came back from New Orleans and gave me three days to let him know what I want to do, but I am still as confused now as before. I don't know what to tell him. Especially now . . . I didn't expect the news of Rodney's marriage to hit me like that. If I am truly ready to move on to another relationship, why is it affecting me like this?"

In New Orleans, Eric was beside himself. He had not heard a word from Tangie since she left. More accurately, since he had given her an ultimatum, he thought anxiously. He wanted desperately to make things up to her. The gifts he'd sent were to let her know that he was thinking about her and was sincere about loving her. But from her silence, he had to conclude that he had miscalculated. Instead of bringing them together, he had pulled them apart. She hadn't called, and the tenuous hold he had on his ego was crushed. He felt liked he had risked too much.

Eric paced around his hotel room. He was wearing the carpet thin in front of his television.

All he could think about was how he managed to screw up the only thing that really mattered in his life. Now he was left with the task of trying to forget her. There was no one else to blame because he had set the terms of the ultimatum, and now he would have to abide by them. His arrangements to return to Quantico were all set. He would be teaching foreign and U.S. agents. He was excited about his new opportunity. It was a good move to make out of the field, but he didn't know how he would handle being so close to Tangie and not in a relationship with her. By 6:00 P.M., he would be arriving at Dulles Airport to begin anew. Ready or not, he thought wryly.

Tangie went into the kitchen, brewed herself some macadamia-nut coffee, and pulled the Archway oatmeal cookies out of her cabinet. She wanted some comfort food and there was nothing better than oatmeal cookies.

She sat down at her kitchen table with coffee and cookies in hand when suddenly a chill went through her entire body. Tangie realized that she had been so preoccupied over the last couple of days that she hadn't spoken with Eric.

Chapter 13

Negative thoughts continued to chip away at her confidence. Would she really be safe with him? All she seemed to have now was questions and no ready answers. She needed to talk to Eric to clear the air, but she also needed to know what to say to him. Tangie decided a run would help her put things in perspective. The oatmeal cookies were fine, but a run would be even better.

Any schedule or exercise regime she'd had before had been shot to Halifax as soon as she landed in New Orleans. Now she was going to have to be much more disciplined. She'd worked too hard to get in shape to go backward. After her run and she'd cleared out some of the cobwebs, she would call Eric in New Orleans. They really did need to talk, especially after her leaving like she did. She had been able to admit to herself that she'd been somewhat immature and she needed to set things right with him.

She knew she needed to be up front with him, and their relationship couldn't be predicated on any more lies. After this Rodney marriage debacle, she needed honesty, trust, and dedication from Eric. Would she ever really be able to love freely without waiting for the other shoe to drop? She thought about that as she laced her sneakers. She knew that kind of relationship wasn't fair to her or Eric. She wouldn't force him to pay for Rodney's mistakes. She hoped Eric would be patient with her while she figured things out.

Tangie walked and ran around her neighborhood, following her familiar route for the better part of two hours. Sweat poured down her back and soaked her running outfit. As usual, the more she ran, the more she pushed her body, the better she felt. Working out was really the best medicine when she felt out of sorts. In pushing herself, striving for that next level, she felt in control again—even if only for a short time. For the first time in days, her thoughts were exclusively of Eric and she had more clarity. She pictured his face and sexy body; just the thought of him raised the temperature up several degrees.

Tangie couldn't resist a smile as she imagined how it would feel for him to make love to her. Closing her eyes she could feel his touch caressing her body, kisses devouring her lips, the sexy, heady smell of his cologne . . . she felt her body aflame with desire and she throbbed at her core. Breathlessly she said to the air, "Eric, how do I find you?"

When Tangie returned home, she called her mom after a long hot shower. She was hoping for some of that sage wisdom that Hattie was known for. "Hi, Mom, it's me, your long-lost daughter."

Hattie breathed a sigh of relief. She had been trying to give her daughter space, but the suspense was killing her. "Hi, baby, I thought I was going to have to send out an all points bulletin for you."

Tangie laughed tentatively. "No, that's not necessary, it's been a rough couple of weeks and I just didn't want to worry you unnecessarily. Anyway, I'm okay, I'm really okay."

"Fine then . . . out with it. What's been bothering my baby? You haven't been the same since you came back from that den of iniquity," she stated in her trademark matter-of-fact manner.

Forty-five minutes later, Tangie had shared the whole story, starting with Eric in New Orleans and ending with trying to find him again.

"How about you try contacting the stores where Eric purchased your gifts?"

"Mom, you're a genius! I'm going to get right on it. I'll call you later and let you know how I make out. Mom, thank you. I love you."

Tangie hung up quickly, ready to start calling around. She collected the cards and wrapping paper from her gifts. She had always been a class-one pack rat, which in this case worked to her advantage. Her enthusiasm was quickly doused, however, when no one would give her any information, citing privacy rules. She also called directory assistance in New Orleans and Virginia to no avail; there was no Eric Duvernay listed anywhere.

Finally she called Quantico, but after being transferred five times, she hung up in disgust. Tangie just hoped she wasn't too late. Surely, after she and Eric spoke he would understand her hesitation to have a relationship with him.

He's probably just working on a big case, she thought optimistically.

Tangie had been back to work for several months

now. She hadn't heard from Eric, but she wasn't giving up hope yet.

"He'll call when things settle down," she told herself as time continued to pass by.

Her return to work had proved to be therapeutic. She felt more in control of her emotions, and work gave her less time to miss him. Tangie continued to work on one project after the other. The marketing team was even having a hard time keeping up with all of the products that she wanted to introduce. After one of her marathon meetings she returned to her office to find her phone ringing. "Hello, Tangerine Taylor speaking."

Without preamble, Candy said, "I am not going to beg to see my best friend. You have been working like a possessed woman! You need a break."

Candy had felt like she had to make a date with her friend lately, and today she was calling to demand that they spend some time together. "Okay, brat, how about we meet this evening?"

"Sounds good, how about a light dinner at Bennigan's, just salad and wine? I'm really trying to stay away from the heavy stuff. I haven't had red meat in three months."

"Sure, just as long as you quit trying to convert me. I love to eat meat, so don't ask me to give it up."

Tangie teased, "Why do I have such spoiled friends? I'll see you at 6 :00 P.M., girl."

Candy felt sorry for her friend. She could tell she was having a tough time dealing with the separation from Eric, but she didn't know what to do for her. She hoped the two would find their way back to each other; at least she hoped so for Tangie's sake.

During dinner they kept the conversation light and

the visit short. Candy had a sinking feeling in the pit of her stomach for her friend.

Tangie's visit with Candy didn't do anything to brighten her mood. They both walked on eggshells, something they didn't usually do with each other.

Tangie needed answers. Her love life was in limbo. She had declined all requests for dates and social invitations.

More important to her was where she and Eric stood. They needed to spend time with each other to see if their attraction was as much emotional as physical.

Several months after her trip to New Orleans, Tangie sat on her couch with her feet tucked under her body. She picked up the phone more than a dozen times . . . even though she wasn't even sure where to begin. She wanted to call FBI headquarters or directory assistance again to find him, but tonight she decided enough was enough.

Eric sighed in disgust. He had to confide in someone. He didn't know if he was coming or going most of the time.

He called his friend and fellow agent Ben. "You know, man, I was doing just fine in my life without Tangerine Taylor. Now look at me. I'm all messed up, living like a monk. I can't even look at another woman without comparing her to Tangie. I hate this," he confessed miserably.

Ben listened to his friend patiently. "If you feel that strongly about her, then you need to talk to her."

Exasperated, Eric continued, "What did I do so wrong? She knows how much I love her and want to be with her. I can't believe I didn't even as much as get a Dear Eric letter."

"Okay, brother . . . now you are starting to sound corny. Take my advice, find her, find out what happened, and move on, for my sake as well as yours."

"All right, all right . . . I'll call her last-known home number tomorrow. Let me get outta here. I need to think about what I'm going to say. I'll call you tomorrow . . . or maybe I won't," Eric said with a telling wink.

"How about the truth, man, it still works best!" Ben quipped. He kind of enjoyed seeing his man-of-steel friend felled by a woman. "Don't chicken out on me. You need to get some resolution in your life. Your concentration has, how should I say . . . been lacking. Don't get me wrong, you do a good job, but I know you have been draggin' in here some days and you look like death warmed over. Do us all a favor, find her, and get things back in line. I'll see you tomorrow."

Ben patted his friend on the back and watched him walk out the door.

Eric spent a very long night at home trying to sort things out. He wanted to be sure whatever approach he used with her didn't make the situation worse. He decided that he would force himself to wait and call tomorrow from the office. If he called tonight and found she wasn't at home, he would torture himself trying to figure where she was and with whom. Work was definitely safer.

In his desperation, Eric had purchased the latest copies of *Essence, Ebony,* and *Cosmopolitan* magazines, looking for relationship advice.

An Important Message From The ARABESQUE Publisher

Dear Arabesque Reader,

Arabesque is celebrating 10 years of award-winning African-American romance. This year look for our specially marked 10th Anniversary titles.

Plus, we are offering *Special Collection Editions* and a *Summer Reading Series*—all part of our 10th Anniversary celebration.

Why not be a part of the celebration and let us send you four more specially selected books FREE! These exceptional romances will be sent right to your front door!

Please enjoy them with our compliments, and thank you for continuing to enjoy Arabesque.... the soul of romance bringing you ten years of love, passion and extraordinary romance.

Linda Gill
PUBLISHER, ARABESQUE ROMANCE NOVELS

P.S. Don't forget to check out our 10th Anniversary Sweepstakes—no purchase necessary—at www.BET.com

ARABESQUE
BET BOOKS

A SPECIAL "THANK YOU" FROM ARABESQUE JUST FOR YOU!

Send this card back and you'll receive 4 FREE Arabesque Novels—a $25.96 value—absolutely FREE!

The introductory 4 Arabesque Romance books are yours FREE (plus $1.99 shipping & handling). If you wish to continue to receive 4 books every month, do nothing. Each month, we will send you 4 New Arabesque Romance Novels for your free examination. If you wish to keep them, pay just $16* (plus, $1.99 shipping & handling). If you decide not to continue, you owe nothing!

- Send no money now.
- Never an obligation.
- Books delivered to your door!

We hope that after receiving your FREE books you'll want to remain an Arabesque subscriber, but the choice is yours! So why not take advantage of this Arabesque offer, with no risk of any kind. You'll be glad you did!

In fact, we're so sure you will love your Arabesque novels, that we will send you an Arabesque Tote Bag FREE with your first paid shipment.

Call Us TOLL-FREE At 1-888-345-BOOK

* Prices subject to change

THE "THANK YOU" GIFT INCLUDES:

- 4 books absolutely FREE (plus $1.99 for shipping and handling).
- A FREE newsletter, *Arabesque Romance News*, filled with author interviews, book previews, special offers, and more!
- No risks or obligations. You're free to cancel whenever you wish with no questions asked.

INTRODUCTORY OFFER CERTIFICATE

Yes! Please send me 4 FREE Arabesque novels (plus $1.99 for shipping & handling). I understand I am under no obligation to purchase any books, as explained on the back of this card. Send my free tote bag after my first regular paid shipment.

NAME _____

ADDRESS _____ APT. _____

CITY _____ STATE _____ ZIP _____

TELEPHONE ( ) _____

E-MAIL _____

SIGNATURE _____

Offer limited to one per household and not valid to current subscribers. All orders subject to approval. Terms, offer, & price subject to change. Tote bags available while supplies last.

Thank You!

AN014A

Accepting the four introductory books for FREE (plus $1.99 to offset the cost of shipping & handling) places you under no obligation to buy anything. You may keep the books and return the shipping statement marked "cancelled". If you do not cancel, about a month later we will send 4 additional Arabesque novels, and you will be billed the preferred subscriber's price of just $4.00 per title. That's $16.00* for all 4 books for a savings of almost 40% off the cover price (Plus $1.99 for shipping and handling). You may cancel at any time, but if you choose to continue, every month we'll send you 4 more books, which you may either purchase at the preferred discount price. . . or return to us and cancel your subscription.

THE ARABESQUE ROMANCE BOOK CLUB
P.O. BOX 5214
CLIFTON NJ 07015-5214

THE ARABESQUE ROMANCE CLUB: HERE'S HOW IT WORKS

PLACE
STAMP
HERE

He lay curled up on his couch reading intently with his beagles at his feet. He was willing to do whatever it took to understand the female psyche. He had tried talking to his dad, but after he teased him mercilessly, Eric gave up. He was on his own in this one, he would just have to figure it out and make it work.

The next day, armed with a plan, he called Tangie's home number. "Damn . . . I wonder what that's all about," Eric said as he put the phone down. There was a recording saying that the number was no longer in service. But before he could wonder too long, Eric was pulled out of his contemplation by the insistent knocking of Agent McMillan. He entered his office accompanied by two members of the military police.

Eric's heart sank. This was going to be serious.

Agent McMillan spoke first. "Sir, you need to come with us. There's been an accident at Hogan's Alley."

"What happened? Who was hurt?" Eric questioned.

Agent McMillan and the two military police personnel were growing impatient.

"Sir, we'll explain on the way. We need to get to the MC immediately. We are expecting the MEDEVAC any minute. One of your trainees, Officer Morrow, was shot in an accidental discharge."

"Let's go." Eric was already walking out of the door.

Eric's blood ran cold at the thought of losing one of his guys. Lieutenant Morrow was a British officer on loan to the Academy, sent to learn about the U.S. system. He was part of an exchange system that dated back to the days of Churchill.

Eric's mind raced, on the way over to the Medical Center. Morrow had always been a competent trainee and officer. He did well on his skill levels and got along with his peers. There had been a single inci-

dent with another British soldier, but it seemed to resolve itself quickly and there weren't any other
problems. Eric just hoped the discharge was accidental, but the feeling in the pit of his stomach told
him otherwise.

Eric was anxious. He didn't like the sound of what
the agents and MPs weren't saying.

"Tell me what you know so far," he demanded.

"Sir, all we know is that Lieutenant Morrow was in-
jured and that somehow Officer O'Malley is
supposed to be at the range."

The foursome spent a short but anxious ride over
to the Medical Center, and when they arrived they
were escorted to a private waiting area immediately.

Eric's stomach was in knots. This scenario did not
bode well for the soldier.

The hospital commander, Navy Captain Myrna
Dell, and Dr. Hight, one of the surgeons, met with
them almost immediately. Dr. Dell wore a grim expression on her face that gave them the answer to
their first question.

"Agent Duvernay, I'm sorry to have to report that
Lieutenant Morrow went into cardiac arrest shortly
after arriving and we were unsuccessful in reviving
him. He's gone."

Eric sat down on the nearest chair. His mind raced.
This couldn't be happening.

The doctor continued, clearly disturbed by something. "Agent Duvernay, were you aware that
Lieutenant Morrow also had several recent injuries
to the abdomen? These injuries had begun to cause
scar tissue, which exacerbated the damage caused
by the GSW. I'm afraid your trainee was running
out of time anyway. Because of these special cir-

cumstances, there will have to be a full-scale investigation into this matter."

"I'm sure you can appreciate how sensitive this matter is," Dr. Dell continued. "The British embassy will
send over an attaché. We need to know what we're
working with."

Eric had the feeling that all hell was about to break
loose.

Chapter 14

"Agent Duvernay, you are ultimately responsible for your trainees and you've apparently had a situation going on for some time. The family of that victim and the British government want answers and they want them now. That means I need them yesterday. Am I making myself clear?"

The base commander had even considered placing Eric on administrative leave until the completion of the investigation, but he knew he needed him in order to get to the bottom of the situation.

"Sir, I understand perfectly. I have been asking a few questions myself. I think I can be more of an asset assisting with the investigation than being on AL. I know my people, and we can get to the bottom of this shortly. Just give me a little more time, that's all I'm asking."

"You've got forty-eight hours before OPR gets here. Make the best of it, I don't want to lose control of this thing. I want a report on my desk in twenty-four hours."

Eric breathed a sigh of relief. "Thank you, sir, you won't regret this."

The Office of Professional Responsibility was a necessary evil, usually called in for incidents of safety violations. A shooting or an accident during training was just such an incident. Eric had checked the training roster, and both men should not have been at the same training site. Lieutenant Morrow was in the right place, Hogan's Alley, which was a specially designed site to give agents real-life training scenarios.

However, O'Malley wasn't scheduled to be anywhere near the site, and after Eric's checking and rechecking assignments, it was looking awfully suspicious.

The sinking feeling had returned to the pit of Eric's stomach. This did not feel good and his intuition was sending out warning bells.

During the next few months, Eric and a team of investigators found out that they didn't know what was going on in the unit after all.

He had been so consumed with work that he had to put all hopes of finding Tangie again on hold. Right now, his first priority was to the Academy and the families of the two men.

What he couldn't understand was why the unit allowed the animosity to progress to such a dangerously high level without informing the command.

What did that say about his leadership? he thought glumly.

The widow of Morrow was seeking compensation for herself and her two children, the British government wanted answers, and Irish representatives wanted an opportunity to meet with O'Malley, who had been sitting in a military jail for two months.

The whole terrible incident had turned into an international three-ring circus.

Eric dragged himself home after another fifteen-hour day. His condo in Manassas seemed like a hundred miles away on the drive home. When he finally came home, it was all he could do to make a cold sandwich and go to bed.

He took out a cold beer and put the can up to his head. The coolness temporarily quenched the fire that seemed to come all the way up from his belly. He had never dealt with such a frustrating and sad case. Eric sighed heavily, sinking deeper into his couch. He wanted desperately to call Tangie. Times like this he wished he had her in his life to share his ups and downs, someone to come home to and rehash the day with.

He did pick up the phone though, not to speak to Tangie, but the only other person that seemed to help him get centered.

"Hi, Dad, it's Eric."

"You don't think I know my own son? How are you doing, old man?"

"I'm fine, just wanted to give you a buzz. I know how you old people tend to feel neglected. I was just thinking maybe we could go fishing sometime soon? We haven't been out in a while. And I want to go by Mom's and maybe Aunt Kari's graves."

As his father, Samuel, listened to Eric, worry furrowed his brow. He was curious before, but now he was downright worried. Eric never wanted to go to the cemetery unless things were really bad.

"Okay, son, spill it," Samuel demanded.

Eric said hurriedly, "I'd like to talk . . . reconnect, that's all. We haven't gone fishing in at least six months and I'd like to spend some time with my old man. Is that a crime?"

Samuel's tone softened. "No, son, it's no crime, I'd

love to. You want to take the *Whispers* out? She could use a good workout. Manny has been keeping her in good shape, but a boat belongs on the water, not in dry dock."

"Yeah, that'll be great."

Samuel added, "I'll stock the galley just in case you don't catch anything. I don't want you to starve out there! Saturday work for you?" Not waiting on an answer, he said, "Besides, you haven't been out in a while and I'll bet you don't know your starboard from your aft."

"Oh, I think I smell a challenge. Care to wager on who catches the most fish?" Eric responded, laughing at his father's good-natured ribbing.

Eric paused, his tone becoming serious again. "Pop . . ."

"Yes, son?"

"Thanks."

Samuel rubbed his jaw absently. "Any time, my boy. I'm always here for you. I'll see you Saturday, sonny."

Eric cradled the phone in his hand a minute longer, thinking about his dad. He called him sonny again, which meant Eric didn't do a very good job of hiding his feelings. His father knew him like the back of his hand.

Some agent I am, he chided himself.

He went to the living room and looked through his photo album. He looked at the pictures of his aunt, his mother, and Rebecca. He couldn't bring himself to part with them. He probably had more pictures of his mother in his timeworn album than his father, and he had memorized them all.

He ran his index finger over a picture of Rebecca

from their honeymoon. He was headed down a path that he didn't need to go down. Familiar disquieting feelings invaded his consciousness. *Why does every woman I love leave me?*

Chapter 15

Tangie was having another banner day. She couldn't concentrate and she felt discombobulated and miserable. She'd goofed again at work, misdiagnosed a problem, and treated one of her staff members unfairly. She hoped she didn't run all of her new staff away. They had been remarkably patient with her and she owed them.

When she pulled into her numbered space in front of her town house, she felt like jumping for joy, only she didn't have the energy to jump anywhere.

Finally! she thought, as mercifully she reached the sanctity of her bedroom.

Taking her shoes off, she walked over to the phone. She expected the usual messages, but to her dismay, no one had called.

Tangie didn't know how long she could keep up this front. As each day went by, she became more upset. It was becoming more and more difficult to convince herself that he would call soon, that he was just really busy, but he hadn't forgotten about her. It took several months, but she finally concluded that Eric wasn't going to call and she had let a good man slip through her fingers. Miserably, she thought, he was probably involved with someone else by now.

Around 8:00 P.M. Candy came by her house. "Girl, what's up with your phone? I kept getting this weird recording saying the number had been changed to an unlisted one. I couldn't get you on your cell either. What's wrong, you hiding from someone?"

"Shoot! My cell phone is on the nightstand in the charger. I'm always forgetting that darn thing. Come on upstairs, I was just about to get into something more comfortable." Tangie headed toward her bedroom as the two continued talking.

She sat down heavily on the edge of her bed, putting her face in her hands; she breathed out loudly when she raised her head.

Candy went over to the sitting area, watching her friend with concern.

Tangie tried to regroup. "Okay, my little pity party is over. You want some turkey spaghetti? I don't wanna eat alone."

"I was going to ask you what we were having for dinner. When have you known me to turn down free food?"

Candy looked at her friend tentatively. "So, have you heard from Eric at all? This is getting weird. I know you two had something special going on before the madness took over all of our lives." She studied Tangie's face. "How are you really handling things?"

Tangie's shoulders shook noticeably as the emotion she had been keeping locked inside came bubbling to the surface. Hot tears spilled down her face.

She confided, "Candy . . . I don't know what I'm doing anymore. I fussed at Serena at work when I was the guilty party; I couldn't concentrate all day! I feel like a complete and total failure. I don't know what to do. I miss Eric so much, how could I have been such a fool? I've tried everything I know to get in touch with him and I can't reach him. It has been so long since we've seen each other or talked, he's probably married to someone else by now," she lamented.

Candy held out her arms to give her best friend a hug. She hated to see her so miserable.

"Tangie, the first thing you need to do is let it out. No one expects you to be Superwoman with all you've had to deal with lately. Just know that I'm always here for you."

Tangie cried harder, sad, mournful tears streaking her face. She felt doomed to be unlucky in love and worse yet . . . celibate too. She ached to be in Eric's arms, to feel his warm touch and have his beautiful mouth on hers.

Candy stayed with Tangie for a while longer. She didn't quite know how to feel about the phantom Eric Duvernay. All she saw was her friend miserable almost since she'd met him. He seemed perfect for her before . . . now she wasn't so sure.

Tangie and Candy talked for a couple more hours, and then Candy needed to go.

"Babe, I would love to stay, but I made plans with Siddiq. Are you going to be all right?"

Tangie hugged her best friend. "Yeah, go on, get out of here. You don't need to baby-sit me, although I love the company. You go do what you need to with Siddiq. Are things cool with you guys?"

Candy grinned happily. "Yeah, we're working things out slowly but surely. If it's not too late when I get home I'll call you, okay?"

"Sure . . . I think after the way I've been looking lately, I am going to give myself a facial and turn in.

Seriously though, now that I've gotten it out I do feel better. I'm not going to flake out on you or anything. Come on, I'll walk you to the door."

Candy sighed. Her heart was breaking for her best buddy. "Hang in there, sweetie. Call me on my cell if you need me."

"Will do. Holler at you later."

Tangie straightened up around the house, then went upstairs. She took a long look at herself in the mirror. She needed a perm, manicure, and pedicure—the works. She usually didn't do her own hair, but after looking at her roots, she decided emergency measures were necessary.

"When they say go on with your bad self, I don't think this is what they have in mind," she told the mirror and chuckled.

She put on Jon B's *Cool Relax* CD and started with her hair. She hummed along with Jon as she put the chemicals throughout her unruly strands.

After she completed the perm process, she took a shower using her signature scent. She blow-dried and curled her hair when she was finished.

Since she was there, she took a moment to inspect her face in the mirror. She noticed the fine lines around her mouth and eyes as well as other telltale signs that she was indeed over thirty. She rummaged through her skin care products until she found what she was looking for. She looked at her bathroom decor; it would be time to redecorate soon, she thought absently.

She put the cleansing mask on, then settled down to do her nails. She planned to use her Bogota Blackberry on them. It was another one of her favorite colors.

As soon as she finished the last nail, the bell rang three times in succession.

"Ugh, girl, if you only knew how close you are coming to getting it." She shrugged on her robe, fussing all the way, and padded to the door.

She threw it open without bothering to look through the peephole. "Candy, girl."

When she saw who was at the door she yelped, "Ahhh, Eric!"

Eric stood in her doorway smiling that devilishly mischievous smile.

He looked down at his watch. "I think that you are well past your three days. I couldn't wait any longer."

Eric didn't care about the face cream. He only cared that he was finally seeing her. He reached for her, gently pulling her to him. He captured her lips in a searing kiss. He ignored her initial protests and was satisfied when she moaned and melded her body to his.

When he finally released her, she pulled him into her living room and flew up the stairs to her bathroom. Tangie took one look at her reflection in the mirror and screamed in embarrassment. *Eric, how could you?* She hurriedly washed off the pink mask and put on a simple shirt-dress to go back down to him.

When she returned he was making tea in her kitchen; he looked like he owned the place. He seemed to find a way to be comfortable in any surrounding. Eric was thoroughly pleased . . . he hadn't been sure that she would see him at all.

When Tangie saw him she had to convince her knees not to buckle. The man was sex appeal on two legs.

As soon as she passed the living room the smell of her cucumber melon shower gel tickled his senses. He inhaled deeply, thinking back to when he first met her. *Some things don't change.*

Tangie put her hands on her hips. "Eric Duvernay, where have you been? I have been trying to reach you now for months. To tell you the truth, I had just about given up."

He brought the herbal tea he had made over to her breakfast bar. After he'd set the mugs down, he cupped her face in his hands. "Don't ever give up on me, Tangie. I've missed you so much."

"Then why are we talking?" she asked.

Eric looked at her. "You are so beautiful. I don't think I will ever get enough of you."

Desire electrified the air around them. She didn't know who moved first, but she was in his arms again. The tea was forgotten. . . .

That familiar fire started at her core. Eric deepened the kiss. Tangie felt her knees go weak. His strong arms tightened around her; he stroked the small of her back. She held on to him for dear life. She pressed her body closer . . . closer. Soft moans escaped her lips. Soon there would be no turning back; the bed was mere steps away.

There was no mistaking his desire for her . . . she felt him strained against the fabric of his jeans. It would be so easy to give in to temptation. . . .

Tangie finally broke the kiss that had them both begging for oxygen.

She leaned her forehead on his muscled chest. He felt so strong and so wonderful—she didn't want to ever leave this place. But common sense took over. It had been several months since New Orleans; she had a lot to tell him about and she needed to hear about his life.

Tangie breathed heavily against his chest. "Eric, as much as I'm enjoying this, we need to slow down. Let me warm up this tea and I'll meet you in the family room. By the way, hello. We kinda skipped that part."

Eric smiled. "Yeah, I suppose we did. How are you, Ms. Taylor?"

"Much better now, Mr. Duvernay." She could look into those dark brown eyes all day. "Have a seat, I'll be right with you."

Eric walked into her family room. With her open floor plan, he could still see her moving around in the kitchen and he loved the view. She hadn't changed too much since New Orleans. He could tell she had been working out. She looked toned and healthy. He could watch her graceful movements all day, he thought.

She'd let her hair grow out too. It was almost to the middle of her back. He imagined how during love-making he would run his hands through her tresses. Those kinds of thoughts did nothing to alleviate the tight pressure he was already feeling in his groin.

Tangie set up a serving tray. She had just put the last item on it when she realized that he might be hungry. "Eric, do you want something to nibble on?"

"Sure, but I can wait until you get here."

"Mr. Duvernay, did I fail to mention that I am not on the menu?"

The buzzing of Eric's pager interrupted their light-hearted repartee.

Eric closed his eyes. "Not now!"

Tangie put the tray back down on the kitchen counter. She had to assume it was about a case.

She looked at him impassively. "Duty calls. I'll be in the kitchen until you're done."

Eric nodded affirmatively.

Tangie watched him for several seconds before turning away. *Is this the way it's always going to be?* she questioned. Interruptive calls in the middle of the night, during dinners, making love, being together, all for the next case? She wasn't sure she was ready for that. Her own job was demanding enough. She just didn't know if she could handle his too.

"Agent Duvernay." Eric listened for several seconds before letting out a string of curses that would make a seasoned sailor proud.

He was already moving toward the door when he called out, "Tangie, I've got to go. I'll call you as soon as I can. Thank you for seeing me tonight."

Tangie was so outdone all she could do was wave.

She poured out his mug of tea, drank her own, and then prepared herself for bed. It was almost 11:00 P.M. Tangie decided she would watch the nightly news, then turn in.

Despite the abrupt end to the day she was glad he came over. She smiled to herself. *At least some of my prayer was answered.* She would know for sure when he called her again.

She would call Candy in the morning to give her what she hoped was the good news.

Chapter 16

"Candy, I don't want you to scream or act crazy at work, but I need to tell you something."

"Ohh, girl, what's going on? It's sounds juicy by your tone."

"I told you not to act crazy now. Eric came over last night after you left. He had been thinking about me and trying to figure out what to do about us, but his schedule was really crazy at work."

"Tangie, are you messing with me?" Candy asked, incredulous.

"Believe me, no one was more surprised than me, girl. I had my pink facial mask on when I answered the door. I thought it was you. I couldn't believe he was standing there . . . it's been over six months with no contact from him."

Candy was almost over the shock. Now she had questions. "Okay, now what does this mean? What happened last night?"

Tangie knew what was coming, so she prepared herself for the inquisition. "We talked Candy. Okay, so he kissed me until my knees were weak, but we talked. I have missed him so much, I was so nervous. I mean, I didn't know if I had just gone off the deep end with him . . . made a relationship out of something that wasn't there. Call me crazy, but when I looked into his eyes, I knew that it was real, everything that I have felt for him these past several months is real . . . very real."

Candy listened quietly before asking, "And now the plan is?"

"Well, my dear, I suppose the plan is he will call me and we will take it from there. We were interrupted by work so we didn't get too far."

Uh-oh. Something in Tangie's tone set off Candy's alarm bells. "Okay, give it up, what's the untold story, Tangie?"

"I've got a meeting in ten minutes. Can you meet me for dinner at the usual place at 6:00 P.M.?"

"Sure, I'll be there. Are you okay?"

Tangie sighed. "I'm fine . . . just need a sounding board, that's all."

"Okay, see you at 6:00."

Tangie took a moment to collect herself. Since her promotion to vice president, work had seemed nonstop. There were meetings, conferences, new product forums, and focus groups. Her department had grown significantly under her tutelage. Her drive and determination had propelled her rapidly through the ranks.

She leaned back in her red butter-soft leather chair. She wondered if she could really have it all. The man she loved, career, and children?

When she returned from the conference room, there was a message on her private line.

It was from Karen, her receptionist.

"Hi, Ms. Taylor, this message came for you and I thought you might appreciate it in your private box."

Tangie smiled, intrigued. She sat down in her chair and waited for the message to play.

"Hi, Tangie, I just wanted to call to tell you how much I miss you already. I thoroughly enjoyed last night and hope we can see each other again soon. This is my direct line. . . ."

Tangie copied the number into her private Rolodex system and also in her Palm Pilot.

She grinned like the Cheshire Cat the rest of the day.

At 5:30 P.M., she let out a sigh of relief. It had been a long day, but she could finally start to close down. She called Candy's cell phone to let her know that she was running about twenty-five minutes late. Then she sat back in her chair, and with nervous fingers she dialed Eric's number. She was disappointed when she just got his voice mail, but it was getting late so she decided to go.

She met Candy at Bennigan's at about 6:30 P.M. Candy had arrived only moments before Tangie had.

"Hey, girl, I took the liberty of ordering the wings. How are you?" Candy asked.

"Whew! What a day. I am so beat, I don't think I could cook if you paid me. Thanks for ordering. I think I am going to add a salad to that."

"You sound like I feel. Take a minute to collect yourself."

Tangie sat back for a moment. She lifted her feet halfway out of her shoes and relaxed.

"See now, you look better already."

Tangie grinned. "You're right. I just needed a moment. Eric called while I was in a marketing meeting. He left me a message with his number. I called him back before coming here, but got his voice mail too."

Candy looked at her friend in anticipation. "So tell me about last night. Does he still look like you remember?"

"Yep, even better. I swear that man is good enough to eat. I loved running my fingers through his curls when he kissed me." Tangie flushed with the memory.

"Oh, Tangie, look at you. It is so good to see you happy again. If he makes you blush like this, why did you sound so hesitant on the phone?"

Tangie paused before answering her friend . . . tucking errant hairs behind her ears.

"Candy, I was so excited about seeing him. I mean, it was like a dream come true and I know he wanted to be with me too. When he got that page . . . something in me felt scared. I just kept thinking about New Orleans . . . how he lied to me. I guess I was having flashbacks about all the stuff that happened since . . . I know I shouldn't do this, but I don't know if I can trust him again."

"Tangie, come on!"

"I know . . . I know . . . I've got to let it go. I can't keep blaming him for being undercover. I know intellectually that he was just doing his job, but emotionally . . . it is something else. Candy, I don't want to go down that road again—self-doubt, not trusting. Being with Eric would be wonderful, but it's so scary."

"Girl, it's okay to be scared, but you can't let fear ruin your life. Don't cheat yourself out of having something wonderful with Eric. I don't think he means you any harm and besides, you said yourself, your feelings are real. Trust that . . . let the rest work itself out. Come on, let's eat."

"Hey, you get no argument from me on that score. We can pick this up later. Honestly, I do feel better . . . I just needed to get some things off my chest."

Between bites, Candy replied, "You know, I'm always here for you. Do me a favor, just call him if he doesn't call you. Keep leaving messages for each other if you have to—I don't think that I can take the drama of another long separation between you two."

Tangie smirked. "Yeah, you're just what I need, my selfless friend who is just thinking about my best interests. You are truly altruistic!"

The next two weeks were very trying. She and Eric managed to talk on the phone each night, but had been unable to see each other. Tangie was beside herself with anxiety and questioned if they should continue or just move on without each other. She spoke regularly with Candy or her mom, but the feelings of uneasiness would not abate.

She was preparing herself for another lonely Friday night when Eric called. "Hi, babe, I know it has been pretty witchy lately, but are you up to hanging out tonight?"

"Hi yourself. It seems like ages since I've seen that handsome face of yours. Do you mind coming over though? I am too tired to do something out of the house; besides, once I finally see you I don't want to have to share you."

"You flatter me, Ms. Taylor. That being the case, would you mind opening the door? I miss you too much to stay away another second."

Tangie looked out her family room window. Eric was in his car in front of her condo.

"Eric Duvernay, we've got to stop meeting like this. Let me make myself presentable and I'll be right with you. Give me about two minutes."

"Take your time, I've got a couple more calls to make. I don't want to be disturbed once I finally see you, hold you in my arms."

Tangie wanted that too.

She dashed upstairs to change. She had been wearing a pair of ratty sweats and a faded T-shirt. She had showered after work, but didn't do much more than that.

Tangie rummaged through her closet frantically. She settled on a green and gold caftan that Siddiq and Candy had given her. The fabric was loose and free flowing, which was perfect, because comfort was the order of the day.

She gave her face and hair the once-over and went down to answer the door. Candy and Eric would have to come up with a better system of ringing her bell—they both rang it three times in succession. She would have to break her old and new friends of this grating habit.

She was in his arms before he was in the door.

His kisses were fiery and passionate. Tangie had no defense against the barrage of delight that had her weak in the knees. Eric knew her body so well . . . knew how to ignite her flame. She would have to be careful with him . . . very careful.

He released her, saying, "Now that's a fitting end to a bad week!"

"That's what I call a proper hello. Are you ready to

come in yet? I think we have given the neighbors enough of a show."

"Oh, I'm just warming up. They haven't seen the real show yet."

"And they never will. Get in here, Mr. Duvernay." Tangie led him to her kitchen. She put the kettle on for tea and took out some homemade cinnamon rolls she had in the refrigerator, which she warmed in her microwave. "I made these last night to munch on over the weekend. They're good, but not too sweet."

He looked very comfortable, seated at the breakfast bar. "Sounds perfect."

His voice was deep and sexy when he spoke to her again. "Come on, sit with me while everything gets ready. I just want to look at you."

Tangie felt her skin become heated. "Eric, it's dangerous how you turn me to mush. I seem to have no self-control when it comes to you."

"I'm going to take that as a compliment. I remember telling you something like that in New Orleans. I don't want to have a pity party, but when you left, Tangie, I felt like someone ripped my heart out. I don't ever want to go through that pain again. Promise me you'll always talk to me."

Tangie felt a panic attack coming on.

Her nervousness was evident when she spoke again. "Eric, we need to go slow. So much has happened lately and I am really not ready to plunge myself into something that's moving so quickly. I know I'm behaving like a chicken. Can't we just take this a step at a time?"

Eric released a long breath. "Tangie, I'll be as patient as you need me to be. I am not going to lie to you and say that I like it, but I'll be patient. I'll try not to push, but you should know that I want you in my life. Permanently. I am getting too old to beat around the bush. Tangie, I love you and I want to be with you."

"Eric, I—"

"Tangie, I won't push, I promise. I'm here when you're ready. You'll get no more ultimatums or pressure from me."

Tangie gave him a weary smile. "Thank you. Can I ask you one favor?"

"Anything."

"Just hold me for a minute. Let me feel you against me."

"Come here," he whispered. His voice was thick with desire. She was going to make his earlier promise very difficult to keep.

The microwave sounded, signaling that the rolls were ready. Tangie reluctantly disentangled herself from Eric's embrace. "I should get that. It seems when it comes to eating we are always getting interrupted. Let's do it while we can." No sooner had the words left her mouth than the phone began to ring. They both looked at it and laughed.

Tangie threw her hands up in the air. "Help yourself. I'm sure this will only take a minute."

She quickly crossed the room to answer the phone. She glanced at the caller ID and smiled.

"Hi, Mom."

"Hi, baby girl. What are you doing?"

Tangie felt heat to the tips of her ears. "I've got company right now. Can I call you later?"

"Sure, I was just checking in with you. Call me at some point this weekend."

"Don't worry, Ma, I'll call you tonight before your

regular bedtime. I know I have at least until you've exhausted all the sports news on-line," she teased.

Hattie laughed. "Well . . . you're right about that. I'll catch you later. Say hello to him—whoever he is."

How does she know that? "I will, Mom. Love you."

Tangie chuckled. "Well, that was the irrepressible Hattie Taylor. You're in for a treat when you meet her."

She returned to Eric, who was cutting the rolls. She loved having him in her kitchen . . . he seemed so natural. She came up behind him and encircled his waist.

He stopped what he was doing to pull her closer. He inhaled the light fruity fragrance she wore. "So when do I get to meet the parents?"

"We haven't even had our first date yet. I don't even know if you're presentable," she teased him mischievously.

Eric turned around to face her. Her gave her a sound kiss before asking, "What do you think? Presentable enough?"

"Hey, just because you can kiss a woman senseless doesn't mean she can take you home to Mama. You got those buns ready yet?"

Eric flicked the dishcloth at her. "Yeah, I got those buns ready. Are you ready for these buns?"

Tangie heard the sensual challenge in his voice. "Come on, I think we'd better eat. You are getting delirious."

He followed her to the dinette table and sat down with her. "So you say I haven't taken you on your first date yet? Where would you like to go? I am game for anything . . . anywhere."

"Hmmm . . . sounds tempting, but the next couple of weeks are going to be ugly for me. I have to run to LA for a week with my team. We are previewing some new products. Anyway, we have a lot to do to get ready, so my nights are pretty well committed. How's your schedule in two weeks?"

Eric shifted uncomfortably in his seat.

She looked at him. His dark eyes were uneasy. "Okay, spill it!"

"I'm going to have to go to Ireland for at least a couple of weeks, probably more like a month. It has to do with a training incident that happened several months ago. There's a civil suit going on, which is about all I am able to say. Believe me though, this has nothing to do with being undercover or covert operations. In some ways I wish it did. This is political and much more frightening."

Tangie was silent. They were looking at about six weeks before they would see each other again.

"So did you come here tonight to butter me up because you knew you were leaving?" she asked angrily.

Eric reached for her hand. "No, Tangie, I came here tonight because I want to be with you. I need to be with you. I promised you in New Orleans that I wouldn't lie to you again. If there's something going on at work, I'll just let you know that I can't talk about it. I deal in matters of national security, but nothing matters as much as you. Tangie, you've got to stop doubting me."

"Eric, I don't doubt you . . . I think I doubt me. I don't know what to think. I just know that for as long as you are gone again, I'll feel empty inside," she told him honestly.

"I don't even want to consider a long separation again, but we've hit the high points of our careers. In a few years we'll be begging for excitement again."

Eric tried to laugh, but it was no use. There was a permanent damper on the evening.

"Come on, I am inviting myself to your family room. Let's talk while we snuggle. I just want to have you close to me."

Tangie brightened slightly. "That sounds like a plan, after that disappointing news. Let me just grab some water. I'll meet you in there."

Tangie straightened their small mess and brought two bottles of cold water to her small cocktail table. Eric sat on the couch so that Tangie could position herself to be cradled in the crook of his arms. They sat next to each for several seconds just enjoying the time and space. Their hearts beat in unison . . . they breathed in unison . . . no words were necessary.

Eric stroked the small expanse of skin on her arm that peeked out of the caftan. Tangie's breath quickened in reaction to the small movement.

He noticed the small change in her; he felt himself harden in concert with her reaction.

Tangie looked into his eyes. Desire shone bright in his mahogany orbs. "Eric, I'm not ready to make love to you yet."

She moved to be in his arms, pressing her body close to his. He embraced her, loving the feel of her body against his. Eric kissed her deeply before responding. "I know, but would you let me make love to you? I just want to taste you, Tangie."

He teased each nipple with the pad of his thumb. He made gentle circles first, then squeezed the buds. Tangie felt her body's reaction in her core. Moisture began to pool between her legs. Her nipples strained against the fabric of her garment and yearned to be free, free to be enveloped by his hot mouth.

Tangie arched her back toward him, giving him greater access to her. He gently slid a hand along the soft skin of her thigh. She moaned with every touch.

His fingers found her wet center, and he continued gently probing her through the silk of her thong. He took off the thin covering in a single motion. Tangie's body responded to his every command. She was pulling the caftan over her head before she realized what she had even done. The air hitting her exposed skin did nothing to cool her ardor. She wanted nothing more than to be his. Eric granted her wish. He took a hard nipple in his mouth, loving it gently at first, then nipping it with his teeth. He felt so good; she wanted more. She called out his name. He continued his assault on her senses. He moved from her nipples and kissed the smooth skin of her abdomen. His fingers continued to move against her wet silky folds. He moved gently, but more insistently until he gained access. He caressed the bud of her clitoris until Tangie began rocking to his rhythm. Eric increased the pressure until he could feel her about to have an orgasm. He positioned his body over hers to suck her nipples at the same time as he worked below. Tangie bucked wildly, calling out his name repeatedly. He felt her passionate release as she held on to him while her body shattered into a thousand pieces.

After several minutes her breathing returned to normal. "I like the way you snuggle, Mr. Duvernay."

Eric slipped his fingers into his mouth. "And I like the way you taste, Ms. Taylor. Do I get seconds?"

Eric's mouth took over where his fingers had been. He licked her feminine juices, which were threatening to spill out over the couch where they were sitting. He loved her with his mouth until she came for him again. She was exhausted and very well sated after he finished with her. It would be a long uncomfortable drive back to Manassas . . . he would have to seek his own relief at home. No amount of cold water would soothe this ache.

Eric had stayed with her long enough to tuck her into bed. It had taken every ounce of his willpower not to slip under the sheets with her. He watched her as she drifted into a deep, comfortable sleep. He did a security check around her house out of habit, locked her door, and left quietly.

It was almost 2:00 A.M. when he settled in for the night.

Tangie and Eric spent Saturday and Sunday together as well, during the rest of the weekend enjoying movies and reading together. He came over to her place each time becoming more comfortable with each visit.

Sunday night before he left, Tangie presented him with her key. "Take this so you won't have to lean on my doorbell. You can let yourself in as long as I know you're coming."

Eric was pleased. "Tangie, are you sure?"

"Yes, I am sure. It's just a key. Now, go on. We both have to get ready for another hectic workweek."

"Thank you, Tangie. I'll have a key ready for you when you get back from LA." He kissed her soundly before leaving.

She tasted her musky essence on his tongue from their earlier activities. It was going to be real tough not to see him for so long after their weekend of ecstasy.

Chapter 17

They continued their nightly routine of calling and sending e-mails to each other, but their separation proved to be far longer than anticipated.

Eric called her from Ireland after she returned from her business trip. "Tangie, sorry about calling so late your time. I have bad news. The judge in this case has ordered a recess for two weeks to review some documents, but I can't leave. I'm going to be here for another month while this mess gets straightened out."

"Eric, no. I can't bear the thought of not seeing you for over two months . . . not now."

"I know, sweetheart. I feel the same way. Did you get the package I left for you? I left you keys to my place."

"Yes, I did, but now it looks like it will be a while before I get to see it. Are you doing okay over there? You sound tired."

"I'm fine. I just miss you and wish I didn't have to be here. Listen, I've got to go, we are about to reconvene. Tangie, I love you."

Eric had to hang up before she could respond.

"I love you too," she said to the dial tone.

Later in the evening, she received a call from

Candy. They had not spoken in days, which was unusual for them.

"Hey, girl, it's Candy. You remember me, right? Best friend since kindergarten?"

Tangie chuckled. "Oh, are you the one that was voted Drama Queen for four straight years in high school? Oh yeah, I remember you. How have you been, crazy woman?"

"I've been fine, but I miss my crazy friend. I take it things are going better with you and that handsome Duvernay guy? When am I going to get a chance to meet him, by the way?"

Tangie paused. "I don't know. You'll have to ask his wife. I'm just the mistress."

"Tangie, what are you talking about?"

"Oh, girl, calm down. I am talking about his job. He is married to it! Right now, he is overseas and he doesn't really know when he will be back. Which, if it is in another month or so, will be horrible timing. Remember that convention I told you about last year? I didn't have the heart or the time to tell him that it starts about the time he returns. I'll be out of town for three weeks because of the convention and the training I am doing in Philly. This is turning into a big mess."

"Sounds like you guys are having a long-distance relationship living in the same state."

"You know what, as crazy as that seems . . . that about sums it up. We're getting ready to go into a heavy workload for the next few months, and to tell you the truth I don't know when we are going to have time for each other. I was looking forward to this schedule before he came back into my life. Some events I even planned as a way not to mope around.

Now I think I'll be moping because he's back and I can't see him. I want you to meet him, but when you will—your guess is as good as mine."

"That sounds serious. What are you going to do?"

"Try to wait it out, see what happens over the next few weeks."

Tangie and Eric arrived at the door at the same time. She was leaving with suitcase in hand and he was arriving.

Tangie looked at him in surprise. "Oh, sweetie, didn't you get my e-mail? I am on my way to Providence for two weeks. Then I'll be in Philadelphia for another week. I'm running late now, I'll call you when I land, okay? Give me a quick peck before I go."

"I'm sorry, I thought that you were leaving next week. Damn, this is tougher than I thought it would be. Trying to meld two busy schedules is murder!"

Eric did kiss her, though it was anything but quick.

"You don't play fair, you know that I have to go. I don't want to get caught in long security lines."

"Then let me drive you. We can spend some time together on the way to the airport."

"I would love to, but my boss, Cliff, will be here any second."

Cliff arrived before Eric could protest. He kissed Tangie again, then helped her with her luggage.

He sat in his car for several minutes after Tangie had driven off. He tamped down any doubt . . . ignoring what his subconscious screamed at him. "Things will work out!" he said aloud.

Eric drove home angrily. This was not working out the way he'd imagined.

When he got home he unloaded his own trunk and went inside. It seemed that he spent so little time in his home it was foreign to him. Eric dreaded the emptiness that surrounded him whenever he was away from Tangie. In the short time of their reconciliation she had taken over his heart; he didn't feel whole without her. He dragged himself up the stairs. His father had the dogs temporarily, and the house had an eerie silence. He checked the house until satisfied that it was secure, then went to catch a quick nap before Tangie called.

However, the time difference and exhaustive schedule had taken their toll on him. Eric's catnap lasted over eight hours. He missed two calls from Tangie during that time.

He called her at the hotel as soon as he got himself together. He was so tired he felt groggy.

"Hi, Tangie, sorry I missed you. I was in a dead sleep when you called. How was your trip?"

"I thought you might be tired, that's why I tried you twice. Are you feeling better now?"

Eric yawned. "A little, but I think I am probably going to be no good for a couple of days. I have to go in tomorrow and do my debriefing, but I am getting out of there as quickly as I can. I think I've earned a few days off."

"I know the feeling. Things are just gearing up with me and I'm exhausted. I was burning the midnight oil while you were away. I think we'll all be happy after these next few months. There's a lot going on . . . talk of mergers and moving departments. I don't foresee being able to take time off for a while, unfortunately. You'll have to remind me what a weekend is like for normal people."

"Are you sure you can't squeeze in any time for one of those normal people? You really wreak havoc on my psyche when I can't see you."

Tangie chuckled. "Okay, so now I have to make you the king of drama, with Candy as your queen. You sound as pitiful as she does . . . She wants to meet you, by the way. As far as my schedule goes, I don't want to sound difficult but it just really depends on what happens over the next couple of weeks."

Eric shifted the phone from ear to ear. He tried not to imagine Tangie next to him on his king-sized bed. "Considering the last six months that I've had, I can understand that. Do you have your laptop with you?"

"Of course, never leave home without it."

"Then I guess it will be back to daily e-mails and nightly phone calls."

Eric yawned again.

"All right, sleepy. Get some more rest. I'll send you words of my undying devotion before I shut down for the evening. I love you."

"Love you too. I'll look for you on-line later. Have a good time and as always, be careful."

"Always am, my secret agent man. Have a good week . . . don't let them work you too hard while I'm away. I want you fresh and ready to go when I get back."

"By your command. Good night."

Tangie's return was marked by another lengthy separation. Eric was tasked to do training for commanders in the Middle East. He would be out of the country for six months.

Eric was waiting at her place when Cliff dropped off Tangie. "Hi, beautiful, did you miss me?"

Tangie smiled radiantly. "Eric! What a pleasant surprise. I didn't think I would see you tonight. Don't you have an early morning run?"

His rakish smile had her heart beating staccato.

"Yep, but I couldn't stand another minute away from you. So did you miss me?"

"Give me a second to open this door and I'll show you just how much." Her gaze met his headlong. It would be mere seconds before they were in each other's arms. Anticipation made her nervous. It took two attempts before she was able to get the door open.

Eric brought her suitcase in before disappearing again.

When he returned he brought her a huge bouquet of red and white roses. "Every time you see them I want you to remember how much I love you."

Tangie threw her arms around him. "Come here, Secret Agent Duvernay. I don't need anything but you to remind me how much you love me. All I want is you." His soft black waves felt like silk against her hand.

"I'm here, Tangie . . . always will be."

She inhaled the heady masculine scent of his cologne. He was wearing Tuscany again. He knew how to wear her down. Tangie was ready to give him her body. Physically she had always been ready, but emotionally not until now. "Give me a minute to freshen up? I feel hot and sticky."

"So do I," he teased.

Tangie grinned. "Have you always been this incorrigible?"

"Yep." This time both dimples were evident when he smiled.

She kissed him before going upstairs . . . then left him to his own devices while she went to freshen up.

Fifteen minutes later, she found him in her kitchen. That was quickly becoming his favorite room in her house. He loved the homey atmosphere. Eric was in the process of making pasta salad when she joined him.

"That's looks great. Are you always so handy in the kitchen?"

"Told you in New Orleans, I am a man of many talents. I thought you might be a little hungry. Airplane food, such as it is, doesn't really qualify for balanced nutrition."

"I am a little hungry. Thank you. Do you need me to do anything?"

"Nope, just sit back and let me serve you. What would you like to drink?"

"Well, since we are having pasta, how about some white wine?"

"Perfect. How about you start that chilling? This will be done in a sec."

After he had put everything in the refrigerator, he and Tangie sat on the couch in her family room to talk.

"You know this is a very dangerous place for us."

Eric laughed. "Yes, I know, but so comfortable."

He stroked the side of her face. He loved the feel of her skin . . . she was so soft and beautiful; he knew he would desire her always.

"Why do I get the feeling that you are holding something back? More than intuition, I see it in your eyes. What's going on, Eric? We promised each other honesty."

Eric rolled his shoulders to loosen the knots of tension he felt. "You know me too well . . . There's something I need to tell you, but I'd prefer to wait until later if that's okay with you."

"My imagination is already doing double time. . . ."

Eric paused for a moment. "You're right, may as well get this over with. My job as an instructor has been rather eventful since I came back to Virginia. I have done more as an instructor than when I did undercover work, it seems. Command has asked me to do training with some foreign officers, which is an honor, but it's for six months."

Tangie looked worried.

"Honey, I am going to have to go to Egypt for six months."

A steady stream of hot tears flowed down her face. Tangie had made the decision that she felt was best, but it didn't stop her heart from breaking. She had to end her relationship with Eric. *Now I know why people say love is not always enough,* she thought sadly.

"Eric, I can't do this anymore. We never see each other."

He reached for her. He wanted to hold her in his arms, but she pulled back.

"Tangie, don't you think I hate this too? I want nothing more than to be in your arms every night, but I have a responsibility to the Bureau. I can't just walk away from that. I've already given up field work. . . ."

She bristled. "No, don't you dare lay that at my feet. I never asked you to give up undercover work for me. We've both made our own choices. I can accept responsibility for mine. Can you?"

This evening was definitely not going as planned, he thought.

"Tangie, we don't have to do this. I didn't mean to lay blame on you about anything. Honey, I would do anything for you. Don't misunderstand me. I just need you to be patient with me. We've spent so much time looking for each other—I've wanted someone like you in my life—always. Tangie, I love you. Six months or six years apart won't change that. We can work through this. As soon as things slow down at work, why don't we take a vacation? Spend some time hiking or camping by a lake?" He knew he was starting to sound a little desperate, but he didn't care. As long as Tangie didn't walk out on him.

Tears still streamed down her face, and she wiped at them angrily. She shook her head. "No, Eric, I can't. I won't. It took everything I had to learn how to trust you, to put my faith in you and give you my heart. I need more than you can give me. I know that you love me, but we need to be together; otherwise it just isn't enough."

He reached for her again and again she pulled away.

"Please don't do this to me, to us. Tangie, I can't go on an emotional roller coaster. If this is your decision I'll abide by it."

Chapter 18

Before Eric left that evening Tangie asked for her key back. Eric put it in her hand. He walked out the door without a word. The hurt and pain that she saw in his eyes spoke volumes.

When she felt that she had run out of tears, she called Candy, who chastised her for giving up so soon, especially after waiting so long to be with him again. But she would not be deterred. Tangie and Eric had been trying to work things out for over six months now.

They had been on the phone for over thirty minutes and despite her best efforts, Tangie wouldn't budge.

"Candy, how much longer do I wait? How long would you give Siddiq? I can't do this. I want him too much. I loved having him in my kitchen . . . I almost felt . . . when we are together it's like we are the only two people in the world, but it only seems to last for a minute. If it's not my job, then it's his. I am tired; I can't do this anymore. I'm starting to feel like I did when Rodney started flaking out on me."

"Are you absolutely sure you aren't punishing Eric for your past relationships?"

"No, Dr. Phil. This is about the way I feel right now

and it's not about baggage from my previous relationships. I am totally over everything that happened with Rodney. This is about trusting that I am not going to get lost in the shuffle . . . that the next big case takes him away from me for good. This is about not feeling comfortable and hating the uncertainty."

Tangie blew out an anxious breath. "Do you see where I am coming from?"

"No, because to me, you work at it until there's nothing left. I think you're giving up too easily, and frankly I think you're going to regret it later."

The bottom line for Tangie was she wanted more than she felt Eric could give to her, and at this point in her life she wasn't willing to compromise. She would never ask him to give up his job. He had already stopped doing undercover work for her, but she wouldn't be second best to it either. She had been down that road with Rodney. She needed a man where she could be the number-one priority.

She had a demanding job too; so she didn't see where she and Eric could come up with a compromise. Tangie felt it was better to cut her losses before any more time passed . . . she wasn't getting any younger.

Furthermore, Candy's wedding was weeks away and Tangie felt jealousy worming its way into her heart. She and Eric didn't spend the kind of time that Candy and Siddiq were able to—Candy never questioned her importance to him. This man was defying family, tradition, and religion to be with her.

It made Tangie realize that she wanted the type of commitment from Eric that moved heaven and earth—and that's exactly what he could not promise her.

Despite urgings from her mother and Candy not to

do it, Tangie severed all ties with Eric. Many times her fingers dialed his number, but she refused to give in to the inner voice that begged her to give him one more chance. She also refused his calls. She knew if she talked to him she would give in. She just hoped that in time the pain would lessen. Somehow, she doubted that this would be an easy process.

Weeks into his assignment, his phone calls were unreturned. It was difficult for him to even call because his training missions usually ran all week long. When he had a break, he would write letters to her or just collapse in the bed in his small room. This was a no-frills assignment. Not like others he had been on where he had time to explore the culture. Security was heightened in the region where he was conducting training with high-ranking military officials. He had few privileges and precious little free time. He looked forward to returning to United States soil and hopefully to Tangie. Though those odds were looking pretty slim.

He gave it one more shot when he returned after being out of the country for a little more than six months. He promised himself one last phone call or message before he gave up. Eric was exasperated to get her answering machine again. "Tangie, when we found each other again I only asked one thing of you and that was for you not to give up on me. It seems that's exactly what you've done. I love you, Tangie, and I know you love me. If you honestly don't want to try to work things out, then I won't call again. I want to hear from you more than anything in this world, but I will respect whatever decision you make."

Eric had enough faith in their love for both of them, but he refused to take on the sole responsibility for the relationship. If he couldn't make Tangie happy . . . he would let her go. Again.

Chapter 19

Eric sat at his desk. He had been back for a month now and had heard nothing from Tangie. The case he had been working on was a mess and had been time-consuming. He supposed he could have tried harder to reach her, maybe even called earlier. He was more convinced than ever that if Tangie had felt the same way about him as he did about her, she would have attempted to call him more often or at least tried to meet him halfway.

Tangie was adamant about not moving in with him or taking any steps to move the relationship to the next level. Her ambiguity was driving him crazy.

Eric's heart had had enough. He didn't want to step back into the world that he'd experienced when Rebecca died. He was now out of the game; as much as he loved her, he wouldn't allow his heart to become Tangie's doormat.

Nope, he thought. Ms. Tangerine Taylor would just have to go on without him and he without her. Oddly enough, after finally making that decision, he felt little better. He knew he couldn't go around feeling uptight and anxious all the time. But where did that leave him?

Eric wouldn't call Tangie again. She was too unsure

of him, doubted he could make the type of commitment to her that she wanted. Tangie would never understand his job or understand how he could be so committed to her and the job.

Eric decided to take time to focus on himself, get back into tiptop shape, and concentrate on being a better instructor. The world was becoming a much more dangerous place these days. There were bombings in the Middle East, Europe, and the United States too.

To many, the value of human life had gone down to nothing. Men would cheat their own mothers for another dollar. Kids were shooting each other over tennis shoes.

Yeah, he needed to focus on the job and taking care of business. Training had become more important than ever to the Bureau. Eric had a responsibility to the agents and soldiers that he worked with on a daily basis.

The dismal situation with Morrow and O'Malley had shown him that he needed to stay on top of things and that he couldn't afford to let his guard down *again*. Maybe if he had been more focused, he would have seen it coming. He should have known better and that's what happens when you get distracted. He made a vow to himself that he wouldn't work any more seventy-hour workweeks, but he would definitely put certain feelings on hold. That was the plan, anyway. . . .

Tangie knew he was back, but she refused to call him. There was too much in the way of their relationship. She had joked with Candy about being his mistress, but the analogy fit. He was married to his job—he wanted her as his part-time lover. The last separation was the last straw. What would be next? It was better to let it go. She would get over him. Eventually. Tired of moping around and being stressed out, Tangie began a physical fitness routine to rival any the armed forces had to offer. She went to the gym nightly and worked out on the bikes and free weights. She began to develop a tone and strength in her body that matched how she felt emotionally. It had been several months since she had last seen Eric Duvernay, or whatever his name was. She wanted a relationship, a commitment from him that superseded his job. Tangie wasn't up to being his mistress, she wanted more from him. If she couldn't have it, she was prepared to move on. She learned to let her other interests take her mind off of her broken heart.

Her routine was standard until this evening. She decided to go into the basketball room to see if she still had any of her high school moves. To her surprise, the room was almost empty, and she didn't pay any attention to the young man practicing three-point shots. She grabbed a ball and towel and proceeded to play by herself. She was vaguely aware of him, but couldn't make out any of his features. She just concentrated on playing basketball. She was making baskets from all angles and was starting to feel the old vibe back, from when she had played in the city championships for three years. Tangie was totally in the zone now, missing few baskets and feeling on top of the world. She dribbled, faked out invisible opponents, drove the ball down the lane, went up with a perfect arch, and released an air ball.

To her chagrin, she heard a delighted chuckle behind her. Cheeks flaming with embarrassment, she turned around to face the second most gorgeous man she'd ever seen in her life!

She was three feet away from the poster boy for *Ebony Man*. Her mouth dropped open instinctively, her body warming in all the right places. Tangie's mind screamed, *Oh no, not again.*

Before things could get any worse, she closed her mouth and quickly stalked off the court. She left the gym and never looked back toward the courts.

Later on that night Tangie told Candy about her little incident. "Girl, you could have bought me for a penny. I was so embarrassed, I don't know if I can show my face in that gym again."

"Okay, cut to the chase, was the brother fine? From your breathless description of what happened, I'd guess so. Does this mean you are finally over Eric?"

"Oh, shut up . . . yes, he is fine. He is the true meaning of tall, dark, and handsome. He is six five, coffee-brown complexion, big nut-brown eyes with flecks of gold, with lashes from here to DC. Oh yeah . . . he's fine and we haven't even discussed that body yet."

Tangie giggled nervously. "And even though he had on baggy shorts and an oversized T-shirt, I could tell he is definitely something to look at. But as you know, I'm not trying to go there—"

Candy interrupted excitedly. "Ohh, girl, sounds like he is a contender."

"Like I said, I'm not interested in pursuing a relationship with anyone, not because of Eric, but because right now I'm just concerned about me. I'm taking time out for myself and I don't want to be distracted. Besides, I made such an ass of myself, I don't ever want to see him again. But I guess I can't avoid the gym forever. I'm not going to give up my routine . . . maybe just my goal of playing for the Wizards next year."

"Tangie, you are so crazy! So how was it before the embarrassing episode? You want some company next time you go? I need to drop about ten pounds before this wedding."

Tangie cringed a little at the thought of Candy's wedding, but did not let on about her feelings. She said lightly, "As long as you're not coming just to check up on me, no problem. I could use the company. You think you can keep up with me?"

"Oh, please! Spare me. I'll meet you tomorrow at 5:30 P.M. Be there. I've got to run. My mom and I are going over wedding colors tonight. Holler at you later."

"Bye, girl, see you tomorrow."

Tangie made herself a simple dinner of salad and pasta and got comfortable. After dinner she took a nice long bubble bath. She was surprised to find herself slightly aroused at the thought of . . . She started to feel that familiar tingle. "Man, why did I have to attempt to play basketball? I was doing just fine not thinking about men." Her mind traveled back to the full, deliciously kissable lips that smiled, no, laughed at her in the gym. Tangie groaned, as the feelings of longing became stronger. She squeezed her thighs tightly together, trying to force away the pulsating feeling in her core.

In her aroused state, conflicting images of Eric and "tall, dark, and handsome" flashed in her mind and she felt invisible hands touching her in all the places she wanted to be caressed. No one had made her feel like a woman since Eric, and even then, they hadn't consummated the relationship.

New Orleans, Tangie thought bitterly. It had been the start of new pain.

It seemed like a hundred years ago. Was she really so blissfully happy with "Mr. Duval" there or was it just a case of what might have been? As long as Tangie concentrated on her feelings of anger . . . feelings of longing disappeared.

Thinking out loud, she said, "You've got to stop feeling sorry for yourself. You can't begrudge Candy's happiness. She's your best friend."

Tangie breathed in and out heavily . . . deep cleansing breaths that signified that she was ready for change. She wasn't going to stop living just because her best friend was about to get married and she wasn't in a relationship. She was smart and attractive and when her time came, she would be ready. In the meantime, she had family, friends, and work . . . and for right now that had to be enough. With that new resolution she felt better and tried to focus on other things.

Tangie ran more hot water in her bath, soaked for another forty-five minutes, and then curled up in bed with the newest Tom Clancy novel. Jack Ryan would keep her mind occupied. She needed the action and drama of a good espionage novel. At midnight, she closed her book and snuggled into her bed.

Tangie smiled. It was an ironic smile, for there was no joy in the gesture. Funny how she enjoyed the drama and fast-paced action of a good spy novel, but that life had cost her the man she loved. She went to sleep with thoughts of Eric on her mind once again. Everything came back to Eric.

* * *

Candy toyed with one of her decorator pillows as she talked. Siddiq knew it was a sure sign that she was nervous.

"I don't know, babe. I am really worried about her. Yeah, she says she is fine, she smiles at the appropriate times, and appears to say and do all the right things, but . . . I know her."

Candy smoothed out the comforter as she talked. "Something is definitely wrong and she's not talking. I didn't know if she feels uncomfortable because we are getting married or what. She's keeping secrets again. I can't figure my best friend out, and that really worries me."

Not sure she was finished, he replied quickly, "I know you two may fuss and fight but you love each other so much you always find a way to work things out. Don't worry about it. When Tangie is ready to talk, she'll come to you. Doesn't she always?"

"But, honey—" she started to protest.

"I know you're right, but I just wish she were as happy as we are now."

The poster boy for *Ebony Man*, better known as Kevin DePalma, sat in his bedroom listening to some jazz. Miles Davis was playing to an audience of none, as Kevin was so distracted. His thoughts kept traveling back to the lovely and delightful young lady he had teased at the gym. He was amused by what he had seen—a most charming young woman making a complete fool of herself. Oh, but she was nice to look at, a well-toned, lean physique, and he liked that in a woman.

He could tell she took good care of herself, and she

didn't appear stuck up or prissy. That was a big turnoff for him. Kevin noticed much more about her than he wanted to admit to himself. He really didn't want to get involved with anyone at this point. He'd been hurt a few times and now was focusing on his health and getting back into a league. He decided, however, if he saw her again . . . maybe it wouldn't hurt to go out for a bite.

The next day, Candy, true to her word, met Tangie at the gym. They went through their normal workout, all the while talking pleasantly. Tangie's heart fluttered each time she thought about that beautiful face. She tried to shake those thoughts loose and concentrate on her workout, but every so often her mind would wander.

Too often her eyes would betray her and look toward the gym door. Candy noticed too, but decided not to tease her about it. She would let this one play out since her friend seemed genuinely interested in someone else.

After about an hour in the gym, Candy and Tangie finished whipping their bodies into shape and headed out the door. Before they reached the archway, they heard a rich-timbered voice.

"No basketball today?"

Candy smiled and Tangie cringed. She replied through tight lips, in her sweetest sarcastic tone, "Any time you think you can handle a little one on one, call me."

Candy put her gym bag down to watch the show. She wanted to see what her friend would do.

Kevin replied, "Oh . . . I do like a challenge. I'll even

make it easy on ya. How about a game of horse? It's a simple game and I'm sure a woman with your skills can handle it. Make you a deal, loser buys dinner."

Tangie headed back toward the court without giving it a second thought. Over her shoulder she said, "You're on . . . let's go! Hmm . . . a big, juicy, tender steak would be nice."

Tangie and Kevin played the sophomoric game as if each shot would win the NBA championship. Tangie's heart beat a mile a minute as she attempted to sink the winning shot.

She misfired when Kevin cleared his throat loudly just as she was about to release the ball. She turned around angrily and spat out, "That wasn't fair and you owe me dinner!"

Holding the ball, he responded casually, "Ah . . . a sore loser, I see." He barely concealed a wide grin behind his hand. "Okay, you've got me. Steak, you say? What time should I pick you up and from where?"

Tangie realized things were moving a lot faster than she had anticipated. Her fun and games had progressed to an entirely new level.

What had she just agreed to? What about Eric? Who was this guy anyway?

Thinking she needed to get control of the situation again, she said quickly, "Hey, why don't I just meet you in Georgetown?"

Tangie continued, "How about 8:00 P.M.? I have an errand to run. We'll act European tonight, okay?" she said, referring to their late dinner hour.

This time he didn't bother to conceal his smile. "Sounds perfect, I like the restaurants in that area too. Let's meet in front of the Mall to decide where to eat."

Tangie practically glided home after leaving the

gym. She was in the shower before she realized that she hadn't even said good-bye to Candy. As a matter of fact, she didn't even remember seeing Candy after she went to play ball with Kevin.

Candy had watched Tangie and Kevin for a few minutes before quietly easing out the door. Not that it would have mattered with those two; apparently they only had eyes for each other. Candy could have left marching to the tune of the marine song and they wouldn't have noticed. And . . . that worried her about her friend. She knew Tangie was still very much in love with her workaholic Eric, so would Kevin just be a rebound lover?

Candy's phone rang; it was Tangie calling to apologize.

"Hey, girl, sorry about deserting you. I guess I got a little caught up," she said sheepishly.

"How are you, Ms. Basketball, what's going on? Tell me all about him."

Tangie was flushed and excited when she told her friend about her date. "You are so silly . . . His name is Kevin; he is very handsome, which you saw for yourself. He doesn't play fair, I'm having dinner with him in an hour, and I'm scared to death. Anything else you need to know?"

The tension was evident in Candy's voice. "What did you say? Dinner at 8:00 P.M. and how did this happen? I didn't think that you would move that fast. Do you even know his last name? Don't you think you need to take it more slowly?"

Annoyance punctuating her words, Tangie responded, "I don't believe this. *Ms. Get on with your life* doesn't want me to go to dinner. What's the deal, Candy?"

"Okay, okay, ease up, I'm sorry. I just don't want you to get hurt. Kevin appears to be nice and he is very handsome, but you don't know him. I'm just begging you to be careful. Make me a deal . . . leave your cell phone on and I'll call at 9:30 P.M. to make sure everything is okay. Say the word and I'll come rescue you. Siddiq is meeting with his brothers tonight to ease their minds about our wedding, so I'm totally free."

Tangie relaxed as she blew air out of her mouth slowly. "Candy, you are a nut, but you've got a deal. Listen, I gotta go, babe. I'll call you tonight if it isn't too late."

"Girl, if you know what's good for you, you'd better call me or I'll be sitting on your couch when you get home," Candy said, laughing.

Tangie groaned. "I'll call, I'll call. Bye."

Tangie and Kevin arrived at the Mall at the same time. After they had selected a nice, quiet restaurant, they watched each other cautiously as the hostess showed them to their seats.

Kevin tried to study Tangie unnoticed. He thought she looked even better in her clothes than in a revealing exercise outfit. Her curves were in all the right places. Kevin noticed that she was wearing an expensive-looking black suede pantsuit. The neckline of her shirt was just low enough to make a brother interested, but left a little for the imagination, he thought.

Before he realized it, Tangie saw the cute yet lewd smile that had crept across his face. Well, two could play at that game. He didn't look half bad in his midnight-blue, brushed silk shirt and black dress pants. She thought he certainly made a nice picture.

Kevin cleared his throat. He told her, "You look nice. I'm glad you made it. I wasn't sure you would show up after my roguish behavior. I apologize for cheating, but it looks like it worked out."

A gentle smile crept along her face. "You are a rogue, but thanks for the compliment anyway. You look pretty good yourself. Do you eat here often? I usually come into town about once a week, but I try to watch this kind of eating. I know I can get out of hand, so I try to make it a treat."

Kevin agreed. "I'm the same way. I try to keep eating out to once or twice a month. Besides, nobody can burn like I can in the kitchen." He gave her one of his devilishly charming smiles. "I live in the Fairfax Towers so I only come when I have time to hang out. This is nice though. I don't think that I've been here in about two months. Maybe the last time was on my buddy's birthday."

He held her gaze when he spoke. She tried not to think about how his eyes possessed the same dreamy quality as Eric's. She continued to make small talk to distract herself from unpleasant thoughts. "I was here a couple of months ago too. I was hanging out with my crazy friend Candy. She was with me at the gym, you know, when you treated me so roguishly," she teased. "So, besides cheating women in basketball, what else are you known for?"

Kevin hesitated briefly. "I do consulting work. I love it because I'm my own boss and I get to travel a lot, which is something that I enjoy doing."

"Looking at you, I would have pegged you as more

of an athlete, maybe director of somebody's physical education program or something like that."

"Very good. Did my being six five give it away?"

Tangie came face-to-face with another devilish grin. "Actually, I was very much into athletics at one time in my life," he said. "I played pro ball in Chile for a year. It was a good experience, sort of like being in a Third World country with all the U.S. conveniences. The countryside is beautiful, unspoiled by man, very natural. At night you see the flames from the snow-capped volcanoes and it's breathtaking."

Tangie could just imagine visiting such an exotic locale. "That sounds wonderful. I've never traveled much, but after my last experience, I think I'm willing to go out more. I really enjoyed the sight-seeing. So make me really jealous, tell me more. What are the people like?"

Kevin chuckled. He liked her quirky sense of humor. "Let me see . . . it's very laid-back and the people there are very welcoming. I had a Chilean girlfriend named Valencia. She was young and had never met a black man before. Her family was interesting. They put up with me and never made me feel terribly uncomfortable. I think they figured she was just going through a phase. We had a good time until it was time for me to go."

He was starting to feel uncomfortable. Maybe it was time to change the subject. Kevin shrugged. "It was a fun, wild time, but fun doesn't pay the bills—for long anyway—and I missed home. I came back and went to Magic Johnson's summer pro-league camp and met some agents, et cetera, but playing professional ball just didn't work out for me. There's a reason they say the NBA stands for 'no babies allowed.' It's a lot tougher than most guys realize when they are shooting hoops on the corner. It was a good experience though, and it eventually led to this job, so I'm happy."

"So whatever happened to Valencia?" Tangie asked, not sure why.

Kevin shook his head and shrugged. "Chile was another lifetime ago, and so was she. It was the affair of a younger, less-settled man. Anyway, tell me about you. Tangie is an interesting name."

"Tangerine Taylor, to be exact. I guess my mom had too much fruit while pregnant. Actually, there really isn't too much to tell. After college in the Tidewater area, I came back here and got a job that I love. I am vice president for consumer affairs for a local computer company. In the next five years, I want to be running my own company or at home with my kids. I don't want to have to do it all, like some of my friends are struggling to do. I've always been independent, but trying to be Superwoman really doesn't appeal to me. I'm pretty career-oriented right now, but I don't see that being the case for my entire life. Hopefully board meetings won't be my only fulfillment."

Tangie paused before continuing. She hoped she wasn't rattling. "But anyway . . . that's a long way off. I have time to wait for what I want and I'm not in any hurry. God gives and does in His own time. My mom taught me that."

"Do you go to church in Fairfax?" he asked, interested in the answer. He knew he wanted someone with a spiritual presence and a spirit he could trust. Valencia was a fling, not one to bring home to Mama, but Tangie, she had distinct possibilities.

Tangie was surprised at how easily she and Kevin seemed to flow. Sure she had first-date jitters, but somehow he seemed safe to her. She knew already that she wouldn't mind seeing him again.

Smiling, without realizing it, they both sat quietly.

Whoa, Tangie thought to herself, *lightning doesn't strike the same place twice.*

Across the table, Kevin thought the same way.

After a very pleasant dinner the two exchanged phone numbers and planned to meet again in a couple of days at the gym.

Exhausted, Tangie called Candy around 1:00 A.M. for a brief check-in. "Hey, girl, I'm back. I know you couldn't call me. I turned the phone off. I had a very nice time. He was the perfect gentleman—he didn't try a thing. Actually he's led a pretty exciting life, he even played professional basketball overseas."

"Yeah, yeah, yeah, what about the good stuff? What was he wearing, and didn't he even try to kiss you good night? Did you brush and floss like I told you?"

"Oh, I'm sorry, did I dial the number to Hattie Taylor?"

"Smarty-pants, I'm still waiting on the details."

"Candy, I'm hanging up this phone, because you obviously need your rest. I told you, he was a perfect gentleman. Girl, I'm beat, I need to get some rest tonight. Let's do lunch tomorrow, okay? I promise to give you all the details."

"Okay, see ya. I'll call you when I can get away from the asylum."

"Perfect place for you," Tangie teased her friend.

Tangie got herself ready for bed, and this night, Eric Duvernay did not enter her consciousness.

Chapter 20

It was a beautiful autumn day in Virginia. The leaves had turned into a stunning fall mosaic of light and dark greens, browns, golds, purples, and reds. The temperatures remained mild and Tangie was finally feeling like things were going to be okay.

She and her mom had begun their holiday shopping ritual, which always made Tangie feel better. As a matter of fact, the holidays always made her feel as if she were a kid again. She loved buying for everyone, searching for that perfect gift that showed him or her how much she cared.

Candy and Siddiq had postponed the wedding for a few months. They had needed more time to work on family issues, but the date was around the corner. Once again.

Standing in front of her walk in-closet, she thought ruefully for a moment about the gifts she had impulsively bought for Eric. She pushed them to the back.

She wanted to focus on her and Kevin's budding relationship instead.

"I refuse to think about him and get sad. I'm moving on, just as I'm sure he's done," she said aloud, blowing out an exasperated breath.

Tangie had no way of knowing that just a few miles

away, Eric was experiencing similar feelings of frustration over the loss of their relationship. Trying to find someone else had proved more difficult than he thought. There had been Mary, Janet, and Maria. All races, shapes, and sizes. Tangie was something special and in his mind incomparable.

Eric often questioned how such a short-lived relationship could affect him for such a long period of time. No matter the answer, he knew he needed to give it one more chance or he needed to reconcile to himself that the past was the past. He couldn't go on the miserable way he was. He was a young, vibrant man who had a lot to live for and it was about time he acted like it.

Eric surprised his father with a second call a few months later. They made another date to go fishing and shoot the breeze. Eric enjoyed spending time with him. Work could be so demanding and he didn't have any real outlets. He didn't want their relationship to suffer too . . . he and his dad were all that was left of the Duvernay clan.

Eric stood up in the boat watching his father intently. He wondered why the older man had never remarried. Surely there had been plenty of opportunity in the decades following his mother's death. Did Duvernay men only mate once?

Samuel looked at his son, the pride and worry evident in his large brown eyes. His son was his own spitting image. Eric owed his curly tresses and milk-chocolate complexion to him, but the feature that was most striking was their unique and expressive eyes. Many a battle had been won by their dangerous power.

Samuel Duvernay grunted loudly. "Okay, boy, out

with it. What's this all about? I let you get away with it last time and I see your disposition has not improved with time."

Samuel felt he had given him enough time to come to him with his problems. It was time to take the bull by the horns or Eric was going to go straight into the abyss he'd faced with Rebecca.

They had been on the water for over a couple of hours and not even a nibble. It had provided good time for introspection, but Eric knew what he needed most was to unburden his heart. He took his time before delving in.

Eric sighed heavily. "Let's sit." He watched the beautiful glassy water of the lake. "I'm in love, Pop, and I don't know if I'm making a total ass of myself. I met her over a year ago in New Orleans while I was finishing up my last SCU case. We had known each other only a week when I realized that she was the one." Eric cast another sideways glance toward the water.

"She's left me twice . . . the first time when I told her about my job and the second time when she felt my job was more important than she. Everything that I have tried to get her out of my system with has failed miserably."

Samuel looked at his son thoughtfully. Of course, it had to be a woman. Nothing like love to bring a man to his knees. "Sounds pretty bad. What all did you tell her to scare her away, son?"

Eric gave a wry chuckle. "As much as I could. She knows the gist of what I do. She'd been through a bad breakup and felt I betrayed her trust. I think she lumped me in the same category as the other deadbeats in her past. At this point I'm not so sure I don't deserve that label."

Another heavy sigh.

"I guess I did, I know I did, but I couldn't very well say, 'Hi, I'm Eric Duvernay and I'm an undercover agent,' now, could I? That's an oversimplification, but the point is, there are things that I can't talk about. I know how important honesty is in a relationship, but in my profession, there is a line to be drawn. I thought she would understand that after we talked, but . . ."

Eric's frustration was growing, his agitation evident by his tone and his fidgeting.

Samuel was delighted. This was the first time his son had shown any passion for life that wasn't based on his job or a case.

"Son, if she has you this tied up in knots, then maybe you are better off without her. A week is a pretty short time to determine that she's the one. What do you really know about her?"

Eric exploded. His dark eyes flashing a fiery mahogany. "What I need to know about her is what my heart says. I love her and that's all that matters. I don't care how long I've known her. When I was with her, it was like time stood still, nothing else existed. She made me feel whole and complete. Nobody has made me feel that way before, not even Rebecca, as much as I hate to admit it. Not like with Tangie."

There, he'd said all of it. His breathing was still rapid, but all the air had gone out of Eric's sails. The minutes passed in silence. Samuel gave his son the space to figure out for himself what he really wanted.

After a while, Eric regarded his father more calmly. "When I looked at Tangie I wanted to be her everything, husband, lover, protector, and father of her children. I still do. She's strong, independent, smart, has a great sense of humor, and not to mention beautiful."

Eric ran a hand through silky, wavy curls. "Sometimes when I'm alone in the house I'll think I hear her laugh or smell her scent, and it's making me crazy."

Samuel placed a gentle palm on his son's shoulder. His eyes misted thinking about his Caroline, Eric's mother. "Son, seems to me you have all the information you need. You only have one choice. Go after her, son, and let her know how much you love her. You two can work it out from there."

Eric took a good look at his father and chuckled. "How do you do that?"

Samuel gave a chuckle of his own. It was great to spend time with his only child. "Practice, my boy, practice."

Samuel sent a silent message heavenward, wishing for Eric's happiness.

Eric replayed in his mind what had gone wrong with their relationship, finally coming to the conclusion that he had been too hard on Tangie. He would have to learn not to treat the people in his life as if they were privates in his own personal army. Like most men, he tended to view things as cut-and-dry. He was learning love didn't work that way. What he needed to figure out was how to find her and after all this time, how to win her back.

"Hell, for all I know, she could be married with two children!" he said aloud.

That would be a terrific blow to his heart and ego, but he had to deal in reality. He was either going to be with Tangerine Taylor the rest of his life, or he was going to have to resign himself to letting go of her permanently.

He would deal with that later. Right now, he just needed to know where she was and what she had been up to. He decided he would call his friend Ben in the morning to get some feedback; besides, it had been a while since he had spoken with his buddy.

"Earth to Eric . . . Eric . . . Okay, I think we've had enough bonding for one day. How about I whip us up something to eat and then you take me home? I've got some just-in-case catfish in the fridge."

Eric reeled in the fishing lines and laughed at their plight. Good thing no one was depending on them for dinner. "You've got a deal. Thanks, Pop, you always come through in a pinch."

That night Eric went to bed with a sense of calm he hadn't felt in a long time. It was amazing to him how much he had been holding in and the amount of tension he'd been feeling. But tonight was different, he'd given in to his feelings. He loved Tangie and if she would have him back, he meant to be with her. This time, he wouldn't make the same mistakes, no ultimatums, and no kids' games. He was ready for a serious relationship; he wasn't getting any younger and if he wanted an Eric Jr. one day he would have to settle down.

Chapter 21

Kevin sat in his recliner listening to one of his favorite jams by D'Angelo, rocking to the beat of "You're My Lady." He held a cold soda in his hand, as he thought about his favorite subject of late—Tangerine Taylor. He had plenty of time before picking up Tangie for their date.

Kevin was surprised at what a good time he and Tangie had been having. She was so easy to talk to, and that body. Was this like or was it lust?

Kevin knew he needed to think about his next move. He would be seeing Tangie today, and while it was still relatively early in the relationship, they had been going out for almost three months, and he didn't want to make any dumb moves. Kevin could tell Tangie was very cautious, always played it very cool. They had fun together. She had a quick wit and a wonderful sense of humor, but something in her eyes gave him pause, told him to be careful with her.

Their dinners had been nice, but now he'd see how tonight's date went. She was the athletic type, so he decided against the traditional dinner and a movie; he wanted to watch Tangie move, see her sweat. His arousal tugged at his loose-fitting sweatpants just thinking about her.

Tonight they were going to one of DC's most exclusive total fitness centers. He still had a lot of contacts in the professional ball arena, which gave him access to a world most people didn't even know existed for professional athletes, company executives, and the like.

They could play a game or two of racquetball, get a massage, and have a couple of the fruit and tofu meals. Kevin treated himself to this spa pampering every couple of months; any more and it could become addictive. He decided that it would be good to share it with someone, especially if that someone was Tangerine Taylor.

His arousal fizzled out as he contemplated darker thoughts. Tangie was becoming more important to him and that was scary. There was so much he couldn't tell her out of fear for his life and hers too. Kevin wondered if he was really safe now. He had a new life, new look, and friends, but was that really enough? he questioned. He knew he could be found. He wasn't a monk . . . he could be traced easily. Maybe he should be more careful in his comings and goings. They had told him that he was ultimately responsible for his own security.

He kept waiting for the other shoe to drop. He didn't know what to make of the article about Bubba Fraser. Maybe he was letting paranoia settle in. Somewhere in the recesses of his heart he knew Valencia would probably pursue him until the day she died, or he did.

He was surprised at how easily he had been able to share his experiences in Chile with Tangie. Kevin rationalized there were obvious gaps, but he had been as honest as he could. Tangie had asked about his for-

mer girlfriends and he had told the truth—Valencia
Rojas-Rios had been a lifetime ago.

Kevin had it all worked out. He would pick Tangie
up right after work and they would change at the
club. On any given night there was no telling who
would show up: political figures, Fortune 500 busi-
nesspeople, celebrities, you name it. It was a very
discreet facility, no press ever allowed. No photos
could be taken of public figures not looking their
best. This was after all a serious workout joint. This
was a place to work out tensions, work off the
pounds, etc. You didn't come to people-watch, the
cost of membership wouldn't allow it. The people
who came here paid for exclusivity.

Of course, Kevin knew the owners. These were guys
he used to play pro ball with. The difference was that
they had been signed to multimillion-dollar contracts. Kevin wasn't bitter though; in the world of
sports there was only so much the player could control. An injury, bad management, bad coaching, all
those things and more were just the luck of the
draw—or the draft.

He was just glad that the guys he considered brothers had real class and knew what being a teammate
really meant. No, Kevin could appreciate their success, no sour grapes, just genuine affection and
admiration, and of course love of the game. Whenever he went, he was treated like family and he hoped
Tangie would enjoy herself in his special place.

Tangie had a hard time concentrating at work. Her
stomach had been full of butterflies since Kevin's call.
He had not given her any sort of indication of where

they would be going and was making this evening very mysterious by asking her what she had in her trunk.

What kind of question is that? she thought, but she'd told him what she usually carried.

It contained what it always did, spare tire, emergency kit with jumper cables, blanket, water, and her workout clothes. She pressed, but he wouldn't give up any answers. She smiled inwardly. He was quite a character. Good-looking, good sense of humor, great body. What woman wouldn't go for the tall, dark, and handsome type, so why the anxiety?

Whatever the attractive and mysterious Kevin De-Palma had in mind, she would work with it. The original plan was to meet at their gym and leave from there, but Kevin had asked if he could pick her up at work. He'd said they needed to get an early start to make the most of the evening. Tangie had been intrigued, because he was being so circumspect. Kevin definitely had a devilish side. So here she was getting more anxious by the second, waiting for Kevin to pick her up.

To pass the time she called Candy. Their relationship had been slightly strained due to Candy's stress over her impending nuptials. "Hey, Candy, whatcha doing, girl? I've only got a few minutes because I'm waiting on Kevin to pick me up."

"Well, what did I do to deserve this call? You've been rather rude to me since Mr. DePalma entered your life, but as you well know I'm the bigger person in this relationship, so I guess I'll forgive you.

"Okay, now that that's done, give me the real dish. How are things going? Is he a keeper? Are you through brooding over Eric, and most importantly, what did you get me for my wedding?"

"Girl, you've got issues. I've been taking your advice. It's been a few months, and we're still taking it one date at a time. Of course I'll be sure to call you when I decide whether or not he's a keeper. As for all of your other questions—forget it, I'm not answering them."

"Whatever . . . where are you guys going tonight?"

"He won't tell me, it's a surprise."

"Not even a hint? Think back, Tangie, what exactly did he say?" Candy had on her radar now. She was intrigued.

Tangie knew better than to let the girl get going. "Crazy girl, nope . . . I'm just going to have fun, wherever it is. I won't promise to call you tonight, but tomorrow I know we have our wedding shopping date. Just be ready at 10:00 A.M. I'll be there to meet you. See you later, gotta go."

"Tangie, you are such a tease, but I know you've got to go. I can wait until tomorrow to hear all the juicy details. After all, I am a woman of remarkable restraint. Bye."

"Oh yeah, Candy, remarkable restraint. I'll see you in the morning."

The rest of the afternoon breezed by after talking with her friend, and before she realized it she was sitting next to Kevin in his midnight-blue Navigator.

Tangie noticed Kevin was a smooth driver. He negotiated DC traffic like a hot knife through butter. But what the heck did he want from her trunk? She had allowed Kevin to rummage through it, taking out what he needed. He didn't let her know what he was doing, so Tangie decided to put curiosity on hold and enjoy the mystery.

He looked especially good tonight and the Gerald

Albright CD he had on was playing with her emotions. Tangie felt desire warming her body, making her taut nipples press against the silk fabric of her blouse.

She tried to concentrate on the scenery of the road and where they were going. She found herself in neighborhoods she'd never known existed and in another twenty-five minutes she was in front of what looked like a very nice office complex.

When they went inside, Tangie's eyes feasted on the most exquisite workout facility she'd ever been to. It was every athlete's dream. The fitness center was fantastic, ultramodern with wait staff and personal trainers. It held every machine known to man; each area housed closed-circuit televisions; there was the Energy Bar and Café; and apparently no amenity had been spared. It was like a five-star hotel, only it was cool to sweat.

Tangie was visibly awed by the splendor. She noticed several high-powered officials walking into different rooms and tried hard not to gawk. She turned to Kevin. "Was that . . . ?"

"Yes, it was," he said, smiling at her.

Tangie gushed, "Kevin, this is fantastic, how'd you ever find this place?"

Kevin watched her face, pleased that she was not disappointed. He mentally patted himself on the back.

He joked, "Can't tell you, you're not authorized."

Tangie gave him a pointed look. She noticed that he had her gym bag in his left hand. "You are truly sneaky," she said, poking him in the shoulder.

He feigned injury. "You are such a brute, or is that brut-ette?"

He and Tangie went farther into the complex, where he was greeted warmly by the guard on duty, and he gave her a full tour. There was an indoor golf course, a tennis area, racquetball courts, two swimming pools, and at least half a dozen rooms for the different aerobics classes. Tangie had her choice between the cardiovascular room, weight room, and massage area. It all looked so good that she didn't know where to start. She momentarily forgot about Kevin, she was so enthralled with what she saw.

He watched her, letting her soak it all in, then suggested a routine.

They worked out for an hour, had a massage, then a dip in the coed whirlpool. At the Energy Bar and Café, he treated her to a delicious salad with various greens and herbs. They also had a thick nutrient-filled fruit drink.

She asked curiously, "Are you sure about all these calories? Did I just ruin my workout?"

"Would I do that to you, woman? You're fine. Nothing we ate contains that many carbs or processed sugar. Besides, after the way you played racquetball, I'd say you'll be burning calories for the next week. You've got quite a competitive streak in you. I'm impressed."

"Okay, indulge me one more time."

Kevin ordered dessert for them. "A friend turned me on to this, a tofu and soy brownie. I know it doesn't sound very appealing, but you've got to at least try it."

Tangie hesitated before taking a small bite. It was different, but she loved it. "Ummm, these are good. The tofu isn't dry at all. I'm going to have to get the recipe."

Smiling from ear to ear, she thought, *Okay, he really knows how to treat a woman. I wonder if that extends to other areas.* She hoped he didn't have any idea about her thoughts. Her hormones were trying to take over again. Desire welled in her and Kevin was becoming more and more attractive to her. Where was this thing headed? she wondered.

Kevin looked around for a distraction. She was getting to him. He wanted her more than ever, but didn't want to make a mistake by pressing his luck.

A nice date does not love make. *Just take it easy, don't let the wrong head control you!*

He said casually, "There's a buddy of mine over there. Do you mind? I just want to holler at him for a minute; then we can be on our way. I've kept you out long enough."

"Oh, sure, invite him over."

Tangie's eyes followed to where Kevin was waving. Tangie used more discipline than she thought possible and stopped herself from gawking; she even managed to be cordial and in control as she was being introduced. A short while later, they left the complex arm in arm, all smiles.

"That, Mr. DePalma, was a lot of fun. Definitely not a traditional date, but a lot of fun. Are you always so imaginative?"

Kevin pulled her closer and whispered, "One day you'll have to let me show you."

"Oh, and now you're a big flirt too."

Kevin looked around quickly. He had the strangest feeling that he was being watched, but shrugged it off. He didn't want to let paranoia ruin his wonderful evening. He helped Tangie into the SUV and they were on their way back to her office.

Kevin and Tangie were so taken with each other that neither noticed a dark blue Mercedes sedan start its engine the moment they left the parking lot.

The sedan followed them back to Tangie's where she could retrieve her car, watching their exchange intently.

Kevin pulled Tangie into his arms and gave her a light, gentle kiss good-bye. Tangie wanted more, but didn't push. The kiss was odd. As excited as she was, she thought she would feel more, especially the way he had turned her on before.

"Thanks for such a good time, it was an unusual date, but great. Let me take you out next time," she said.

"Okay, but let's not make this a contest of the oddest date, all right?" Kevin teased.

"No, but we could make it a fun contest," she suggested.

They kissed again, this time with a little more interest. Tangie allowed his tongue to explore her mouth and pressed her body closer into his. Warning bells went off in her head. She wasn't sure she was ready for this, but she was trying. She broke the kiss and turned to get into her car.

"Tangie, I really enjoyed myself with you tonight. I'll call you later," Kevin said huskily.

Take it slow, man, his mind cautioned. Unfortunately his body hadn't heard a word. He wanted her. The ride back to his place would be a long and uncomfortable one. His well-endowed manhood strained against the fabric of his sweats and he shifted uncomfortably in his seat. He tried to readjust himself. Kevin was too uncomfortable to notice anyone else around him and he missed the same blue sedan that had been at the athletic center. When he watched Tangie to make sure she got out of the parking lot safely, he didn't notice anything out of the ordinary. He watched for a moment before he turned up the volume on his KC and Jojo CD. He needed something upbeat, especially with the mood he was in.

Being distracted cost him some very important details. Kevin missed Tangie being photographed repeatedly with a high-powered zoom lens and her license plate number recorded. A black sedan followed Tangie to her condo while the blue one continued to monitor Kevin. His information was recorded as well. Now that the men in the sedan had an address and license plate, they would watch for a couple of days and get to know their routines.

The men had mapped out a preliminary plan, and since Kevin was the main target, he would go first. . . .

Chapter 22

Agent Spates anxiously dialed Eric's phone number. He hated what he had to do, but he knew he needed him too much. Listening to the phone ring, he hoped he could count on his friend one last time.

Spates knew Eric was happy out of the undercover game and teaching at Quantico. He had proven to be a solid instructor and the higher-ups were pleased with him. Spates didn't want to upset the balance that Eric had been trying to achieve in his life, but he wouldn't make the call unless he had to.

Now, because of this case, Spates had to bring him right back in. Eric had certain talents that were often necessary, but hard to find in a good agent. He had been involved in a lot of unusual cases, but this would require all of his considerable skills. The report on Spates's desk was very troubling.

The Bureau and local police had finally been able to get a bead on the murder of James "Bubba" Fraser. The case had been cold for several months, but a break in an immigration case had given them much-needed information. Fraser's death had been linked to several others of players for an international basketball team. The Bureau had established jurisdiction over the state police, and the Special Corruption

Unit had been specifically requested to monitor and intercept the foreign nationals suspected of killing the ballplayers.

Spates now had the task of identifying the agents who would work on this particular case. And he knew the best man for the job would be the most reluctant. . . .

Eric had been in his office poring over some class material when his phone rang. He finally answered on the fifth ring, annoyed at being disturbed. "Duvernay here," he answered tersely.

"Eric, it's me, Spates, we need to talk."

Eric closed his eyes. A feeling of dread spread through his body. He knew Spates wouldn't call unless he had to, unless a mission required him to. Eric knew that the senior officer understood his stance on going back into the field. It had to be pretty serious and pretty risky if he was being "recalled." He willed the queasiness in his stomach to go away and leaned back his chair to listen. "Go on, you've got my attention."

Spates continued, hesitantly. "I've heard good things about you. I'm glad that you are doing well. Eric, you know I wouldn't have called if I didn't need you. All I'm asking is that you meet with me. Can I count on you?"

Eric was serious about trying to get his life back on track with Tangie, but he knew he couldn't turn down the SCU. The Bureau meant a lot to him. His undercover work had been his lifeblood, and no matter what they wanted, Eric would give it, albeit more reluctantly.

He let out a jagged breath before agreeing to a 7:30 A.M. meeting with Agent Spates at the Hoover Building. Tonight he would prepare himself to reenter a world and a life he thought was behind him. Until he dealt with whatever problem Spates was going to present to him, he would get focused, temporarily putting Tangerine Taylor out of his mind. Distractions, as he had learned early on, could be deadly in his line of work. He put his quest to reclaim her love on hold. Again.

Eric contacted his assistant. If he was going to be out of the loop, someone would have to step in to teach his classes. He finalized plans with other office personnel to take care of unfinished projects and walked out, not knowing when exactly he would return.

That evening, he prayed for strength. He had a bad feeling about this case without knowing what it was about. Sometimes intuition was more important than fact in his business. His mind shifted to autopilot. He concentrated on finding the core group of agents commonly referred to as the E-team. They had worked together on so many cases that they knew each other better than family. These agents were the handpicked group that he would trust with his life.

Wherever they were scattered, Spates was going to have to locate them and bring them in on the case. That would just be one of Eric's conditions when they met to reinstate his undercover status. He didn't know what the case was about or where they were going, but he knew who he wanted to have by his side. They would all learn about the mission profile together.

It took four days of pulling strings but Eric's team

was finally put together. He'd had to pare the team down because of agency commitments, but he was satisfied with his choices. Each agent was selected because of the special skills he possessed but also for the ability to keep cool under very stressful situations. All of them knew it must be an important case if they were pulled from their other duties, but more importantly, that Agent Eric Duvernay was leading them.

In the conference room, Special Agents King, Anderson, Banks, and Thomas waited anxiously to hear about their new assignment.

When Agent Spates entered the Haig Room, they were all visibly relieved. It was disconcerting to be told to drop everything and report to Washington.

He noted their reactions. "Hey, don't look so serious, guys. Excuse me, Agent Thomas. Look around. With all this expertise in the room, we can handle anything that comes our way—right?"

"Right, sir," they all said in unison.

Agent Spates was pleased with Eric's choices. He had selected the best in munitions and explosives, computer security systems, and hand-to-hand combat. These young agents combined with Eric's ability to lead and bring out the best in his people made a formidable crew.

Eric walked in and was seated, which completed the group. He nodded to each agent, grateful that each was present. Some of the tension eased out of the room as soon as they saw him. There had been some concern that he had been out of the field for an extended period of time, but all that was resolved when they saw him. He looked fine, but more importantly, they recognized the signature Duvernay control. He still looked like he had the edge, and that was a good sign. Eric smiled at Agent Thomas. Nope . . . there was no one quite like her. Thank goodness!

He studied the rest of his team. Banks, Anderson, and King looked good and seemed no worse for their experiences. He liked that, and he was looking forward to having a personal moment with each of them. Being with them, he felt some of his own discomfort dissipate.

Spates watched the silent interaction of the group from the head of the conference table. He was satisfied that he had made the best decision bringing Eric in and having him reassemble his group. He thanked them for coming before he began.

Pointing to the briefing board, Spates addressed the assembly.

"Now that everyone is here, let's begin. In 1994 a splinter group of the Colombian Cartel was destroyed. The group was based in Chile and had their own unique distribution system. While they were never as high-profile as the Colombians they learned very well and were every bit as precise, as business-oriented and as deadly as their Colombian cousins.

"Valencia Rojas-Rios headed the group over there. We suspect that she was made the matriarch as repayment for her husband's wrongful death. There was a case of mistaken identity and Senor Rios was killed by his own people. It is rare that mistakes are made like that, but it happened and Senora Rios was compensated and sent off to Chile in 1990. Mrs. Rios ran a very tight organization, but in late 1994, early 1995 she was infiltrated and eventually our agency counterparts were able to bring them down. Mrs. Rios escaped, but her organization, was gutted. Her only child, a niece she was caring for, was lost in a shoot-out with agency personnel."

Spates waited as pictures of the family were loaded for the presentation.

"It was a multimillion-dollar-a-year cocaine operation and Rios was known for her lavish style. After her fall, reports indicated that she wasn't able to reach her nest eggs before the noose came down on all of her assets. She had been sighted in various countries in 1996 or so, but no one had paid much attention to what she was doing . . . until now."

New pictures were loaded of homicide victims before Spates went on.

"A pattern of mysterious deaths has emerged. The most recent was an ex-basketball player named 'Bubba' Fraser. Intelligence indicates that in 1994, the cartel used a basketball league as mules. The players, mostly United States players who couldn't get NBA contracts, traveled from country to country and provided the means for the cocaine to be distributed. Fraser played on one of those teams. It appears that everyone was involved. The coaches, players, trainers, on down to the water boys."

A picture of the team was shown next.

"Our big break came when an anonymous call exposed the organization. The call actually came from one of the players who was not involved and wanted help getting out of the country. Kevin Lopez became our informant, and after the busts were made he was helped out of the country by the U.S. embassy.

"In the last six months everyone associated with the ball clubs has turned up dead. Everyone, that is, except Kevin Lopez, now DePalma. He is a local boy who lives in the Alexandria/Fairfax area."

Spates referred to the briefing material on the table.

"If you look in your packets, you'll see that a coordinated effort from the state police departments was extremely helpful. No pattern could be determined until we starting getting information in from various PDs. They sent us information on their most bizarre and vicious murders. We noticed a commonality with several of the names. Once the link was found to the league, the Bureau was given authorization to begin surveillance on the remaining team members. We were too late for Mr. Fraser, but we won't be for Mr. DePalma. Agents from the Virginia field office have been watching him for a couple of days. Seems he's got company from Chile already. Valencia Rios does not waste time. We know he is the next mark, so we need a plan, and we need it fast. . . . Okay, any questions so far?"

Eric asked, "What kind of company are we talking about, how many, and do we have a base location for the Rios operatives?"

Spates responded, "Since the surveillance began he and his lady friend have been tailed by a late-model blue Mercedes. That type of car is standard issue for her operation. Our boys have been very discreet but they get the sense that something will be going down very soon. They will fax a copy of the pictures to us later this afternoon. We should have them after lunch."

Eric had some concerns about the SCU's involvement in the case. Local operatives should have been able to handle a simple pickup case. "Sir, why is the SCU involved in this one? Isn't there another unit that can apprehend Rios?" he asked.

The senior agent was visibly annoyed by the question, but he answered professionally. He realized that Eric didn't want to be involved, but they all had orders to follow.

Spates nodded his head. "I'm sure there is, but we were requested. The agency doesn't want it since it's domestic and no one else really wants it because the cartel is involved. You only have to see the results of one Colombian necktie to get leery. Their enforcers are fast, thorough, and extremely brutal. So like I said, we've been asked and I've accepted on our behalf because I know your unit has the expertise to handle this efficiently. We will not allow Valencia to set up a base of operations on U.S. soil. Since she is here and obviously has cars, firepower, and operatives, we have to assume she also has some law enforcement assets. The SCU is probably more appropriate for this case than originally anticipated. I expect top-notch work from everyone and that's usually what I get. Problems?"

The agents looked at each other and in silence communicated that they were ready and willing to take the case on.

He told the group that they would reconvene in two hours, at which time he wanted to hear ideas for designing a mission.

Eric sat quietly as his team members left the room.

He mulled over the case in his mind. Would this really be the last time he worked for the Special Corruption Unit? How many times would the Bureau call him for one of their emergencies? At this stage of his life all he really wanted was a wife and children.

He realized he was tired of chasing the bad guys. This had to be the last time, the last mission, he thought solemnly. He had a woman to go after. Tangie had stolen his heart, and it was time to settle it once and for all.

At 3:00 P.M. the small group reconvened. They already knew they were taking the assignment, but Eric asked them each how it would affect them just in case. He respected them enough to let them out of an assignment if necessary. There was no sense taking agents into dangerous territory if they had reservations about being there. As expected, they were confident and ready to get on with it.

While they were putting the finishing touches on their preliminary plans, an agent arrived with the long-awaited surveillance photos. Everyone took their copies and sat down. Eric shuffled through a few pictures nonchalantly, but then he looked down at the next picture in the stack and dropped them as if his hands had been scorched.

Incredibly, he was looking down at the smiling face of Tangerine Taylor, who was being held by Kevin De-Palma. The blood in his veins turned ice-cold. The other agents stared at his ashen face and wondered what in the devil was going on.

Agent Spates took a good look at the pictures. All he could manage to say was, "Sweet Lord." The other agents were baffled now and irritated that no one was explaining what was going on. Eric excused himself after a few tense moments, leaving Spates alone to explain to the group what they had seen.

He took a deep breath, then addressed the agents. "What I am about to share with you in no way changes the mission or the plans that have already been made. First off, you all have worked with him and you know Agent Duvernay is an excellent agent and leader and he will persevere no matter what the circumstances.

"However, you all should know this case just became very important to him. The woman in these pictures is his ex-lover Tangerine Taylor."

Spates paused, letting the shock wear off before he continued.

"It doesn't take a profiler or psychologist to see from his reaction that he still cares a great deal about her. I'd say he has more reason than ever to want to be involved, but emotion has no place in these situations. I know I don't need to tell you all to watch each other's backs—you'll do that anyway. But I need that assurance from you, all of you, that this operation will be done smart, clean, and with no collateral damage, if you know what I mean."

"Sir, yes, sir. That's the only way to do it," said Agent Thomas, leaning back in her chair. Her face gave no indication of her innermost thoughts.

Spates stood, signaling that the meeting was finished. He needed to find Eric. "Thank you. We are going to adjourn for the night. We've covered a lot and I know you all want to get settled in to your accommodations. Go get some rest . . . I have a feeling that you'll need to take it when you can get it. Our timetable has just been moved up. I'll see you four back here at 0800 hours."

Spates retreated to the sanctity of his office. He called in a couple of his senior agents to discuss the situation. He still felt that Eric was the best, but now that emotion had entered the scene, he hoped he wasn't believing blindly.

Chapter 23

The Rios Cartel had been watching Tangie and Kevin for days, waiting to make its move. Their routines and habits were monitored until they were clearly identifiable.

The man spoke in rapid Spanish.

Carlos said, "We've got him. He is always with the same woman. Juan is watching her."

Tomas responded, "Keeping watching him, but don't do anything until I tell you. Senora Rios will let us know when to pick them up."

"Yes, boss."

Tomas contacted Juan next. "Do you see the woman?"

Juan was watching her as he spoke. He used a powerful lens to take pictures of her every move. "Yes, she just pulled into her driveway."

"Good. Finish getting your information, then report into headquarters. Senora Rios wants to talk to us."

Tomas was pleased. Ms. Rios would appreciate their swift handling of the surveillance. She always rewarded good work, and that was good for him and his men. Their families would be taken care of very well.

* * *

Valencia Rios was a middle-aged woman, with jet-black, naturally wavy hair, which she wore in an elegant upswept style. She was of medium height and petite build. She possessed striking features and a fair, flawless complexion. Ordinarily she would have been considered beautiful. But her obsidian eyes held such dark foreboding that the effect was marred.

She leaned back into the softness of her Italian leather custom-made chair. She was pleased with the progress that her people were making. Valencia stroked the arms of the chair and smiled. Juan had called her with the good news. His progress meant she would soon realize the goals of her sacrifice. *Soon, very soon,* she thought.

Her home in the New Mexico desert was designed to look like a European palazzo, complete with courtyards, small servant quarters, and long meandering garden paths.

One look at her spacious private library and one could see that everything was in place and in order. She didn't tolerate chaos or ineptitude in her surroundings, her organization, or any part of her life. For any transgression, her men knew that there would be hell to pay. For that reason they were thorough, unrelenting, and highly efficient.

Valencia felt the rush of power and control. She was a force to be reckoned with, and soon those stupid American boys would know it. Her plan was finally being realized . . . *Revenge, what a sweet-tasting fruit,* she thought.

Valencia had only one thing on her mind these

days—vengeance. Her world, the only life she had ever known, had been stripped away from her. Worst of all, it had been taken away by a coward! No matter, she thought . . . she would find the mole in the organization and that would be the last day of his life.

Chapter 24

Candy and Siddiq, after months of talking and counseling, seemed to have found a way to work out all of their differences. Their wedding promised to be a most interesting and intriguing affair. Candy and her handsome fiancé wanted to be sure to respect each other's family and background during the ceremony and they'd made certain unorthodox compromises. Siddiq's family was from The Gambia, a small country neighboring Senegal. They had planned an exquisite ceremony, that beautifully combined the two religions. It was going to be as much about culture as religion.

Candy's biggest concession had come with the wedding gown. She chose to follow Gambian tradition and wear a black dress. She and Tangie had had plenty of discussions about that decision.

They also chose the traditional Gambian wedding day of Thursday. The bride, groom, and wedding party would dress in traditional African clothing. The vows would be in English and Mandingo, and two religious leaders would officiate at the ceremony.

Afterward, Siddiq's family would go to the mosque to pray for the couple, then bring kola nuts to her family. While they prayed, Candy's family would wait to receive them at the reception hall. They decided on a traditional wedding feast, which would consist mainly of beef Banaken. The family would sacrifice a cow and it would be cooked starting early in the morning. In this case, the sacrifice was going to be made via the slaughterhouse with the purchase of a whole steer. The meat would be prepared with rice and vegetables in a red sauce of tomatoes, eggplant, bitter tomatoes, bell peppers, and hot peppers. And as was the tradition, there would be enough food to literally feed an entire village. Unless some of Siddiq's distant cousins attended, there would be enough beef to last until the next week. Fortunately, good news traveled fast and plenty of the "village" would show up at the hall.

They had even worked out how to raise the kids, when the time came. They would expose them to both religions and let them choose.

Tangie and Candy spent yet another Saturday shopping for the wedding. They seemed to spend every waking moment planning for the wedding. The coordinator had quit about four weeks into the process, so it was up to them. Candy was so high-strung about the wedding she was making everybody crazy. She had turned into this never-satisfied beast.

Tangie decided that she would give her one more day of interrogating dress clerks, wedding cake vendors, and florists. With a two-week countdown, decisions had to be made, and after dragging around the mall all day, Tangie had entertained thoughts of quitting too.

Today's mission was to find the proper dresses. The seamstress had also quit, so it had to be off the rack. They were going to the mall to select two dresses to wear—one white and one black. The black was for the traditional ceremony and the white was for the reception.

If it weren't for Tangie handling certain other areas, everyone else associated with the wedding probably would have quit too.

After finishing their last-minute shopping for the tenth time, the two left Landmark Mall and headed to a restaurant for a quick bite. They devoured two baskets of Buffalo wings, talking excitedly about the bridal shower and the honeymoon. Kim and Tangie were in charge of the shower, which they promised her would be a wild and wicked affair.

Candy was almost beside herself with curiosity about the entertainment. But they were both keeping mum, which was driving her crazy. "Tangie, I know I have been a little tense these last couple of days. I just want you to know how much I appreciate you being with me through all of this. And I think that the dresses we picked out today are perfect. I mean it."

Tangie smirked. "Just forget it, you are not getting any information out of me. Kim and I will do you proud and that's all you need to know."

Candy looked at her. "You know I can always hire a best friend for this wedding."

"No, you can't, they would quit too. Just concentrate on what you have to do. We've got the dresses, we've ordered the flowers. The only thing left is for you to look at pictures of more cakes and let *me* handle the order. I don't even want to see you with a phone in your hand for the next two weeks. Otherwise the next person who quits will be me!"

Candy looked at her in mock horror. They finished eating, and soon Candy realized she wasn't going to get anywhere with the tight-lipped Tangie.

Tangie shook her head, smiling. Her friend was truly one of a kind. "Come on, girl, let's get you back to your car. I need to run." Tangie and Kevin had made a date to see a late movie together and she was hoping to get a nap in before they went out.

The pair said good-bye in the parking lot and she headed home. Tangie thought she had noticed the same dark blue Mercedes at the restaurant and the mall, but shrugged it off.

She dismissed the uneasy feeling that began at the base of her neck and took the short drive back to her town house. She gingerly pulled into her parking space, looking around cautiously before getting out of her car. She breathed a sigh of relief when she didn't see that dark sedan or any other cars. Breathing calmly, she thought it was a typical quiet Saturday afternoon in her neighborhood.

Tangie quickly entered her house and locked the door behind her. The sigh she was about to release turned into a scream. Too late, she realized she was not alone, but before she could react strong arms grabbed her and something foul was clamped over her mouth and nose. Soon . . . there was just blackness. . . .

"Agent Duvernay slow down . . . you can't just go charging over there, we're in the middle of an investigation."

"Are you going to stop me?" Eric asked as he was almost out of the door.

Eric didn't care about protocol, he had to see Tangie. He raced to his car after leaving the briefing and headed toward her town house. Eric's palms had begun to feel clammy from cold sweat. The blood flowed so quickly through his veins that he thought they would burst. All he could think about was Tangie. He prayed he would reach her before any harm could come to her. He blamed himself for staying away so long. If pride caused him to lose the woman he loved he would never forgive himself. All of a sudden, the months that they had spent apart meant nothing. He had stronger feelings for her now than he had had in New Orleans. It seemed that absence had only made his heart grow fonder. He knew now that she was his soul mate and he had to find her in time. He just wanted Tangie to be safe.

Eric broke just about every traffic rule there was, but all that was on his mind was getting to Tangie. The feeling that something was desperately wrong started in the pit of his stomach and crawled all over him. He felt sickened by the thought that he might be too late.

Eric ran past Tangie's car in her parking space and burst through the door.

The scene that met him made the hairs on his arms stand tall and his flesh crawl.

"Is this Candy Carlson?"

"Yes, may I ask who this is? I don't know anyone from this number."

"Ms. Carlson, this is Agent Duvernay. Have you seen Tangerine Taylor? Is she with you?"

Eric tried unsuccessfully to keep the anxiety out of his tone.

"What has happened to Tangie?" Candy cried into the phone. Panic gripped her so strong she felt faint.

Eric was disheartened. He didn't want to believe the evidence. He wanted Tangie to be safe with her best friend, but that was not the case. When he spoke again he was all business. "I'm sorry, Ms. Carlson, I can't give you any information. This is part of an on-going investigation. We are just checking into her whereabouts. I'll be in touch as soon as we have more information." His tone softened before he hung up. "Candy, I know she is your best friend and you love her. I shouldn't be saying this, but I love her too. I will find her."

Candy sat holding the phone in her hand, stunned. She had to call Siddiq. There couldn't be a wedding until she knew Tangie was safe and at home again.

Chapter 25

Tangie smelled perfume, very expensive perfume, as she was coming to her senses. Through the fogginess that the drugs had left, she wondered where she was and why her entire body hurt.

It was dark and she was cold. Slowly her senses awakened. She could smell, but something was very wrong. Tangie wanted to shrug her shoulders to get some of the tension out of them. She tried to move, but with sickening horror she realized that she was both blindfolded and bound.

"Ah, my little bird is awake," Valencia said in Spanish as she eyed Tangie with utter disdain.

Tangie's high school Spanish didn't afford her an understanding of Valencia's highbrow dialect. And though she didn't understand what had been said, she knew the words had dripped off the woman's tongue like icicles from a winter's tree. The tone made Tangie shudder involuntarily.

Tangie tried to concentrate on her surroundings, her instinct for survival seeming to heighten her senses. She tried to distinguish each smell, sound, and sensation. She didn't know who her captors were or what they wanted, but they had another thing coming if they thought she would give up without a fight. Every nerve ending in her body prepared for battle. The woman with the perfume was moving. Tangie could smell the scent as it gently wafted through the air.

Valencia watched her captive with interest. When she spoke again it was in English. "How are you, my dear? I trust that my men did not hurt you . . . sometimes they get overzealous."

She acted as if they were old friends, her familiarity disconcerting to Tangie. Especially since her tone had been so hateful with her first comments. Tangie didn't understand this sudden change.

"Well, I suppose you are wondering why you are here. And who I am." Her slightly accented English gave Tangie pause. Why was she being held captive by this Spanish-speaking terrorist? She worked for a software company, for goodness' sake! What value could she possibly provide for this woman?

Tangie listened in silence, trying to figure out what was going on. She had no idea what this crazy woman was talking about. None of this was making sense to her and her head hurt something fierce! She silently wished the woman would remove the blindfold and give her some water. The drug they had used on her made her throat dry and scratchy.

Valencia seemed to be enjoying herself. In syrupy sweet tones she continued, "All this must be so troubling for you, but this really isn't about you. You, my dear, are . . . how do you say in America . . . you are simply a means to an end."

She paused briefly, letting her words dig into Tangie.

"You are the victim of your unfortunate choice of a man. Did you know your lover, Lopez, was a coward?

He ruined my life, my family, my business, and now he is going to pay. I've got him now and when I finish with him he will wish he were dead, just as I have, all these years."

Almost apologetically she added, "Lopez is really not worth your life, or should I say DePalma? I simply needed you in order to get to him. He will learn first-hand what pain and suffering are all about. He'll learn to watch helplessly while someone he cares about is in pain."

Valencia smiled again, though Tangie couldn't see the malevolence in the gesture. "Yes, your lover will learn to appreciate what I have been forced to endure over the past few years. I've lost almost everything thanks to that American pig and traitors in my organization . . . now it is time for my revenge." Valencia gave a short derisive laugh.

She walked over to Tangie and removed the blindfold. Tangie was shocked at how venomous this beautiful, sophisticated woman was acting. They stared at each other, neither moving nor making a sound for several minutes.

Tangie was genuinely scared now. She had to assume that Kevin was also being held by this crazed woman. Looking at Valencia, she further assumed that this mess had something to do with Kevin's time in Chile. The woman's features were decidedly South American.

She felt her entire body stiffen as she listened to the worst bloodcurdling screams she had ever heard in her life coming from a nearby room. She drew her body in closer, as if to escape the ghastly sounds. Tangie looked at Valencia and then quickly turned away.

When Valencia offered no explanation or comment, Tangie turned more into herself and tried to create a little ball of protection.

Valencia watched the young woman silently. She acted as if the screams they were listening to were commonplace. She seemed to be enjoy the pitiful sound of the man's torture.

Tangie had to find a way to escape—from what her captor said, she would be next. Fear and panic were quickly taking over her senses. She didn't know if the man being tortured was Kevin or someone else. Tangie finally exhaled when the screaming stopped. Valencia left the room without another word.

A cold feeling of dread snaked its way through her entire being. Tangie's life meant nothing to Valencia. Furthermore, she didn't know if Kevin was dead or alive. She silently prayed for strength.

Chapter 26

Nerves ran high as the team took their positions around the Rios compound. The intel had proved to be invaluable from their informant. Without it, they all knew they might never have caught a break with the case. Eric had been nearly crazy with worry when he reached Tangie's apartment and she wasn't there. There were visible signs of an intrusion and even though the apartment was empty, Tangie's car was in the parking space. There had been a slight struggle evidenced by the overturned plant in the foyer and scuff marks on the flooring. Whoever had her had obviously had to drag her out. Tangie hadn't left of her own volition. He'd also found a cloth with a Halcyon-like drug on it. He knew Tangie was in great danger.

Eric rushed back to headquarters and assembled the team. He had told them failure was not an option. After two days of round-the-clock research, they found out that Tangie and Kevin had been taken to a remote subcompound in New Mexico. They had squeezed every informant dry for the information— they knew time was running out.

Eric put the plan of attack together on the plane

ride to New Mexico. He had one focus—to bring
Tangie back safely.

Thomas had to hand it to Eric; he was one cool customer. She had to admire him for his skills. After
reading about Valencia Rios, she would be glad when
the case was over. Valencia was bad news.

From their positions around the compound, Duvernay and his four-person team watched in anger
and abhorrence, as the mutilated body of Carlos,
their key informant, was dragged from the main
building. While the two guards were occupied, Anderson moved into first position. He was just inside
the corridor where he put his magical computer skills
to use. He disengaged the monitoring and security
systems and signaled to the others how many guards
he had visual confirmation of. After doing so, he
moved down the hall to continue his security checks.

A Rios guard made the mistake of crossing too
close into Anderson's path. In two quick movements
he broke the man's neck and moved his body out of
the way.

Agent Banks, who had been watching the two
guards, sent two poison darts to their necks silently.
Within minutes, they would face the same fate as Carlos. The poison was lethal, but not immediate.

Thomas moved into the house and began to sweep
the second floor. She froze at the third door she came
to. Behind it, she heard a man speaking Spanish with
an American accent. Thomas assumed it was DePalma
from the bits of information she was hearing.

"Valencia, let Tangie go, she has nothing to do with
this. You have me and you've made your point, let

her go. You can do whatever you want with me," Kevin pleaded.

"Dear Kevin, always so naive, of course I will do anything I want with you. What makes you think you can bargain for the little *punta?*" responded Valencia.

Thomas moved on. While taking down Valencia was the primary goal, she wanted to see if she could find Tangie. Besides, as long as she and Kevin were talking, Thomas could come back for Valencia.

Eric and Anderson continued to sweep the downstairs, taking care of three more guards and securing the small staff of the house in the kitchen's deep freezer. King performed perimeter checks and took care of the outside guards.

Back in the house screams were heard coming from a second-floor bedroom.

"Valencia, leave her alone, what are you doing to her?" Kevin demanded.

Valencia seemed to enjoy Kevin's reaction.

She smiled wickedly as she watched Kevin's reactions war within him. She had left him unbound on purpose; he would never try anything, for fear of repercussions.

She thought, *What a coward.*

Kevin couldn't stand to hear Tangie's screams. He bolted into action and hurled himself into Valencia to immobilize her. The two were in an all-out struggle. Though his six-five physique was enough to intimidate most men, Valencia's heart was hard with revenge and she fought against him bitterly. She summoned all of her strength to free herself from Kevin. Her fierce eyes turned a darker shade of black as she reached for the gun that she had hidden in her desk drawer.

Fighting to regain control, he realized too late there was a gun leveled at his chest. He lunged again for Valencia, causing the weapon to fire as the two scuffled around the room, breaking furniture as they went.

The commotion distracted the two men guarding Tangie and they went running down the hall to Valencia's aid. Agent Thomas met Eric in the hallway and they both headed toward the noise. Before Valencia's men reached the doorway, Eric and Thomas felled each man with a bullet to the forehead; they dropped liked heavy stones.

Thomas burst into the room where Kevin and Valencia were embroiled in a free-for-all.

She yelled, "DePalma, get down."

Thomas squeezed the trigger in the next instant and opened fire on Valencia. Two of the bullets hit Valencia in the chest, piercing her through the heart. Valencia fixed Kevin with one more demented smirk before her body hit the floor.

The Rios family was officially out of business.

Kevin thought he would be ill. Adrenaline and bile rushed through his body, making him feel sick to his stomach. He sat down at the desk and put his head down briefly before jumping up. Finally, he looked at Thomas. His hands and body shook. "Where's Tangie?" he demanded.

Thomas ignored the question and responded, "Sir, we are federal agents. We have secured this location and you are safe. We need to get you out of here as quickly as possible."

Kevin looked at Valencia and at the agents in front of him. He sat immobilized for several seconds. The whole scene was surreal and he felt almost as if he were having an out-of-body experience.

Thomas sought to reassure him. "I'm sure she's safe now. Agent Duvernay will find Miss Taylor. Sit down now so that we can take care of your injuries."

Agent Banks gave Thomas a first-aid kit to attend to Kevin's wounds.

The Special Corruption Unit believed in no loose ends, and this case was no exception. The team prepared the house for implosion. No trace of the SCU's handiwork could be left behind.

Eric ran down the hallway in search of Tangie. The hairs on the back of his neck stood up as he neared the room the two men had come running from. Eric's mouth was dry and his pulse was beating rapidly as he opened the door. Savage curses poured from his lips. He was afraid to think what might have happened to her. He would never forgive himself if anything . . .

He searched frantically, expecting to see her as soon as he opened the door.

Tangie removed the blindfold and tried to orient herself. She needed a plan and quickly, but before she could make up her mind about what to do she heard footsteps coming toward the door. She hid in the large closet, praying that it wasn't Valencia's two thugs returning. She held her breath and looked around for a weapon. She twisted a wire hanger into a short spear. Her plan was to gouge out eyes or anything else she could find when those thugs returned.

She crouched down low in the closet. She was poised to strike whoever had the misfortune of opening the door. Tangie closed her eyes for a brief second and fervently prayed for strength.

The door opened. She held her breath and concentrated, steeling her body to make the assault. She opened her eyes—ready.

She nearly fainted when she saw him standing in the room. She closed her eyes again, shaking her head to make sure she wasn't hallucinating. But this was no illusion. It was him, it was really Eric. She flung open the closet doors and ran to him. Without a word she plunged her body deep into his chest.

Eric was immobile for a few seconds before his instincts kicked in. She was there, holding on to him for dear life. He was almost overcome with emotion. He squeezed her more forcefully than he intended, causing her to wince slightly. He was so glad to see her that he didn't know what to say, so he just held her. Neither spoke.

Comforted by his embrace, Tangie's body finally gave way to the tension she'd been holding and she started to shake violently. After several minutes, she looked up to see his beautiful brown eyes watching her.

"Is that the way you treat the man who has come over two thousand miles to rescue you?" he said.

Tangie opened her mouth to speak, but no words came out. Her mind couldn't process any more. Two days of being a prisoner and a year of heartbreak had taken their toll on Tangie. Eric could do nothing more than hold her as she cried uncontrollably, her body once again shaking with emotion.

There was no mistaking the love in Eric's eyes as he looked at her—savoring her sweetness. Eric was so glad to finally hold her. Tangie meant the world to him and he would spend the rest of his life proving that to her if that's what it took.

Even in these worst of circumstances, he never wanted to lose this moment with her; she was safe in his arms where she belonged. He thanked God she had not been harmed and that all the horrible things he had imagined weren't true. He continued to hold her close, rocking her as if she were his newborn child.

The other members of the team found Eric and Tangie in each other's arms standing in the middle of the room. No one seemed to notice Kevin trailing behind them.

As she finally noticed him, Thomas's gut told her he had feelings stronger than just friendship for Tangie. But one look at his stricken face and she knew he realized with the scene unfolding before them that he didn't stand a chance with Tangie. Something in Thomas tugged at her heart. She took Kevin aside. "Are you all right? I mean physically, anyway?" she asked.

Kevin looked down at the floor. . . .

He was feeling sorry for himself, but he didn't want anyone else's pity. "Yeah . . . just fine. I'm glad you guys made it. How in the world did you find us?" he mumbled. "By the way, thank you for saving my life."

Kevin stole another glance at Tangie and Eric. His heart was breaking with every second. He wanted to get out of there now! Instead, he turned his anger toward the very people responsible for saving his sorry life. "Agent Thomas, how did this happen? How did Valencia even get into this country?"

Thomas spoke firmly. She knew how Kevin was feeling. "Sir, we aren't at liberty to discuss the details

right now, but we will be able to discuss some of this
with you when we get back to Virginia."

Kevin knew that it wasn't the most gracious behavior, but he had been through quite a bit in the last
week. He had just come to terms with his feelings for
Tangie and was on the brink of telling her how he felt
when this disaster struck them.

He felt terribly guilty for involving Tangie in his life
and having her face these problems with the people
who were after him. And to top it off, she was in love
with another man and hadn't bothered to tell him
that. He felt as if he were watching a soap opera unfolding, only it was his life.

Valencia had been taken care of, but he would
probably have to be moved again and given a new
identity. No one knew how many more lunatics Valencia had working for her or what they might have
in mind. No, his life was pretty much over, as he knew
it. There would be a lot of changes to deal with from
now on, and losing Tangie was just one of them.

After what seemed like a lifetime of questions and
answers, Kevin and Tangie were finally able to have
a moment alone. The tension that filled the room
was almost palpable.

Tangie stammered, "Kevin . . . I . . . I . . . don't know
what to say. I should have told you . . . I thought I'd
never see him again."

"You don't have to say anything, Tangie. I know
when the ball is not in my court, and seeing you with
him lets me know exactly where I stand. I guess we
never got around to him, huh?" Kevin said more
harshly than he intended.

He looked deep into her eyes, afraid of the hurt he
might see. "I am so sorry for dragging you into this

mess, I never thought there was a chance that you would get hurt. Can you ever forgive me?"

Tangie ignored his earlier comment. There would be plenty of time to deal with all that later. Right now, she needed to know he was safe.

"Kevin, I don't blame you, she was insane, but what will you do? Where will you go? Are you going to be safe back home?"

"No . . . I'm not going back home. I don't know where, it depends on what the government has to offer. It's okay though, I've got a lot of decisions to make. The FBI is going to relocate me and I'll get a fresh start someplace new."

"Oh, Kevin, nooo," she responded, her voice cracking with emotion.

"Tangie, look at me. We both know this is for the best. You need time to focus on the feelings that you have been trying to bury all this time."

"Kevin—"

"No, don't." Kevin put his pointer finger to her lips. "I just hope he knows how very lucky he is. You are one very special young lady and you deserve the best. I'm just sorry that it didn't turn out to be me."

"Kevin . . . I don't have the words . . . I never in a million years would have predicted something like this. I can't think about my relationship with Eric right now. So much has happened."

She paused to look him directly in the eye. "Promise me that you will be happy." She embraced Kevin tightly, melding her body into his.

Kevin broke the embrace, before his emotions and his body gave way to his true feelings. He shoved his hands in his pockets and walked away from Tangie.

He was making the best decision for both of them, but it still didn't stop the deep ache in his heart.

Tangie stood alone in the room awhile before Eric finally came back. She didn't realize he'd overheard the last portion of their conversation.

Eric could see the pain in Kevin's eyes as he said good-bye to Tangie.

Would he see pain in hers too? Just how far had their relationship gone? Maybe he wasn't sure he really wanted to know. Eric knew he couldn't bear to lose her again. Living without her had tested his sanity before. If he lost her now . . .

He knew he didn't want to live without Tangie as the center of his life. He entered the room and practically whispered her name. He waited nervously for her to turn to him. Moisture glistened in her eyes as Tangie faced Eric. Looking at him after all the time that had passed made the scene surreal; she wasn't sure if she wasn't just waking up from a bad dream. How many times she hoped and prayed to see him again . . . and now . . .

She looked deep into his eyes before trusting herself to speak. They had so much they needed to say to each other.

Her voice was barely above a whisper. "Eric, I need some time to sort things out. This has all been so crazy, with Kevin . . . that obsessed woman and those awful men . . . now seeing you after all this time."

Tangie fought hard to control the emotion in her voice. Her eyes sparkled with unshed tears that threatened to spill out over her long lashes any minute. She was fighting hard to maintain control, and had resolved herself to get through the next few days with her wits about her. Tangie took a deep breath and continued to fight for control.

More focused, she continued, "There hasn't been a day since we first met that I haven't thought of you, missed you, and . . . I can't do this right now. Please just get me out of here! Give me some time . . ." she pleaded.

The desperation in her voice shook Eric to his core. He had caused her so much pain by not being there for her. He knew he'd never forgive himself for this.

Eric said nothing as Agent King signaled that everything was in place. He led Tangie to a government vehicle that was waiting outside to take them to the plane. It would take them to Quantico and FBI headquarters, where they could give a full report of what happened.

Eric turned to Thomas. "Make sure Ms. Taylor is comfortable. I'm going to ride in the other vehicle." Thomas gave him a questioning look, but decided not to press the issue. Just follow orders. From what she could see, Tangie and Eric both looked the worse for the wear.

As quietly and quickly as they came, three government vehicles whisked them off to the landing strip for their flight back to Virginia. They all turned when they heard the explosives being detonated. In minutes, the Rios compound was reduced to unrecognizable rubble. A local team would come in and make sure that everything was taken care of completely. The government would seize the land, and maybe in a year or two a school or an office building would inhabit the space.

The team took great satisfaction in knowing that the Chilean Cartel was finally finished on American soil. Agent Spates was extremely relieved when he got the call from Eric that all had gone well. The E-team had been successful one more time.

Tangie, Eric, and Kevin, each in different vehicles, remained quiet during the drive to the plane. It would be a long, sad trip back across the states.

The team felt it had been a complicated but successful mission and rescue; however, instead of celebrating victory like they usually did, the tension was unmistakable and the air charged with negative energy. Thomas and King looked at each other before going to their respective vehicles, both shrugging their shoulders. "Don't look at me, I just work here," King said.

As the team proceeded down their trek, they wondered what in the hell was going on!

Thomas had the feeling that this was more the beginning than the ending. She knew Eric very well and she had never seen him pursue a rescue quite like this one before. Tangerine Taylor was one lucky woman. Kevin DePalma was no slouch and she was ready to give him up for the commander, or so it seemed. Thomas felt a certain kinship with DePalma; once she had been in the very same position as he. She recognized his vulnerability, a sensation she never wanted to experience again.

Chapter 27

When the team arrived at the rendezvous point they began to board the plane. The bodies of Valencia Rios and her key henchmen were stowed in the cargo area and then they prepared to leave.

Eric, who was checking on the last few details, was the last to board. Since this was one of the smaller aircraft in the government fleet, the only seat available was right next to Tangie.

He noticed that King, Anderson, Banks, and Thomas had refused to make eye contact with him as he looked for a seat. They had set him up and purposefully forced him to sit next to Tangie.

Eric approached her slowly before gingerly sliding into the vacant seat. Tangie refused to acknowledge the love she saw in his eyes when he looked at her. It was too soon to deal with their relationship. Tangie needed time to think and sort out her feelings. She knew she still loved Eric . . . she felt it the moment she saw him again, but what was love without trust? She knew she could trust him with her life, but her heart was another story. After two years, could they really forge a strong relationship? She didn't want to be with him out of some sense of gratitude; she had to sort it all out!

She was so exhausted from her ordeal she fell into an uneasy sleep. She had tried to stay awake, tried to think of what to say to Eric, but her body had reached its limit. Soon after the plane was in the air, she was dreaming.

Eric watched Tangie in tense silence. He knew that she was having a nightmare. It was only natural that she would have some reaction to the kidnapping. She was suffering the aftereffects of her ordeal. It would take time to heal those wounds, but the hurt would eventually stop.

He started to reach for her but stopped. He might make her more scared. Tangie twisted and turned in the cramped airplane seat, struggling against invisible demons. Tears streamed down her face.

Eric couldn't take it any longer. Whispering her name, he drew her into his embrace. Planting butterfly kisses in the wake of her tears, he repeated softly how much he loved her and would always protect her. She seemed to relax in the safety of his arms. He held her close, afraid to let go of her ever again.

Despite two days in captivity, she was still as beautiful as he remembered. Her unbrushed hair fell in a silken, disheveled mess around her shoulders. He wanted to kiss her lush mouth, caress her soft skin, and make her feel loved. She was beautiful, the most beautiful woman he'd ever seen; to him she would always be. Eric drew life from her spirit. He wouldn't accept that their relationship was over.

Tangie awoke three hours later, still enveloped in Eric's tender embrace. Instead of pulling away from him, she allowed herself to snuggle closer. They had a lot to talk about, but for right now she needed him. For this moment in time, she wasn't going to let pride get in the way . . . she would let him take care of her.

Following the debriefing at Quantico after all the questions were answered, she was given clearance to go. Their interaction had been all business at the base until Eric offered to take her home. She accepted, desperate to get home. Eric led her to his Acura, and in silence they began the journey to her town house in Fairfax.

When Tangie arrived home her mother and Candy were waiting for her. Eric had called Mrs. Taylor when they arrived safely from New Mexico. Tangie ran headlong into their waiting arms and began crying anew.

Candy stayed with her friend for a week. She helped her make arrangements for a new security system and offered her a shoulder to cry on whenever she needed one. After the third night, when Tangie was finally ready, she and Candy spent time going through what had happened. Tangie explained about the cartel and Valencia's determination to get revenge. From what Tangie understood and could talk about, Valencia had been planning for years how to get revenge against those she accused of ruining her life back in 1994.

Tangie pulled her hair back and sat cross-legged on her couch. Her pink T-shirt and pant pajama set made her look more like a teenager. She enjoyed her tea before launching into her ordeal.

"This is so wild! So where exactly did you and Kevin fit in to this diabolical plan?"

Tangie sighed heavily. "Well, apparently Valencia had managed to find out where everybody was that had been on Kevin's old team. She and her crew tracked them down one by one and killed them. As far as I know Kevin is the only one left."

Candy took another bite of her muffin. She listened to Tangie with rapt attention. "That's so incredible and so sad. How did Eric know how to rescue you?"

"Some of that is classified, but what I can tell you is she had been planning for a while and they were able to put a mole in her organization. He died while I was in New Mexico—I really owe him my life too. Without the information he provided, Eric would never have found us in time."

Tangie alternately cried about her captivity and rejoiced that she was okay. Soon the shock of the ordeal would wear off and she would feel normal again.

The two friends embraced tightly.

Tangie shuddered, remembering Carlos's screams as Valencia's men tortured him.

"She was truly crazy, she twisted the love she felt for her family into something ugly and unrecognizable. I know it's bad to speak ill of the dead, but I'm so glad she is gone!"

Candy found herself shuddering too. She knew Tangie needed time to get it all out of her system. Candy encouraged her to get her feelings out.

"Is she gone . . . or really gone?" Candy asked dramatically.

"Yes, Ms. Drama Queen . . . she's dead. She died in a shoot-out with one of the agents. Now, that's all I can say on the subject. You aren't cleared for any more information."

"Okay, but it sounds like it might make a great book! I can see it now—*My Life As a Hostage*. All that murder and mayhem, you know I love that kind of stuff."

"Yes, Candy . . . I know you love that kind of stuff. You probably would have told Valencia she was over the top and to calm down a bit," she teased.

Candy sniffed in mock indignation. "I can't help it if nothing exciting ever happens to me. I have to live vicariously through the drama of my friends. You and Kim keep me quite entertained. I'm hungry, you want to help me make chicken taco salads?"

"Sure, maybe if you eat you won't be able to ask any more questions."

Candy looked serious for a moment. "Tangie, I'm so sorry about what happened to you. I didn't know what was going on. I just thank the saints that you made it back to me. Come here, girl, and give me a hug. You are my best friend in the world. Even whatshisname couldn't hold a candle to you."

On their way to the kitchen, the phone rang. Tangie kept walking, ignoring it as if it didn't exist.

After a few days of talking with Candy, Tangie was able to put her relationship with Kevin in perspective. He had been a pleasant distraction, but she knew she really wasn't in love with him. She was sorry that his life was going to be turned upside down again. Tangie knew she had to concentrate on herself. It was time to stop being a victim and regain some control.

Candy told her that she had to leave at the end of the week. She felt comfortable with her friend's progress, and Tangie needed to begin to deal with her feelings. Besides, she knew there was one very anxious young man ready and willing to take over the protection of Tangerine Taylor permanently. Candy and Siddiq had postponed the wedding after Tangie's kidnapping and now they were impatient to get things back on schedule.

After she and Tangie had finished their taco dinner, she brought up her impending nuptials.

"Siddiq and I have set a new date for the wedding. I know we haven't talked about it much, but we have a lot of plans to put back in place. You're starting to look and sound like your old self, so I think it's about time I mosey on out of here and let you get back to your life."

Candy took a breath and studied her friend's face. "Are you still planning on going back to work next week?"

Tangie held the butterflies at bay. She was going to be alone again.

"Yep, Cliff and I talked yesterday. He wants me to take it easy, but I need the distraction. I don't want to be cooped up anymore! I'll take it easy, and when I get tired I'll just back off. I really do feel much better. Thanks for taking such good care of me."

"Not a problem, I know you would do the same for me."

Tangie said softly, "In a heartbeat. Listen, there's something I need to say and I hope you can forgive me."

Candy looked intently at her friend. She didn't like her ominous tone. "What's up, girl?"

"I feel really bad about you and Siddiq postponing your wedding. I have a confession to make. I was so jealous! You know I only want the best for you, but I always thought we would be planning our weddings together, and since I knew that wasn't going to happen I got a case of the green-eyed monster—bad. Then I got kidnapped and you guys put your plans on hold for me. I feel so guilty. I really don't deserve you."

Candy was touched. "Now who's being the drama queen? I always thought we would plan our weddings, baby showers, and everything else together too. Don't beat yourself up, I'm sure I would have felt the same way."

Candy looked at her friend seriously. "Tangie, look at me. We may not be able to plan our wedding together, but there's a gorgeous young man who'd like to help you plan one soon enough. Now if you would just stop being so stubborn and listen to your heart, you could get started. Tangie, do what's best . . . give him a chance."

She looked at her friend, exasperated because she knew she was right.

Tangie sighed. "What makes you such an expert on Agent Eric Duvernay?"

Candy responded, "Don't you worry about that . . . You just take heed to my words. Anyway, you're getting in my way. Go lie down or do whatever you invalids are supposed to do while you recuperate."

"Yes, Mother," Tangie snickered. "I am feeling kinda tired. I'm going to take a short snooze. I love you, girl."

"I know, I know . . . I'm the best thing since sliced bread. I'll come get you in an hour."

While Candy had been helping her friend recuperate, she had time to check out Eric. He had hovered over Tangie as if she were a piece of fine breakable china. He called every day to see how she was doing, even though Tangie wouldn't take his calls.

Soon he and Candy fashioned their routine and she felt as if she had known him all her life. She even asked his opinion on some wedding details. By the end of the week, there was no doubt in her mind that Eric was the right one for Tangie.

The day before Candy was set to leave she got a surprise phone call from Eric. He wanted to talk to her specifically.

"Hey, Candy, how you doing, girl?"

"Fine as usual. How's my buddy doing?"

"I can't complain. Is our patient doing better today? Are you still leaving tomorrow?"

Candy sat on a kitchen stool. "We had a good long talk last night. She's come a long way. I know she's going to be fine. Not as fine as if she had one fine young secret agent man keeping her warm at night though." Candy hesitated. "Don't give up on her, Eric. My friend is nothing if not stubborn."

"Well . . . that's part of the reason I called. I need to borrow you for a couple of hours. Can you get away?"

"Not today, can it wait until I move out of Tangie's place?"

Disappointed, he said, "Okay, I'm just anxious, that's all. Can we hook up in a couple of days then?"

"You bet, call me at my home to confirm."

"Tell her someone who cares called to ask about her."

"I always do, Eric. She won't admit it, but she looks forward to your calls, even though she won't talk to you yet. Give her time, she'll come around."

Candy got more comfortable before continuing.

She didn't feel guilty ⸻
business. Tangie was too ⸻
and Candy wasn't going to l⸻

"Tangie's eyes brighten ever⸻
knows that you are on the phone. ⸻
right thing by calling her every day. K⸻
know that you care."

"Thanks, Candy, I needed to hear that. I⸻ e her
and I am willing to wait as long as it takes. I haven't
always done things that I am proud of, but I have
never done anything to hurt her intentionally—I
hope you know that."

"Don't worry, Eric, if I thought you weren't one of
the good guys—you would truly have hell to pay."
Candy chuckled.

Eric was warmed by the sound. "I'm glad she has
you for a friend. I want you to know that I am very
sorry about what happened to her. I almost lost my
mind when I heard she had been kidnapped."

"I'm just glad you were there for her, Eric. And I
think deep down she knows she was too."

"Thanks again. She is lucky to have you for a
friend. I mean that. I'll talk to you later."

"I'd say we are all lucky. Bye, handsome."

Chapter 28

Eric gave himself two weeks to work things out in his mind and let Tangie rest. He thought it only fair to give her a chance to sort out her feelings too, but he was determined to get her back. No flowers this time, no corny poetry.

Eric knew he needed to be honest with her. He would just let her get to know and trust the real him. On Friday of the second week, he called. His fingers nearly shook, he was so nervous.

"Tangie, it's Eric. I really need to talk with you." He anxiously waited for her response.

Tangie's heart quickened at the rich-timbred voice on the phone. "Hello, Eric," she said barely above a whisper. "I've been thinking about you. I don't know if I ever really thanked you for saving my life."

She hesitated before continuing. "I know you called every day while Candy was here. I think you've made a real impression on that girl."

"Yeah, you've got a great friend in her. I'm just glad she was able to be there for you."

He sighed. "How are you?"

"I am doing better. At first it was weird in the house by myself."

If it were up to me, you wouldn't ever be alone, he thought.

His voice became deeper, more passionate when he spoke again.

"As for saving your life, I'd do it anytime, anywhere. Have the nightmares stopped? I wanted to give you some time, but I really need to see you, Tangie."

His voice washed over her like a warm summer breeze. She shivered involuntarily. How she wanted to be in his arms instead of on the phone.

Tangie forced her voice to sound normal. "I think I've had time to put things in perspective. The nightmares are less frequent, but sometimes when I'm napping I'll wake up disoriented. I'm fine though. I've started back to work and I'm not looking over my shoulder so much. I think the alarm system you guys recommended makes me feel a lot safer." Sighing heavily, she added, "I think we should see each other too. I think we need some sort of closure."

His voice tight with emotion, he said, "Tangie, I made a big mistake letting you go earlier. I can't make another one now by saying good-bye to us again. Can't we try to see where this takes us?"

Eric didn't want too push too hard, but he needed her to understand how much he wanted to be with her. "Let's just put all of our cards on the table and let it be. I can't pretend that I don't have strong feelings for you. That I don't—"

Tangie interrupted him before he could finish. "Eric, I can't pretend like nothing has happened. Things are different now—"

Eric interrupted emphatically. "No, Tangie, don't try to trivialize our feelings, I know what you felt for me."

Tangie sat on her bed, slumping her shoulders in defeat. "What do we do about it then? I can't com-

pete with your job. I don't know which way to turn
and I'm all out of answers."

Slowly Eric blew the air out of his lungs. He felt
some measure of success. She wasn't telling him good
bye again.

He thought for a moment. "I guess we go back to
the beginning."

"To New Orleans?" she asked incredulously.

"Not physically, but mentally. Let's hang out with
each other. See what's going on under all these
sparks between us."

Tangie warmed to the idea. Before she could
change her mind again, Eric suggested a date for the
next night. They planned to meet in a nice public
place, preferring to ease slowly into more intimate
settings.

They met at a local restaurant in Georgetown for
dinner. The atmosphere was cozy but busy, and both
felt it was a good place to establish boundaries.

Tangie took great care in getting ready. She wore
an ankle-length black skirt that hugged her in all the
right places. It was sexy without being too provocative
and she finished the look with a burgundy top. She
wore her shoulder-length hair loose, to show off recent auburn highlights. She decided on simple,
natural-looking makeup, except for her berried lips.
She wanted to look nice without giving the impression she was on the prowl. She didn't want to give
Eric the wrong idea. This was not her man-catching
look, as Candy would say.

Eric wore black dress slacks with a loose-fitting
burgundy-striped silk shirt. His face was clean-shaven
and he had a fresh haircut shaping his wavy black locks.

Seeing him made her feel weak in the knees. On

closer inspection, she noticed a few strands of gray that hadn't been there before. *Ummm, he smells so good. How am I going to do this? I can't even look at him without falling apart,* she thought.

"Hi, you look great" His voice, sweet and low, was like a tender caress.

Tangie's body reacted instinctively. She sighed inwardly. "You look great too. Was that on purpose? You trying to make this hard on me?"

"Hey, only if it's working. I'm glad you came out with me tonight. I really have missed you."

There was an awkward silence until the waitress came to take their orders. Tangie ordered a simple chicken Caesar salad and Eric the blackened catfish. They engaged in light conversation during their meal. Eric looked at her appreciatively. There was more that he wanted to say, but didn't. He didn't want to scare her after winning this tiny victory. He would have preferred to confess his undying love, beg her to come back to him, but he wouldn't do that. Tangie would come around, and when she did, he would be ready.

"I can tell you've been working out since . . ." *This feels so awkward. What do I say? Since I let you walk out of my life?*

She bailed him out. "Since we were both too stubborn to see how important our relationship was. We don't have to sugarcoat anything, Eric. I know I messed up."

Eric nodded. "No more than I. Work should not have come between us. I should have realized that I was killing our relationship."

Tangie reached for his hand across the table. "I should have been more patient. That's why I want to take it slow. I don't want to stop and start anymore. I need stability in my life, not adventure and intrigue."

Eric closed his eyes. He couldn't promise her that Spates would never call. "I don't know if this is the best place to talk about this."

"Okay, let's go back to keeping it light."

"Agreed. How's it going with work? Are you still enjoying consumer affairs?"

"Yes, I love the position because it gives me so much more freedom. My staff and I have been trying to come up with some interesting customer benefits. Maybe I'll have something to preview for you in a few months."

Her innocent comment sent his libido into overdrive; Eric felt a very uncomfortable tightening in his groin. He had to fight the overwhelming need to be close to her. When he and Tangie made eye contact, there was no mistaking his desire. Or hers.

Tangie looked down. "What are we going to do, Eric?" she said quietly.

"I'm sorry, Tangie, I can't help the way I feel about you. I'm willing to take it slow. Just don't ask me to lie about how much I want you or care about you."

She was silent for several minutes. She leaned back in her seat before speaking again.

"I didn't think I'd ever see you again. I thought you were sticking to your ultimatum and I'd blown it with you. I wanted so desperately for you to knock on my door, Eric. Stubborn pride stopped me from knocking on yours."

Eric reached for her hand. "Tangie, I wanted to come to you, but I was a coward. I gave up on you without a fight and we both paid the price. I'll never do that again." Eric warred within himself. He wanted the answers to questions he had no right to ask.

"Tell me about DePalma. Were you in love with him?" he asked before looking away.

Tangie knew it was none of his business, but it was more important for them to start clear and fresh. She didn't want him harboring doubt about her feelings. "I'll answer that for you, but I think we should get out of here. People are starting to stare and I think the staff is ready to go home now."

"Where would you like to go?"

"I'm in Fairfax and you're in Manassas. Maybe we could find someplace quiet in the middle." She didn't know if she could trust her hormones around him in a more private place.

"My aunt's loft is just a few blocks from here. We could go there," he offered.

His eyes searched hers, willing her to say yes. "I promise, no games and no compromising situations, just coffee and talk. What do you think? Trust me?"

"Against my better judgment I'll go. I do trust you."

As they walked, they saw lovers strolling down the sidewalks or walking hand in hand in the various shops and stores. Tangie unconsciously moved farther away from Eric. They were both treading dangerous waters. When they reached the loft, they were both feeling nostalgic for the love they once shared.

When they settled down again in his living room they picked up their conversation where they'd left off at the restaurant.

"I suppose I knew we had to get to this one day. I guess I was lonely. Kevin was a nice distraction." Tangie hesitated. "Kevin was a bright light in a very dark tunnel, but on some level I knew the relationship wasn't meant to be." Tangie shrugged.

She took off her shoes and crossed her feet on the couch.

Seeing her bare feet almost unnerved Eric, but he remained motionless, listening to every word. He needed to be able to put Kevin in perspective, to know if he had a hold on a piece of Tangie's heart.

She hesitated for a minute before continuing. "But that's not all you want to know, is it?" She looked into his deep mahogany pools and almost melted. His effect on her was truly unnerving.

Tangie continued, "Did he replace you? No. I thought about you, dreamed about you, wanted to call you all the time. I've got year-old presents in my closet for you to prove it. After missing you for so long and work getting in the way, I couldn't think straight. But that's not all you want to know, is it?"

Eric had the good sense to look sheepish for a moment. He turned away as the heat rose in his face. "No—but the answer doesn't change anything," he added quickly.

Tangie waited until his gaze met her own. "I did not sleep with him. Our relationship might have progressed that far in time, but that's not where we were. We both enjoyed spending time with each other. Unfortunately, I haven't been with anyone since Rodney. You were the closest I've come to any intimacy. That was over a year ago."

"Damn! Tangie, that's been—"

"You don't have to tell me how many years it has been. I have lived every second of it."

He knew he didn't have the right to ask these questions, but he was glad that Tangie answered. "I'm sorry, maybe I shouldn't have asked. I have no right and I'm prying."

"Yes, you are, but I wouldn't have expected anything less from you. Men always want the details of the woman's love life, but don't want to share their own. Besides, I know I don't have to answer. I want to. This is important for us. No more secrets, Eric."

Eric sighed wearily. "Tangie, please don't generalize with me. If I could have told you everything about me on the first day I saw you in New Orleans, believe me, I would have. I fell for you the moment I noticed you." He hesitated before continuing. "You didn't ask, but there have been a couple of women, nothing long-term. I haven't been with anyone in well over a year. My heart was never in it. I've never gotten over you, Tangie."

Tangie was losing the battle. . . .

She wanted to be in his arms, loving him. She needed to go home before she wouldn't say no. "Eric, I've had a really nice evening with you. I can't make any promises for our future, but I'm willing to take it a step at a time."

Eric defied the urge to pull her to him in a passionate kiss. He wanted to show her just how happy she'd just made him. Instead, he suggested that they see each other again.

"You want to go for a drive next weekend? I know some great places where we can air out the Acura."

Tangie's eyes lit up. "I'd love to, just give me a call on Friday. Well, I guess with true confessions over, and I mean that in a good way, I'd better get out of your hair. I'll call you tomorrow. Sleep well."

"My hair is exactly where I want you to be," he responded.

Tangie walked quickly toward the door. She wasn't upset, just fighting the deep and powerful urges of her body. Surely, Eric knew how much she wanted him. From the moment their eyes met in New Orleans she was drawn to him. She had to make her escape before her eyes made a confession she wasn't ready to make yet with her mouth.

Eric rushed to her side. "At least let me walk you back to the car."

When they'd reached her car in the almost deserted lot, he hugged her lightly, then opened her car door. He waited until she was safely on the way before turning back to go home.

Tangie was emotionally and physically drained by the time she made it home. It had been an enlightening evening. They covered a lot of ground. She was almost ready to admit to him that all she wanted was for him to be in her life. But she couldn't. They still needed to iron out some details, figure out some things. She wanted to commit to him. But, not until she knew she wouldn't play second fiddle to the Bureau or the next big case. She was selfish. She wanted to be the number-one priority in his life.

The phone rang again as soon as she put her foot in the bed. Answering the phone, she said, "As much as I love talking with you, I am really beat, Mr. Duvernay."

Her sleepy sultry voice was more than he bargained for. His water bill was going to be very high until they resolved their relationship. "I have one big favor to ask. When you dress like you did before, it makes it really tough on a brother to keep things under control."

"You are silly, but just in case you didn't notice, you have the same effect on me. Okay, we'll make a pact, we've both got to wear our ugliest clothes when we are together."

Eric laughed. The sound warmed Tangie through the phone lines.

"I know you're beat, I feel the same way. I just needed to hear your voice before going to sleep. Tangie, I can't wait to see you on Friday."

"I'm looking forward to seeing you again too. Get a good night's rest, okay? Sweet dreams."

"Can I call you next week to set something up?"

"Sure, that sounds good. I'll be looking forward to it." Tangie chuckled. Didn't he realize that they had already made a date to go driving?

"Good night, Eric. I'm going to sleep now, I am a real bear when I don't get my rest."

Eric sighed. He knew he'd be dreaming of her. "Okay, you win. Good night."

That evening Tangie dreamed again of trying to run away. She was being chased, but this time she didn't feel scared. There were strong arms protecting her. They fought her attackers, defeating them and making her feel safe. She woke up the next morning smiling for the first time in several weeks.

Eric called her on Monday. They both agreed to leave work early on a Friday for their driving date. He had some training assignments coming up and didn't know if his weekends were going to be free for the next several weeks. He wanted to take advantage of any time that he could spend with her. This time he wouldn't let his job come between them.

Tangie had been beside herself all day in anticipation of seeing him again. She didn't know whether she should be so excited about him. Maybe she should back off and think about things more slowly.

Then again, maybe she should just commit herself and get it over with.

By the time the receptionist announced Eric's arrival at the office, she was a nervous ball of energy. She willed her nerves to calm down as she walked to the waiting area. She smoothed her tailored cream silk slacks down with damp hands. She walked to the reception area appearing much more calm than she felt.

Eric sat down in the reception area to wait for Tangie. He flipped through an information technology magazine with keen interest, but he stopped immediately when he felt her presence. Eric sensed her before he saw her or smelled her signature fragrance. As he turned around to face her, his breath caught in his throat. He would never get used to her beauty.

"Hi there, you look great. Are you ready to go?"

Tangie smiled. "I'm glad you could make it. Did you have any trouble with traffic?"

"Traffic wasn't too bad getting here, but it's Friday afternoon and traffic is going to be horrible getting over the bridge."

Tangie arched one eyebrow. "The bridge?"

"Yeah, the old man may have a few surprises up his sleeve." Eric interlocked his arm with hers and headed in the direction of her office. "Come on, let's get a move on."

"My office is just around the corner," she directed him. "Let me get my bag. We can be on our way. Do I have time to slip into some jeans? I want to change into something more casual. Do I get to know where you are taking me?"

Eric gave her that mischievous smile that turned her to butter. "Jeans are fine. Why are women so impatient and don't know how to take a surprise?"

"You win, I'll be a sport. I am trusting you with my life once again," she said, shaking her head and grinning.

"I like the sound of that."

Several minutes later they were headed up I-495 North. Their route would eventually take them to Route 50 along the beautiful coastal waterways of Maryland. Traffic was typical for a Friday afternoon in the Washington, DC, metropolitan area, but made more bearable by the music and the company. Tangie enjoyed the feel of the Acura and its fresh clean smell. Eric pulled out all the stops to make her feel comfortable. She took off her shoes and stretched out a bit more. She reminded Eric of a very satisfied feline. Will Downing was soothing her with his deep baritone and Tangie didn't have a care in the world.

Eric alternated between watching her and watching the road. She was definitely more interesting than the six lanes of cars, but such a dangerous distraction. *She has no idea what she does to me*, he thought. Eric nodded his head to the music. He imagined himself holding her in his arms, as they swayed to the soft sensuous beat. He hoped his fantasy would come true by the end of the evening.

They would be in Maryland's Eastern Shore before the end of the dinner hour. He planned a very nice meal for her aboard his boat, which he hoped his dad had remembered to dock for him. The evening might come to a very embarrassing end if he didn't.

"You look mighty comfortable over there. Just let me know when you want to stop. By the way, I know we didn't really talk about overnights, but that's a possibility if you're too tired to make the trip back tonight."

Tangie slid down farther into the passenger seat of his car, reveling in its plush interior. She'd ridden in it before, but was looking forward to the power of the open road. Eric could swear he heard a little purr.

After another languid stretch, she answered, "Always a man with a solution, aren't you? I bet you were the best little Boy Scout when you were younger, weren't you?" Tangie teased. "Actually, let's just play this by ear. I'll let you know later." She wasn't making any promises.

Switching subjects, Tangie said, "You know, I just realized something, you've met my mom and my best friends, but I've never met your friends or your family. How would you like to do a little dinner party in a few weeks?"

"That's not a bad idea. I'd love to introduce you to my friends and I know my dad can't wait to meet you. I've told him so much about you. Should I invite some of my SCU people?"

"Sure, I haven't seen anyone since the 'incident' and this would be a good way to say thank you again."

Eric marveled at the way her eyes lit up. "I'll put out the invitation, but depending on assignments, it may be difficult to count on them."

Tangie was a little disappointed, having warmed up to the idea "Well, all we can do is invite them. I would love to see Agent Thomas again especially. She must be a very special woman to do the job that she does."

Eric looked uncomfortable for a moment.

Tangie studied him for several seconds. She pursed her lips as understanding threaded its way through her consciousness. "You two had a relationship, didn't you?"

Eric took his eyes off the road long enough to look

into her eyes. "We have a professional relationship. We let it get out of hand a couple of times, but we never had a real relationship. In my previous life, sometimes all you had was your team members. We knew right from the start it wasn't meant to be, and we knew that we couldn't afford to let feelings get in the way of the mission. I care about her a great deal, but not in the way that I care about you. I've never felt for anyone what I do for you, Tangie." Eric sighed.

Tangie watched the road for a few seconds before answering. "I can't imagine what your life must be like when you are on special assignments. The nerves, the loneliness. I understand, I really do. I still want to invite her. She's part of the reason I'm alive today."

Eric reached over and squeezed her hand. "Thank you for that, it means a lot to me."

He was really starting to get to her. The warmth that suffused her body negated any feelings of jealousy or insecurity. Eric loved her deeply. The only thing she didn't know was what she was going to do about it.

They rode in silence for several minutes, each lost in individual thought. They were having a lovely ride and that's all she would deal with right now. They had already wasted almost two years.

The sun was just beginning to set. Traffic was much lighter as people found their exits and moved on. The number of cars going over the bridge was surprisingly light, and they were making great time en route to their destination. Tangie looked at the water under the bridge. The sheer volume made a lot of people nervous, but Tangie didn't mind. Besides, Eric was the one doing the driving. She read the highway sign. They were entering Queen Anne's County.

He drove until he pulled into the driveway of a

lovely two-story Cape Cod cottage. "This is my father's house. It has been in the Duvernay family for almost seventy years. You can freshen up here, but this is not really our destination—just a stopover."

"Eric, it's lovely. I love the gables and the veranda. I can just imagine sipping mint juleps out here."

"Come on inside, it gets better. This is one of my favorite properties."

"Lead the way, I'm right behind you."

"The house has four bedrooms and two and a half bathrooms. You should appreciate the kitchen. It's great for entertaining. I love to cook in there. Sometimes Dad and I get together here with cousins or coworkers. This area is probably one of Maryland's best-kept secrets. You want a cup of coffee or something or a snack?"

"Yes, please. Just let me loose in the kitchen as soon as I finish in the bathroom."

"I'll be in the kitchen," Eric said.

When Tangie returned she couldn't find him. She continued her tour of the house, pleasantly surprised by the tasteful choice of furnishings. Everything was designed for comfort. There were baskets and flowers throughout. It definitely had a feminine touch. This house was decorated with care and love, she thought. The fireplace mantel contained pictures of generations of Duvernays. They had strong genes. She looked at a picture of Eric standing with someone who could only be his father. The resemblance was striking. Eric was a younger version of the very handsome Samuel. There was another picture of Eric, Samuel, and a woman. Tangie guessed it was his mother, judging from her age. She'd probably had something to do with the decorating. Tangie looked from photo to photo trying to figure out the relationships. She was so engrossed she didn't hear Eric return.

He approached her, coffee in hand. "Those photos pretty much sum up the Duvernay clan. I'd like to add my own collection to those soon."

"Thanks for the coffee. I hope you don't mind. I didn't see you, so I continued the tour on my own. This is a very comfortable home. It's a shame you don't get to use it as much."

"I know, maybe in the future," he hinted. "When you are finished I have something else to show you."

Tangie nodded, finishing her drink quickly. She wanted to see more.

Eric clasped her hand. They headed toward the rear of the house.

"Are we going out the back door?"

"In a manner of speaking," he answered, grinning. But it wasn't a car garage at all.

"Oh, Eric, this is beautiful. I think I'm in love with this house."

"Its probably the best feature of the house. Dad and I added it about five years ago. This boat is called *Whispers in the Wind*. We bought it in 1992. Dad and I try to get out every six months for some fishing. Mostly we just talk trash though and go buy dinner."

"She's gorgeous. You guys are lucky to have her. And this house too."

"So you up for a little trip? We haven't finished our drive."

Eric helped her aboard and busied himself getting the boat into the waterway. Tangie looked around in eager anticipation. In minutes, they were cruising down Chesapeake Bay. She joined Eric when he called for her.

"In a few more minutes we'll clear the residential zone and be out in the bay. I have a little snack for us in the kitchen area."

"Don't you mean the 'mess'?" she teased. "I'll go down in a few." She loved the water and the freedom of the open air. "I am enjoying this so much."

Eric set their course and took her down to the dining area. "We have fresh fruit and vegetables, snack chips, salad fixings, and fresh snapper. What are you in the mood for, cooking or driving?"

Tangie looked at Eric with a mischievous grin. "How about both?"

"When you look at me like that, how can I refuse you? Let me wash up and then we can start dinner."

"You got a taste of the depths of my appetite in New Orleans. I can always eat."

"Oh yes, my little Sumo wrestler. I'll be right back."

Tangie prepared a rub for the snapper. She loved grilled fish and had a few culinary tricks up her sleeve. By the time Eric returned, she had turned the kitchen into a work zone.

"You never cease to amaze me," he told her, admiration in his tone.

"Yeah, I could say the same about you. I hope you like it spicy. I'm making a Tangie special."

Eric had prepared a table for two with wine and candles. He lit the two white tapers before Tangie came up. It made a beautiful picture.

They sat on deck to eat their meal. The burnt orange and yellow of the setting sun served as their backdrop. No canvas could capture the sheer splendor of the moment.

They ate at a leisurely pace feeling complete, safe, and fulfilled in each other's company.

Eric let out a sigh of contentment.

Tangie looked at Eric. It would be so easy to throw caution to the wind. She felt so comfortable with him. But she wasn't ready to make love to him yet.

Eric looked at Tangie, and saw conflict warring in her eyes.

They started the return trip late in the evening. It was a quiet drive with both tired from the day's activities. Eric contented himself that Tangie seemed to enjoy his company. It was too soon to give up hope. He would continue to be patient.

The next time Eric called her, they agreed to another date.

"Are you up for a little physical activity?"

"Eric," she warned.

"No, now get your mind out of the gutter. I'm talking about going rock climbing, horseback riding, or walking on a trail in Rock Creek Park."

Tangie arrived at Eric's Georgetown town house at 8:00 sharp. She was almost breathless as she reached for the brass door knocker. It was become harder to quell the excitement she felt when she knew she would see him.

They pulled out of the drive and headed toward the highway. Tangie was silent for a while, enjoying the way the engine purred to life.

By 9:00 A.M. they were turning into the park ready to enjoy a morning horseback ride.

The air was cool, but the summer sun was already

shining brightly. It would be a warm day, but it was a perfect morning for a ride.

They rode for a little less than an hour. The scenery in the park was breathtaking. Especially during this part of the year. Tangie sensed fall coming in the air. Nature was responding to the impending change in season. The flowers seemed to bloom in all their glory, knowing their time was short-lived.

After returning the horses to the stables, they sat near an area of the creek where they could see and hear the water. Tangie felt so peaceful she didn't want this time to end. Eric watched her, perfectly contented himself.

Tangie scooted herself over to him and positioned herself between his legs. He encircled her with his arms and they rocked in a gentle, comfortable motion.

He could swear he heard a purring noise again. They sat quietly, enjoying each other's company, until Eric heard a loud rumbling sound. He erupted into peals of laughter. "Your belly has spoken, I guess it's time I got some food in you."

"Suppose I should have accepted that earlier offer of coffee, huh?"

Eric jumped up, pulling her to her feet too. "I know the perfect place to get something to eat. Come on, follow me."

Before she could respond, they were halfway up the path.

He continued to lead her through the trails. Several minutes later, Eric looked at his watch. It was just after 11:00 A.M. Smiling to himself, he thought, *Do I know my woman or what?*

They walked in companionable silence for another

couple of minutes until they came upon a clearing. "Oh, Eric!" Tangie practically squealed. "This is so beautiful."

There was a beautiful picnic laid out on a table with signs that read RESERVED FOR DUVERNAY PARTY OF TWO.

"Eric, how did you do all this?"

"It's secret government stuff, you wouldn't understand. It's all part of my elaborate scheme to woo you."

He took her hand and led her toward the table. "You like it? There's probably enough food in those baskets to feed a small army, but someone I know with a fantastic figure and a bottomless pit can probably handle it."

Tangie punched him gently in the arm. "You really know how to make a gal feel special. Gee, how did I get so lucky?"

"I like my women with a little meat on their bones. Helps to keep me warm at night," he teased.

"No, what you are is a rat! But you are my rat. Come on, let's see what we've got here." There was pâté de foie gras, Camembert and Brie cheeses, buttery crackers, plump fresh white grapes, and succulent strawberries. To drink, there was chilled white wine and sparkling cider. A cooler contained chicken salad, pasta salad, and veggie sticks with dip. A bread basket held freshly baked croissants, which smelled heavenly.

Tangie snacked on the Brie and crackers. "Tell me whatever I did to deserve such royal treatment, so that I can do it again."

Eric moved closer and stroked her cheek. "You are just you and that's good enough. Don't ever feel like you don't deserve the best."

Tangie poured sparkling cider into two wineglasses and offered one to Eric. "A toast to happiness. May we always have it, whether we think we deserve it or not."

"To happiness," he echoed. "I'm having a good time with you. Are you up for another walk? We need to burn off some of these calories."

"Thank you. Everything was delicious." Tangie took his palms into her hands and kissed each one. "Thank you, little hands, for slaving over hot picnic baskets."

The gesture was meant to be in jest, but it was enough to push Eric over the edge. So much for self-control. He brought her in front of him and wrapped his arms around her softness and warmth. His mouth covered hers. He kissed her thoroughly and completely. Eric drank in her taste until he got his fill. Tangie moaned softly. She pulled him closer. She wanted to feel all of him.

By the time they came up for air, they had an audience. An elderly couple had stumbled into their space. The old man waved and winked.

"See what you do to me whenever we are together? You make me weak in the knees, Mr. Duvernay."

Two weeks later Eric sat in Tangie's comfortable kitchen watching her move around like a culinary expert. Maybe it was time.

Eric noticed immediately that Tangie broke the ugly clothing rule by wearing a yellow T-shirt dress that stopped at least two inches above the knee. She claimed in her defense that she needed to be comfortable in order to cook; otherwise the food wouldn't taste good.

Tangie took cooking very seriously, a pastime for which Eric would pay dearly. Every time she reached for something, he was treated to another view of her lush body. His libido was in overdrive again and causing him no small pain. He alternated between wanting to shake her for being so inconsiderate and wanting to ravage her right on the kitchen floor.

Attempts at benign conversation were thwarted with every move she made.

Tangie turned to ask him a question just after he had been treated to a generous look at her thigh. The way he looked at her made her forget what she was going to say. She didn't miss his obvious lustful examination and approval. His body radiated pure heat toward her.

Tangie walked over to him, sitting at the breakfast bar. "Eric, don't look at me that way, I'm not the dinner."

He covered the distance between them. He had been fighting a losing battle all evening. Eric gently cupped her face in his hands, lifting her lips to his. He gave her a slow, patient, soulful kiss that left her panting. Smiling, he walked out of the kitchen into her living room. He owed her that for the dress.

She changed her clothes, then set the table for dinner. She had prepared baked herb chicken, oven-roasted potatoes, fresh green beans, and topped off the meal with turtle cheesecake. Eric blessed the food and they ate in relative silence. What they said with their eyes spoke volumes. Soft music played in the background and scented candles burned throughout the room, adding to the romantic effect.

It was a wonderful evening except for the burning desire they shared for one another. Heat threatened to scorch them in their seats.

Eric was hanging on by a thin thread. Tangie's bedroom was mere steps away. Finally, he said, "This is wonderful, Tangie. One of the best meals I've had in a long time."

"Thank you. You are easy to cook for. Would you like coffee with your dessert?"

"Yes, but you go ahead to the living room. I'm going to take care of the kitchen. You cooked." Tangie started to protest. "I've got it. Besides, playing in the bubbles is therapeutic for me. It'll just take me a few minutes. I'm good at this. You relax and let me have some quality time with the bubbles. Go on, I'll holler if I need anything. Sit, relax, and pour yourself some more wine. I'll be back with you shortly."

Fifteen minutes later, Eric had returned her kitchen to its former glory.

He joined her in the comfortable family room. "Come here, let me do something for you. How about a shoulder rub or back rub?" he asked tenderly.

"You just cleaned my kitchen, you don't need to do anything more for me. Come closer. Just relax."

She was finally starting to quiet those nagging doubts. She needed to tell him that she wanted to be with him exclusively. The attraction was much more than physical. She loved him more than anything. . . .

Eric's eyes smoldered with desire. His fingers yearned to touch her, he wanted to rub her shoulders and back, but that was just the beginning. . . .

His hands gently massaged her back, sending shivers through her body. His hands stroked her neck, arms, and hips. He gently turned her around to face him and cupped her face in his hands. His kiss was tender and patient at first. Desire increased the tempo. They both were panting when the kiss was finally broken. They were both breathing heavily now. On the precipice, ready to fall off.

"I want to do that every night," he whispered sweetly in her ear. "I love you, Tangie."

Eric looked deep into her brown eyes, staring into her very soul. He took a deep breath, then lowered himself off the couch, onto one knee.

Tangie eyed him suspiciously.

He reached into his pants pocket and pulled out a black velvet ring box.

Her heart raced. Tangie was wide-eyed with shock. Speechless.

"Tangerine Taylor, I love you more than life itself. Will you be my wife?"

Tears streamed down her face as she accepted his proposal. "Yes, yes, yes, I'll marry you. Eric, I love you so much."

Her hands shook as she held out her finger.

Eric rose and embraced her. His heart was beating so fast, he thought it would jump out of his chest. "Whew, you had me worried there." He brushed tender kisses along her face and neck. "You've made me so happy, Tangie. I've wanted this for so long. I don't want to rush things, but can we have a short engagement?"

Tangie pulled away. "What do you consider a short engagement?"

Eric reached for her again.

"You know, when you do that I can't concentrate."

"I can. I find it very easy to focus on what I'm

doing," he said as he planted more butterfly kisses along her chin and neck.

She would have to do something soon or she wouldn't be responsible for her actions.

"Eric . . . Eric . . . Eric . . . we have to stop." She exhaled deeply. "I want to wait until our wedding night."

Eric sighed. The bulge of his arousal was becoming very uncomfortable. He walked slowly and carefully to the kitchen. He leaned up against the refrigerator, willing his body to cooperate.

Eric returned with two ice-filled glasses of juice. They sat at arm's length from each other on the couch. Tangie drank her juice quickly, needing the coolness to quell the fire at her core. Eric watched her as she absently rolled a cube of ice around in her mouth, making little sucking noises.

His temperature rose several degrees. He stood up abruptly. "Tangie, I love you. I'll see you tomorrow, I'm going home to take another cold shower."

Tangie looked puzzled. "What?"

After a quick peck on her cheek, he was out the door.

"I love you," she said to his retreating back.

Tangie's breath momentarily caught in her throat when she looked down at the sparkling three-carat solitaire on her finger. It was absolutely perfect. "I'm getting married . . . I'm getting married," she sang to herself.

Chapter 29

Tangie called her mother first thing in the morning. "Mama, sit down, I've got some news for you."

"Well, don't keep an old lady waiting, spit it out, girl," Hattie demanded.

"Mama, I'm getting married! Eric asked me and I told him yes."

"Oh, honey, I am so excited for you two. Now I am finally going to have some grandbabies to spoil. You two will make beautiful children."

Hattie dropped the phone in her excitement. Her baby girl had finally come to her senses over Eric Duvernay. She had known for a while that the two were made for each other. She just didn't know how long it would take for them to admit it.

"Ma, slow down. We haven't even set the date yet," Tangie said as she giggled. Her mom was like a runaway freight train when she was happy about something.

"Hope it's a short engagement. Near as I can figure, you two have waited long enough. Besides, I'm ready for a good old-fashioned Taylor party. Do you have any ideas yet?"

Tangie sat down at her kitchen bar. "No, Ma, it's all too new. We are going to sit down tonight or tomorrow. He's got a lot of work to do and so do I. I have to admit, I'm a little apprehensive too."

"Tangie, don't you dare try to be practical about this. You two have been through enough, and none of us is getting any younger. Live, child, live! If the man wants to fly you to Rome to get married in the Sistine Chapel, you'd better go."

"Ma," Tangie protested.

"Uh-uh, don't you Ma me. I know that man would slow-walk through fire for you. I saw him after he brought you home from New Mexico. Eric loves you more than anything. I'm not so old that I can't appreciate that kind of devotion."

Hattie paused. "Baby, I know I don't say it often enough, but I am so proud of you. I see the young woman that you are today and I puff out my chest. You are my pride and joy."

Tangie sniffed. Her heart was so full. She had a great mother, great best friend, and now a great man in her life.

After about a week of discussion Tangie and Eric finally decided to have a small wedding in New Orleans. Tangie called and booked flights for her wedding party, which included close friends and family.

Candy had been a little disappointed at not being able to plan a huge celebration with a theme and co-ordinated colors. But she understood their reluctance to plan a large-scale celebration. To a certain degree, she was surprised that they just didn't run off and elope.

With a coordinated effort among Tangie, Hattie,

and Candy, it took just three months to plan and organize their unique celebration. They never wanted to take their love or each for granted again. They decided the marriage would take place in a small chapel close to the restaurant where they first met.

The couple wrote their own vows, which they would share with the world in a short special ceremony. It was important to the two of them that their wedding reflect how special their love had grown, because they had been through so much to get back to each other.

"Are you ready to become Mrs. Duvernay?"

Tangie looped her arm through Eric's as they approached their respective rooms. "Only if you will have me."

Eric cupped her face in his hands and drew her near. He kissed her long and slow. Tangie felt her knees about to buckle. He gently steadied her. "I'll take that as a yes."

At the ceremony, Eric's eyes misted when he saw his bride walking down the tiny chapel aisle in her figure-flattering, white satin gown, under which she wore silky silver panty hose and sleek silver pumps. *She's the most beautiful woman I've ever seen,* he thought as their eyes met across the room.

Tangie felt her heart leap in her chest when she saw her groom standing at the alter. Eric wore a black double-breasted tuxedo with satin lapels. Under his jacket, he wore a gray jacquard vest and tie set. Looking at Eric took her breath away.

Hand in hand at the altar, they forced themselves to concentrate. The blood was pounding so loudly in Tangie's chest, she couldn't think.

Candy gave her the thumbs-up and Tangie's mom

gave her a reassuring smile as she turned to say her vows to Eric.

When she finished, tears of joy trickled down her face. Eric gently wiped away her tears with his index finger. He smiled at her before saying his vows.

As the pastor pronounced them husband and wife, Eric hugged her to him fiercely, capturing her lips in a passionate soul-stirring kiss. She felt her knees go weak again. Eric was there to steady her. He would never let anything break them apart.

The members of their small wedding party whooped and clapped. Eric finally felt like he was whole again. He held on to Tangie, enveloping her in his strength and warmth. Their kiss deepened and lengthened, causing the guests to wonder when they would come up for air.

Finally, with much more restraint than he thought possible, Eric broke the kiss, smiling broadly at his audience. Tangie felt desire course through her body like liquid fire.

As they departed the chapel, rice was tossed wildly at them. They were taken back to the hotel for the reception by horse-drawn carriage. Their first dance as husband and wife felt like a demonstration of torture. The smoldering flames of desire coursed through their bodies. They danced to some of their favorite slow tunes including Whitney Houston's "I Will Always Love You" and Quincy Jones's "Secret Garden." Eric would use any excuse to hold her tight.

When Tangie danced with Siddiq or one of the agents, she would meet Eric's gaze from across the room. More often than not, they wound up in each other's arms locked in a tender embrace. Tangie's body ached for his touch. Eric felt the unwelcome surge of arousal as they danced closely. That they were able to restrain themselves during the toasts and wedding cake was nothing short of miraculous. Mercifully, the reception was short and sweet.

Chapter 30

Tangie and Eric held hands as the walked on board the luxury liner where they would spend their honeymoon. Samuel had booked a suite for them with a private balcony for their two-week-long getaway. On board they had nearly one thousand square feet of luxury at their disposal, but they only needed two feet of space on the bed. It was a four-room slice of heaven complete with a wet bar in the living room and a whirlpool tub in the bathroom. He wanted their honeymoon to be one of their most memorable times together ever.

The cruise ship staff had gone out of their way to make sure that happened. By the time Eric and Tangie entered the room, their clothes were already hanging in the closet and champagne, compliments of the SCU, was chilling in the ice bucket. A huge bouquet of red roses, compliments of Candy and Siddiq Mohammed, filled the room with fragrance. Through the compact disc player an instrumental version of "Unforgettable" played in the background.

The master bedroom was decorated in a neutral delicate pattern that covered the bedding and drapes and matched the towels in the bathroom. The room was elegant and beautiful, down to the decorator pillows.

Eric and Tangie had held true to their decision to wait until their marriage day before giving their bodies to each other. Now they hungered for each other until they felt out of control. The feeling was much more than sexual desire. They both desired a bond that would seal them together physically, as well as emotionally.

Eric pulled Tangie to him, capturing her sweet lips to his. His kiss was passionate, hungry, and anxious. She sensed his thrill of his passion as he plunged deeper, exploring her sweetness. Her soft moans only excited him more. Tangie felt desire well up in her like the burgeoning tide. Her skin felt on fire and it was a flame that only Eric could put out.

They stood in the middle of the bedroom taking in all they could of each other. Her eager response matched his—they didn't even want to come up for air. They gave each other passionate kisses until they were both gasping for air.

"Mrs. Duvernay, you're all mine now," Eric said, taking her hand as they walked to the bathroom. He continued to plant kisses on her mouth, nose, and down her neck. His hands explored the soft lines of her waist and hips, his lips then tracing a sensuous path.

Once there he began to slowly undress himself and then moved to remove her clothing. Tangie trembled at his touch, letting out a ragged breath when he had removed the last piece of clothing. Anticipation was wreaking havoc with her emotions.

Eric filled the tub with hot water and Tangie's favorite cucumber melon bath gel. She smiled mischievously at him.

As Eric gently eased her down onto the bathroom

rug, he marveled at Tangie's beautiful body. He caressed her gently as he trailed soft kisses all over her body. He kissed the soft skin between her breasts. He nibbled or sucked her every inch from her head to the bottoms of her feet. Tangie was lost in the sensation as every part of her was on fire from his touch. After covering her entire body, he began again, paying special attention to his favorite areas.

He stopped to pay homage to her pecan-colored nipples, laving each one to a hardened peak.

Positioning himself on his knees, while she stood, he continued to trail kisses along the taut skin of her abdomen. He found her feminine core with his fingers, massaging her most sensitive area.

She moaned aloud with erotic pleasure. She felt her knees weaken as Eric continued his sweet torture. She couldn't stop the loud cries of delight that escaped her mouth.

He stood abruptly, crushing her to him. As he pressed his mouth to hers, she moved even closer to him, feeling the effect of his full arousal. She stopped caressing his back and began to stroke his most private places, causing him to shudder.

Entering the tub, they washed, they played, and teased each other until the water turned cold.

Tangie wanted to show him how much she wanted to be with him. She rained kisses along his chin and neck while gently stroking his manhood. As she playfully squeezed and released she heard a moan come from deep in his throat.

The hot tide of passion raged through both of them until they couldn't hold back anymore. Eric positioned himself over Tangie, ready to give her all the physical pleasure that they had been denied until their marriage. He nuzzled her with sweet kisses along her neck, but he was quickly losing control. He needed her. Soon.

His voice was strained by passion and desire. "Are you ready?"

Electricity seemed to arc through her. Tangie welcomed him into her body. "Yes . . . Oh, Eric, I love you so much, I can't wait any longer."

She knew exactly how to accept him and he knew just how to make her feel good. Almost instinctively, they found their perfect rhythm and tempo. Their lovemaking was like a well-choreographed dance, well timed, passionate, and beautiful. His expert touch sent her to higher levels of ecstasy than she had ever imagined.

Tangie was so overcome, hot tears of joy rolled down her face. But for her, they were also healing tears, complete tears as the bitterness of the past few years was washed away and she was left with nothing but happiness. She and Eric were finally together!

Riding the tides of passion, she pushed her tongue deep in his mouth, as he made slow, gentle love to her until she couldn't contain herself any longer. Over and over, he brought her to the brink of completion, and she dug her nails deep into the sensitive skin of his back as her body began to quiver in orgasm. Blood pounded in her brain, leapt from her heart, and made her knees tremble. Finally unable to hold back any longer, she screamed a long tortured moan, and totally surrendered to her pleasure.

Eric didn't seem to notice her screams, since his release was mixed with her own. They climaxed together in an explosion of white light and blinding heat.

Neither one seemed to notice that they had missed the big send-off of the boat leaving the dock.

They lay exhausted and sated in each other's arms, succumbing to the numbed sleep of satisfied lovers. The cruise ship sailed off toward the blue waters of the Atlantic Ocean and their Caribbean paradise.

Chapter 31

Several months later

Tangie walked in as Eric put the furniture together. When he saw her he said huskily, "It really is true what they say about how women look when they're pregnant. You are so beautiful, you're glowing."

Tangie blushed in response. Their happiness and the love they shared were reflected in the way they looked at each other every day.

When they were first married they had some fertility problems, but it was finally going to happen this time. They'd had to deal with disappointments and failures, but now Tangie was carrying their twin sons. Her increasing age and stress had made it difficult for conception, but they were a little less than a month away from the boys whose names would be Ivan and Isaiah. They would be named after two very important men in their lives, their maternal grandfathers.

The impending birth of the babies was a turning point in their lives and they couldn't be more proud—or more scared. Eric looked as Tangie practically glided toward him.

She whispered her favorite request in his ear, "Darling, would you rub my belly?"

He scooped his wife into his arms, and as he held her he thought she was the most beautiful mother-to-be in the entire world. He knew the minute he started massaging her growing belly that he wanted to massage other areas of her body.

Tangie smiled at the man she loved with all her heart. She knew she was a very lucky woman to have a second chance at love with him, especially with all they had been through. She had learned to trust love again, to trust Eric again, and had come out the winner.

Tangie sighed, perfectly content to be in her husband's arms, the little gesture stoking the fire in Eric that began to burn whenever they were together. He gently placed her in the nursery rocking chair. He stroked her belly until she practically purred. Tangie loved the way he touched her.

"Ugh," he groaned, "I'd better let you go before we start something we can't finish. Besides, at the rate I'm going the boys will be here before I get these cribs together."

Before he let her go, he kissed her passionately. He knew that he would never be able to get enough of her.

When she was finally able to come up for air, Tangie teased him. "I can't believe my man who can slay dragons and leap tall buildings all while shooting up the bad guys is letting 'ready to assemble' beat him."

"Ha, ha, laugh now . . . but I'll have you know that I'll have this room finished in no time."

Eric knew he was the luckiest man alive and he thanked God for it. They had it all, each other, and very soon, two healthy boys.

Eric stroked the side of Tangie's face. His voice was thick with emotion. "I love you, Mrs. Duvernay."

"And I love you, Mr. Duvernay. Come here and I'll show you just how much."

Dear Reader:

Thank you for choosing to read my debut novel, *Love Worth Fighting For*. I hope that you enjoyed reading about Tangerine and Eric and their adventure toward true love. It has been a wonderful process to bring the Special Corruption Unit to life. I have four stories in mind about the different members of the group to complete the series.

Please let me know what you think of this story and please look for the second story, *Worth the Wait*, scheduled for release in July 2004.

Until then, keep reading!

Take care,
Katherine D. Jones
PMB#36 8775 Cloudleap Ct., Suite P
Columbia, MD 21045

Writeme@katherinedjones.com
www.katherinedjones.com

Katherine D. Jones

Born in Leonardtown, Maryland, not *that* long ago . . . I spent my early years traveling around the world as one of four daughters to a State Department employee. The traveling began when I was twenty days old and was whisked away to live in Cairo, Egypt, then Germany, Zaire, Tel Aviv, Paris, Antigua, and the list goes on. . . .

I have been married for over sixteen years to my wonderful husband, an army officer, and we have two handsome boys.

My writing is reflective of my travels, experience with government agencies, and desire to help women become more aware of their personal power and strength. I believe in strong characters that are firmly grounded in real-world issues and problems.

I obtained my bachelor of arts degree in sociology from Hampton University, Virginia.

More Sizzling Romance From
Francine Craft

__Betrayed by Love	1-58314-152-9	$5.99US/$7.99CAN
__Devoted	0-7860-0094-5	$4.99US/$5.99CAN
__Forever Love	1-58314-194-4	$5.99US/$7.99CAN
__Haunted Heart	1-58314-301-7	$5.99US/$7.99CAN
__Lyrics of Love	0-7860-0531-9	$4.99US/$6.50CAN
__Star-Crossed	1-58314-099-9	$5.99US/$7.99CAN
__Still in Love	1-58314-005-0	$4.99US/$6.50CAN
__What Matters Most	1-58314-195-2	$5.99US/$7.99CAN
__Born to Love You	1-58314-302-5	$5.99US/$7.99CAN

Available Wherever Books Are Sold!

Visit our website at **www.BET.com**.

Arabesque Romances
by *Roberta Gayle*

__Moonrise $4.99US/$5.99CAN
  0-7860-0268-9

__Sunshine and Shadows $4.99US/$5.99CAN
  0-7860-0136-4

__Something Old, Something New $4.99US/$6.50CAN
  1-58314-018-2

__Mad About You $5.99US/$7.99CAN
  1-58314-108-1

__Nothing But the Truth $5.99US/$7.99CAN
  1-58314-209-6

__Coming Home $6.99US/$9.99CAN
  1-58314-282-7

__The Holiday Wife $6.99US/$9.99CAN
  1-58314-425-0

Available Wherever Books Are Sold!

Visit our website at **www.BET.com.**